THE FIRE FIGHTER

Francis Cottam was born in Southport, Merseyside, in 1957. A full-time journalist, he has lived and worked in London for the last twenty years. This is his first novel.

Francis Cottam

THE FIRE FIGHTER

V

VINTAGE

Published by Vintage 2002

2 4 6 8 10 9 7 5 3 1

Copyright © Francis Cottam 2001

Francis Cottam has asserted his right under the Copyright, Designs and Patents Act, 1988 to be identified as the author of this work

This book is sold subject to the condition that it shall not by way of trade or otherwise, be lent, resold, hired out, or otherwise circulated without the publisher's prior consent in any form of binding or cover other than that in which it is published and without a similar condition including this condition being imposed on the subsequent purchaser

First published in Great Britain by
Chatto & Windus 2001

Vintage
Random House, 20 Vauxhall Bridge Road,
London SW1V 2SA

Random House Australia (Pty) Limited
20 Alfred Street, Milsons Point, Sydney
New South Wales 2061, Australia

Random House New Zealand Limited
18 Poland Road, Glenfield,
Auckland 10, New Zealand

Random House (Pty) Limited
Endulini, 5A Jubilee Road, Parktown 2193,
South Africa

The Random House Group Limited Reg. No. 954009
www.randomhouse.co.uk

A CIP catalogue record for this book
is available from the British Library

ISBN 0 09 928640 8

Papers used by Random House are natural, recyclable products made from wood grown in sustainable forests. The manufacturing processes conform to the environmental regulations of the country of origin

Printed and bound in Great Britain by
Bookmarque Ltd, Croydon, Surrey

For Gabriel, my son.
For your gift of life.

One

CROUCHED IN the shade provided by the field gun, Finlay blew on his tea to cool it and waited for the figure approaching him across the sand to resolve itself out of heat shimmer and into recognizable shape. When it did it was the Colonel, so he rose and brushed the sand from his shorts and slopped the tea-leaves out of his canteen.

'At ease,' Colonel Baxter said. He nodded at the teastain on the sand. 'You could have saved me a mouthful of that, Sergeant.' Finlay liked Baxter. He was a popular officer. The Colonel was a career soldier. Command was not a novelty to him and so he never bullied the men. But it was unusual for the Colonel, alone and on foot, to seek out an enlisted man. Now he gestured at the gun in the shadow of which both men stood.

'What's wrong with it this time?'

Finlay thought it would be easier to say what wasn't. 'Calibration, sir. We can't properly calibrate the angle of the barrel. Worn parts. No replacement parts.'

Baxter looked at the gun. 'We had these bloody things at Ypres. They tended to sink in the mud on recoil. But at least when you wanted replacement bits you could go to a factory to get them and not to a bloody museum.'

It was true. Finlay's company had cannibalized their eight serviceable guns from an original twelve. Soon they would be down to six.

'I suppose we have to look on the bright side,' the Colonel said. 'A pessimist would point out that we are short of guns. An optimist would argue that shells are consequently less scarce.'

'Sir.'

'Either way, it is no longer your concern.'

'Sir?'

But the Colonel would not look at him. Finlay was aware of a sand-fly droning close to his ear. Sweat trickled down his temples and a hot wind whipped particles of sand against the skin of his legs. Behind the Colonel, heat made the light ripple across the dunes. Despite his tea, Finlay was thirsty again. His mouth was so dry that he could not swallow when nervousness obliged the reflex. He wondered at the enormity of whatever it was he must have done wrong. The Colonel stroked the near wheel of the gun. It was steel and ridged and shiny-smooth with friction where the ridges ran over the ground.

'We used to pull these with teams of horses,' he said. 'Don't suppose the lorries in those days had the traction or the engine power. Lost an awful lot of horses. Honest beast, a horse. Four years. Two million horses. Hardly bears thinking about now.'

The Colonel's eyes clouded and for a moment Finlay knew that he was back there, at the Salient, his forty-pounders half-swallowed by the sucking ground. The Colonel cleared his throat and returned Finlay's gaze. 'When was your last home leave?'

'Four and a half months ago, Colonel, sir.'

'A lot can change in four months.' Baxter looked at the sky. 'Evidently a lot has.'

Finlay said nothing.

'They tell me you were a fireman in civilian life.'

'I was, sir.'

'A Chief Fire Officer.'

Finlay nodded.

'Why did you not apply for a commission?'

'Borstal, sir.'

'What?'

'Reform school. I was convicted of a juvenile crime and sent away.'

'I see. But you began the war in the fire service. Shouldn't you have been exempted?'

'I have a brother serving in a submarine. Last I heard he was under the Baltic Sea, Colonel. And like you, sir, my father served on the Western Front. Only he didn't come home. I didn't want to be exempted, sir. I volunteered.'

'Why did you join the fire service?'

'Can I ask what this is about, sir?'

'Answer the question, Sergeant.'

The sand-fly was still buzzing around Finlay's ear. His fingers were linked at the small of his back, at ease. He was sweating freely despite the shade of the gun. His voice was harsh with thirst. 'I was a tearaway as a boy, sir. A firebug. The police called me an arsonist and the doctor they sent me to labelled me a pyromaniac. I was just interested in fire, sir. It was something that fascinated me. Still does. I studied the rate and intensity at which things will burn. I suppose in my own way I made a science of fire. And because I know about setting fires, I understand better than most people how to put them out.'

Baxter nodded. 'Thank you. Now I understand.' He cleared his throat. 'I've received an urgent wireless message from Whitehall demanding your immediate return to England.'

'England?'

'You can forget all about calibration, laddie. You're going home.'

'I don't understand, sir.'

'Fire, Finlay. Home fires burning a mite too brightly. The Luftwaffe are fire-bombing London.'

Finlay forgot himself and let out a whistle. 'I hadn't heard anything.'

Baxter smiled. 'Always the same in wartime. Ordnance might be scarce. But we've never any shortage of censors.'

Senior officers did not speak like this to the men. Not even Baxter spoke this freely. Finlay doubted Baxter spoke like this even to his staff officers. He looked at the sand. Odd puckers of damp from the tea dregs, tiny craters, were still visible. He was thinking of his mother in her home in a terrace in Bootle behind the docks. He was wondering what it would be like to be a civilian again.

'Things are grim,' Baxter said. 'Night after night of it. Indiscriminate. No let-up.'

Finlay didn't say anything. Fire was always indiscriminate.

Colonel Baxter put a hand on his shoulder and leaned towards his ear and pressed with his fingers.

'This isn't a soft option, laddie. I imagine it is going to be pretty bloody for you. And no medals. Think about that when you're worrying about your brother's damp socks in that sub under the Baltic.'

This close to Finlay, the Colonel smelled of lavender water and pipe tobacco.

Finlay scoured his mess tin with sand, folded his Primus stove and put his kit away. He buckled his pack. His shoulders were immediately sore under their burden. He was still sunburned from a football game played with one side stripped to the waist to tell the teams apart. When had that been? Two days ago? Sunburn would soon be a memory. His papers were in his tunic pocket and the Colonel had told him to go straight to the airstrip and a waiting Tiger Moth. The airstrip was about a thousand yards from the base and he could hear the engine of the little biplane from that direction through the white-gold haze of heat. He turned once and saw the stiff figure of the Colonel walking back to the base. He felt sorry for Baxter and Baxter's command of half-trained men and obsolete artillery pieces. The guns had not been good enough to breach German trenches twenty-odd years earlier in the war for which they had been manufactured. They had not been good enough to cut the German wire. What chance would they have in the future, in open conflict against advancing German tanks?

Finlay unbuttoned his flies and pissed on the sand. He unhooked his water bottle and drank half its contents. He did not know the rank of the man piloting the waiting aeroplane. But he assumed it would be an officer and so had no idea when he would be given permission to take another drink.

The man in the blue overalls introduced himself as Arthur Babcock. He was about sixty years of age and very pale, with eyes that were nocturnal black and as busy and alert, Finlay observed, as those of a rodent. He led the way down the spiral of iron stairs with an electric torch pointed always at what would be the next step for Finlay's descending feet. Finlay's instinct was to falter and to feel; it was so dark in the shaft down which they travelled and the steps were so dim and so steep in the darkness. But Babcock progressed in front of him, casual, unseen, and finally they stopped on a landing and the thin beam of the electric torch lit upon a door. They were under Liverpool Street station. They were so far down, Finlay judged that only pumps could be keeping them above water. Babcock drew a bunch of keys and opened the door. The door was secured by two mortise locks and a Yale and was so narrow that even Babcock, who was a man with a build consistent with his rodent eyes, had to turn sideways to enter the space beyond. He switched off his torch. Finlay followed him. Babcock closed the door after them. Momentarily they stood in absolute blackness. And then Babcock switched on a wall light and the single room was revealed.

The rear wall was curved, a concave parallel to the curve of the shaft in which the door to the room was set. The two side walls were flat. The room was about ten feet deep and ten wide and about eight feet high. The floor was covered in grey linoleum. Walls and ceiling were panelled in some dense, unvarnished hardwood. Finlay went over and tapped one wall.

'Angle iron and concrete underneath,' Babcock said. 'We used the place for storage when we were building the Central line.'

'That was a long time ago.'

'Completed 1912,' Babcock said. 'On schedule.'

The room was furnished with an army cot, an armchair, a wash-stand and a metal table and chair. There was a shelf of books and a telephone on a nightstand under a lamp by the cot. A green carpet covered the middle of the floor. A green floor-length curtain on an angled rail in one corner pulled back to reveal a lavatory. Two lengths of articulated hose penetrated a foot into the room from opposing corners of the ceiling. Each was stoppered by a copper cap.

'Air pumps,' Babcock said. 'They aren't always necessary and they make a bit of noise. The feeds are a long way apart, just in case one of them should get knocked out. The air might get a bit thin if you're using a Primus to cook on or there's a big set-to above.'

'Set-to? You mean raid?'

'I mean fire,' Babcock said. 'It's fire that will devour your air.'

Finlay nodded. Even here, he could now hear the dull crump of bombs, like a rumour of war, on the streets above.

'First attack of the night,' Babcock said, looking at the dial of his wristwatch. 'Punctual chap, Jerry.'

'Where do you shelter, Mr Babcock?'

'It's just Babcock, sir.'

'It isn't "sir".'

'The instruction film they showed at the Rialto urged me and the wife to build a shelter in our garden,' Babcock said. 'Anderson shelter. Very cosy it looked too. But I spent the last war in the trenches. Our sappers used to dig the officers' shelters fifteen to twenty foot down. Packed tight in French clay. And if they took a direct hit, there was nothing left of them afterwards but vapour. That, and the fact that we don't have a garden, decided me and the wife. We shelter in the Aldwych Underground station. You can usually get a cup of tea and the singing isn't always entirely excruciating.'

Finlay laughed. Babcock did not seem the sort to take his wife to the pictures. 'Babcock?'

'Chief Fire Officer?'

'Do you think we'll win this war?'

Babcock looked around Finlay's new home. 'Maybe we should lose a war, for once. The Germans lost the last one and it doesn't seem to have set them back unduly.'

Above, the crump of bombs receded and advanced across the city with the density and volume of visiting death. 'Is that what you really think?'

Babcock blinked about him. He let out a long breath, as if containing something. 'You'll come back covered in soot from fighting fire and you'll scrub and scrub with the soap in that dish over there and you'll wonder why it isn't getting you clean,' he said. 'And the reason is that it is rendered whale fat and not soap at all. Because there is no soap any more.' He was silent for a moment. 'I don't think we'll win this war, Chief Fire Officer, because I think we've already lost it. We just don't know yet how to admit it to ourselves.'

Finlay said nothing. Babcock smiled. 'Here are your keys,' he said. And he was gone.

He had been wrong about the man who flew the Tiger Moth. The pilot had been a pilot sergeant, not a pilot officer. He had given Finlay a sheepskin flight jacket and fur-lined gauntlets and been happy to share rum from a pewter flask on the high, cold flight. They had landed on a stretch of shore, dim puddles of burning pitch strung out as landing lights, and two commandos in face-blacking and Royal Marine berets had paddled him half a mile in an inflatable boat to a waiting launch. The launch had taken him to a cruiser sitting at anchor on a dark sea and he had climbed a rope ladder to the deck and then been hauled aboard in silence. Aboard the cruiser Finlay was confined to a cabin, his meals brought to him, his smalls laundered, his questions ignored, until they docked at Southampton. He had disembarked and had his papers scrutinized and stamped and had been spoken to at last; debriefed, he was informed, by a man from the Ministry of War. The man wore the uniform of a major and the insouciance of a high-ranking civil servant. He wore exquisite leather gloves which, throughout the interview, he chose not to remove. Finlay was too weak and tired from vomiting to be capable of anger or indignation at his treatment. He was a poor sailor and had kept nothing in his stomach but for the odd sip of water during his eight nights and nine days at sea.

From Southampton, Finlay had been taken to London by car, sharing a seat with the Major from the Ministry. The Major wore his gloves and smoked Piccadilly cigarettes ceaselessly through a tortoiseshell holder and remained silent throughout the journey. The car drove straight to a building on Whitehall and Finlay was told to wait in an ante-room off a larger room which, he saw briefly, was furnished with an ornate desk and a half-circle of chairs arranged to face it. Barrage balloons filled the otherwise vacant sky in the large window behind the desk. After an hour, a woman knocked on the door and entered, pushing a trolley of tea and biscuits. Finlay drank a cup of tea and ate a biscuit. The tea was strong and malty and tasted wonderful. The biscuit tasted of flour dust and fish oil.

Whoever it was he was there to see must have been waylaid, because he saw nobody. When he had been waiting almost three hours in the ante-room, the door was opened by the Immaculate Major. The Major prompted Finlay with a small cough and a gloved forefinger and he was delivered to Liverpool Street and to Babcock, waiting in his blue overalls at the London Underground entrance adjacent to the main-line station, in Broad Street.

Now, Finlay lay down on the army cot in his new quarters. He had slept only fitfully at sea and was very tired. He felt guilty that his fatigue was born of congenital weakness, and not combat, and wondered for a moment whether seasickness afflicted those sailors who served beneath and not on the surface of the ocean. Tom was five years younger than Jack Finlay and he loved his brother so intently that when he thought of him his face clenched and his eyes became wet with the indignant, fierce insistence of that love. Looking after his brother was a promise he had made his mother at his father's grave in 1935, when Finlay had been twenty-four and his brother nineteen. But it felt to him so profound a pledge as to have been sworn in his mother's womb.

The telephone on the night table woke him with its unfamiliar ring, loud in the catacomb room they had provided him with beneath Liverpool Street.

'Fire Officer Finlay?'

'Speaking.'

'My name is Grey.'

'Mr Grey.'

'In half an hour it will be dawn, Finlay. It is important that you know fully the reason you have been brought out of the front line. It is important you appreciate the urgency of the task you face here at home. With this in mind we've arranged a little tour and then a demonstration. Please meet me in half an hour at the Broad Street Underground entrance.'

'Mr Grey?'

'Finlay.' The voice sounded strange: pitched between tedium and anger.

'How will I know you?'

'I'll know you, Finlay. Your photograph is in your file.'

It was ten in the evening by the time the car returning Finlay pulled, lightless, into Broad Street. There was a smell of burn in the air; of ash and cordite and petroleum. It seeped through the heavy doors into the wood and leather of the car interior. But the bombs sounded far away.

'The docks at Chatham,' Grey said by way of explanation. Finlay nodded. 'Sometimes I wonder at the paradox of such a disciplined race as the Hun employing surprise as a tool of warfare. I wonder if it doesn't tax them, psychologically, more than it does us.'

'It's us that's doing the dying,' Finlay said.

Grey nodded. 'That's true.' He was hunched into the seat, his head sunk on his chest and his neck drawn into the collar of his coat. Now he stretched forward and opened his briefcase, on the floor between his feet. He reached into it and pulled out a bottle of whisky, showing Finlay the label as he raised his eyebrows in a gesture of invitation. Finlay nodded. Grey leaned forward and said something that, even this close, Finlay didn't catch, to his driver. Finlay looked at the driver, all that was visible of him a heavy wedge of shaven neck between the coat collar rising above massive shoulders and the band of his chauffeur's cap. The driver pulled up to the kerb and the two passengers stepped out of the car.

'You don't mind if I have a quick rinse?'

'Be my guest,' Grey said. He was seated in the single armchair in Finlay's quarters with his drink, amber, held in front of his face in a tooth glass. 'Didn't you take a shower at the facility?'

'I did,' Finlay said, unbuttoning his shirt half-way down the chest and then pulling it over his head. 'It didn't quite get rid of the stink.' He went over to the wash-stand and poured water from a jug and splashed it over his face and the back of his neck.

'Fuck,' he said, after an attempt at scrubbing.

'Technical hitch?'

Towelling his hair, in only his vest and trousers, Finlay sat on the cot, opposite Grey, and picked his glass up off the floor. 'I was told, but had forgotten, about the soap.'

'Ah,' Grey said. He swilled whisky in the tooth glass, sipped, savoured, swallowed.

'What do you do to get into that sort of shape, Finlay? If you don't mind my asking. Last time I saw muscle like that it was on two darkies contesting a British Empire title at White City.'

'I did gymnastics at Borstal,' Finlay said. 'Parallel bars and so on.'

'Competitively?'

'Yes.'

'Win anything?'

'It kept me away from peeling potatoes.'

'You don't do it any more?'

'I grew,' Finlay said. 'I got too tall for it. The power-to-weight ratio changes.'

Grey nodded. 'Any thoughts on what you saw today?'

'On the streets, or at the facility?'

'The latter.'

'Only that water won't put it out,' Finlay said. 'Hoses will only spread the fire, make the damage worse, inflict higher casualties among the fire fighters. The stuff we saw today has been designed that way. But I think you know all this already.'

'We want you to think about it,' Grey said.

Finlay looked at the whisky in his glass. 'You must have scientists better qualified than me.'

'Oh, we have,' Grey said. 'And we've got them working night and day on perfecting something even more frightful for us to drop on Jerry. We have the boffins, Finlay. But none of them has quite your experience or record of achievement in the actual business of extinguishing fires. We have the scientists, all right. But they don't quite have your power-to-weight ratio.'

'Is that supposed to be funny?'

Grey concentrated his gaze on his glass. 'Let me pose a question. Would you, in an air raid, follow a chap in a white lab coat into a burning building?'

Finlay sipped whisky.

'You are the fellow who put out the fire at Pimlico Rubber.'

'For the loss of five men.'

'When the *Empress of India* caught fire at anchor—'

'An engine-room fire. All I did was close the watertight doors, starve it of oxygen.'

'The fire aboard the *Empress* was first believed to have started in the coal hold.'

'But it hadn't,' Finlay said. 'That much was bloody obvious from the smoke.'

'Just as well it was obvious,' Grey said. 'Wasn't the *Empress* berthed next to a cargo vessel brim-full of petroleum?'

'You know it was,' Finlay said, tiredly. 'It's in the file with my picture attached.'

'What was obvious about the smoke?'

'Copious. Greasy. Billowing. Black. Does everyone have a file?'

'Absolutely,' Grey said.

Finlay awoke with a thick head, unable to remember Grey's departure or much of their conversation. It had been a long day, the sort that concertinas night into something rushed and sudden and entirely without significance. Today he was to go to the Mile End fire station and meet some of the men instructed to obey him. He shaved as best he could with cold water and latherless whale soap and washed and dressed, all the while thinking of what he had been shown the previous day. The latter half of the day, at what Grey had called the facility, had tested rather than dismayed him. He had seen incendiaries before; murderous, stubborn, all but ungovernable. He had seen far worse things in peacetime than the emergency aboard the *Empress of India*, or the blaze that charred five good men to blackened bone at Pimlico.

The *Empress* had been a difficult emergency. Ships containing volatile cargos of glue, saltpetre, industrial alcohol, sulphur, magnesium and crude oil had flanked its berth in the bustling dock. The decision had been whether to close the watertight doors, with the seamen who had been fighting the flames with fire blankets and bilge water still in the engine room, not knowing whether those men were alive or dead. And that had been Finlay's decision to take.

It was not so much the composition of the German fire bombs that disturbed him, or their size, as the quantities in which they were being dropped. They spilled out of the sky in massive, careless clusters, capable of spreading acres of flame. Finlay understood the momentum of fire, what it fed on, how it could succour itself on the surrounding air to nourish its source and to spread. He appreciated its greedy protection of itself and its devouring impetus. These fire bombs would burn fiercely enough to melt steel, smelt iron, turn monuments of brick to powder and proud stone edifices to brittle carbon husks.

He shook his safety razor in the water and saw to his surprise that it had changed colour with rinsed blood from a cut he had not felt himself inflict. In the sunless light of his cell, the water appeared not pink, but violet.

The first part of the day had shaken Finlay very badly. The streets of East London were a catastrophe for which he had tried and failed, between bouts of nausea aboard the boat, to prepare himself. As he climbed through them, he knew it was a failure more fundamental than mere lack of imagination. His mind had failed him. His mind had imposed order on what was insane. He had imagined ruin, but was confronted by something more terrible and profound in the mad upheaval of London after the bombing. A milkman capered, whistling something familiar, over the brick rubble and spilled furniture at the end of a charred terrace to put two pints on the step of a house with no door or windows. From its blasted interior, a seated woman waved to him from a soot-blackened parlour and then returned, rocking in her chair, to the knitting on her lap. Further on, a man in a carpenter's apron sang like a ventriloquist through the nails gripped between his teeth as he hammered a coffin together from the panels of a wardrobe. Beside him was a sack, the blood soaked through it giving definition to the body parts within.

''Aven't found 'is 'ead yet,' the carpenter said to Finlay, or to Grey, as the two men passed him, looking. 'Daresay 'e won't be needing it now.'

They were walking through Whitechapel, headed towards Wapping and Shadwell and the river. On an approaching corner, a fire crew manned a hose pointed at a burning timber yard. The flacid loops of the hose told Finlay that the crew did not command sufficient water pressure to contain the blaze. The fire fighters were old and tired-looking, gaunt with fatigue in uniforms filthy with soot, brick dust, singeing. Finlay looked up. The sky above their heads was spangled black with soot.

'They come up the Thames, using the river itself to navigate by,' Grey said. He flicked ash from the shoulder of his overcoat. 'The black-out tends to be pretty much absolute throughout the city. By contrast, from altitude the river shows silver under moonlight and the stars, even through cloud. Captured air crew describe it as a truly beautiful sight.'

'I'm surprised captured air crew aren't lynched before you get to them,' Finlay said.

Grey ignored this remark. 'They do have strategic targets. They go for the docks, the power stations, the railway termini and any buildings their intelligence tells them might house important personnel. Beyond that, they attack the symbolic targets. St Paul's, the House of Commons and the Tower have all been hit, though none of them has been significantly damaged. When the bomber crews turn for home, desperate to lighten their load, gain altitude, increase air speed, they dump anything left in their bomb bays along the Thames. So life is no picnic these days if you live in Bermondsey or Rotherhithe. If it ever was.'

'Is there air pursuit?'

Grey sniffed. 'There is. Where the night raids are concerned it is almost totally ineffective. We can't see them to shoot them. It isn't even good for morale, since those a show might reassure are sheltering under ground. Waste of aviation fuel, really.'

'Then why do we do it?'

'Indicates to Jerry that we haven't thrown in the towel.'

Someone had hauled a piano, its case rent, its innards exposed, on to the pavement. The two men shuffled around it. That was it, Finlay decided. The antimacassars flapping across rubble, the fragments of plaster hurled into the street with bits of pelmet and wallpaper still attached; the blue enamel washing-up bowls and broken-spined books and bits of body wearing gabardine and floral cotton print. It was the combination of familiar domesticity and martial destruction that jarred. It was the horrible unreality of this encounter between civilian people cowering in their civilian properties and the bombs nightly delivered them. The war he had seen so far had been so neatly choreographed. The armies might have been painted soldiers shuffling across a painted board for all their organization and neatness. For a moment, Finlay was intensely nostalgic for Baxter and Baxter's desert batteries of make-and-mend guns. 'You can forget all about calibration,' Baxter had said to him. He remembered then what Baxter had said about medals.

There was a sudden tearing of the air and a boom behind them and Grey was on the ground. Holding on to his hat, he looked up at Finlay, who was still standing, looking down at him. 'Petrol engine,' Finlay said, smiling. 'Probably a lorry in that timber yard back there. Some poor bleeder just lost a full tank.'

Grey climbed to his feet brushing dust, disgustedly, from his elbows and knees. 'You hit the ground pretty fast, Mr Grey,' Finlay said, still smiling. 'I think you may have done that once or twice before.'

Grey said nothing in response to this remark. He adjusted the angle of his hat brim. He sniffed. In the aftermath of the explosion the air smelled bitter with creosote and burn.

Suddenly the river lay curved in a broad bend before them. It was still not long after sunrise and in the chill a pall of mist hung above the water. The tide was low, the current slack and the only river sound was its soft lap against pilings emerging from the mist. Cranes and gantries, twisted, broken, formed forlorn geometries in front of the warehouse buildings staggered among ruins on the far bank. The superstructure of a sunken tug was visible above the water in one of the deep channels towards the centre of the river. Debris gathered in grey swags, like ghostly bunting, from its ship's rail and blown portholes. Looking up and down the river, Finlay saw that the tug was not the only wreck. Half a dozen boats had been sunk at anchor. At the edge of his vision, almost on the river's bend, a coke barge burned in a rudderless circle under a still column of smoke. There was a sound like a cough and a building with the name of its proprietor lettered large across its edifice sagged and sank on the far bank in a spreading pillow of dust. Dust loured across the water towards them. Grey tapped Finlay on the shoulder.

'Seen enough?'

Finlay nodded.

'There's a pub along here does a decent lunch. Least, it was here yesterday. What say we call a late breakfast an early lunch and I have the car fetched?'

Finlay didn't say anything. The cloud of dust tumbled over itself across the river towards them.

'Feel better with a bit of grub inside you,' Grey said.

The night raid had left the pub intact. It was an inn rather than a pub and Finlay guessed that it had remained pretty much intact for centuries. It was called The Prospect of Whitby. It offered a prospect only of wharves, water, ruin. They sat in a nook to the rear of the pub with a view out over the river through a leaded window. The pub had its own moorings and a Thames barque was tied up there. Its black sails gave the barque the sinister appearance of a pirate vessel. Then Finlay realized that the black was just soot staining the canvas. There were whorls of soot in the grain of the barque's teak deck. The old boat was filthy with spent fire.

Grey ate kedgeree, sucking flakes of fish through a gap in his teeth. 'Why am I obliged to live in a hole in the ground, Mr Grey?'

Grey tutted.

'You were in the artillery. Let me ask you an artillery question. Suppose a tank takes a hit. Shell isn't armour-piercing, just explodes, gouges a bit of plate, tank wheels along on its merry way. What happens to the crew?'

'The crew is dead.' Finlay said.

'How?'

'Trauma. The shockwave from the explosion causes the tank crew's internal organs to rupture and collapse. Superficially, their bodies will be intact. But they are dead.'

'Jerry has an item of ordnance called a blast bomb. Detonates when it reaches a specific altitude. Say a hundred feet above the target. Sends a massive shockwave. Designed to kill personnel and leave property intact. Designed really, we think, to damage morale. It isn't just you, Finlay. We are all living in holes in the ground.

'Our logistical friends refer to human resources. Experts, they tell us, as if we didn't know, are a scarce human resource. We lost too many valuable people to the first period of the bombing. Can't afford to lose any more. Even Winston sleeps in a hole in the ground. And Winston's bomb-proof. Aren't you going to eat something?'

'White,' said White. He sat back down behind his desk. Finlay sat in one of the chairs arranged in a semi-circle facing the desk. The Immaculate Major sat in a chair to Finlay's right. In the big window behind White, the same barrage balloons he had seen that last time he had been here sat plump, suspended in the Westminster sky. Now, though, the view was diminished by a large crack extending across one of the window's panes. The panes wore crisscrosses of brown tape.

'What are you thinking?' White said.

'Just that it must be terribly confusing for your secretarial staff. All these people from the Ministry, named after neutral colours.'

The Major coughed.

'What do you make of Grey?' White said.

'He is the first homosexual I've liked.'

'I suppose you must have met your fair share in Borstal.'

'No. I came across plenty of sodomites. But on reflection I think that was a consequence more of availability than choice.'

The Major coughed again. 'Grey was at Gommecourt Wood,' he said. 'Have you the remotest idea of what that means?'

'I am afraid I haven't,' Finlay said, addressing his reply to White. 'Geography was never my strongest subject.'

There was a pause in the conversation. Finlay was aware of the absence of traffic on Whitehall. Everything on the roads of London had been freight since his return. Except of course for the bicycles. The only cars he had seen so far had been that allocated to Grey and the one that had brought him from Southampton. To his right, he could hear the Major breathing in measured breaths and feel the heat of the anger in his face.

'Armstrong,' said White, swivelling in his chair. He looked at Finlay. Finlay did not respond.

'Carter,' White said. 'Eagan. Gaines. Lampetter. And of course, Tooley.'

Finlay just sat.

'Do you think of those names often, Chief Fire Officer?'

'Never alphabetically. Not until now, anyway.'

'Grey tells me you blame yourself for what happened to the men you led into the blaze at Pimlico Rubber. Just as Grey of course blames himself for what occurred at Gommecourt Wood. But blame is of no use to us. Guilt, remorse; these are crippling handicaps for someone from whom we expect as much as we expect from you.'

'Perhaps you should have left me in the desert, Mr White.'

Beside Finlay, the Major coughed. He has a cough to cover his entire emotional range, Finlay thought. That one signified disgust.

'Grey had you tour the stations?'

'We visited Mile End and Shoreditch and Hoxton and Moorgate stations yesterday afternoon. We would have visited Bethnal Green, but every available man was clearing fire breaks around a lightbulb factory on Old Ford Road with an unexploded thousand-pounder in its goods yard.'

'What was your impression?'

'Excellent men overwhelmed. Where are our ground-to-air defences?'

White looked momentarily lost.

'I saw them in a Pathé news film they showed us in Egypt. Batteries of anti-aircraft guns revolving on plinths.'

The Major laughed. 'Oh, those. Those batteries are at Borehamwood,' he said.

Now Finlay looked confused. White appeared, for the first time, uncomfortable.

'There is a film studio at Borehamwood,' the Major said. 'Very good people. Marvellously sophisticated lighting and camera work. Most of our films are edited there. It's where some of them have to be faked.'

'The ground-to-air batteries are a cinematic trick?'

'They call them special effects,' the Major said.

'"Good men overwhelmed" was the phrase you just used,' White said. 'It is regrettably apt. We can't tell our men in the field that we are not able adequately to defend their families at home.

We are losing this war and if we admit that to our troops, we will have lost it. Would you like some tea?'

'Yes.'

'Biscuits?'

'Absolutely not.'

There was a silence.

'I would have done nothing differently at Pimlico Rubber,' Finlay offered finally. 'I would give a great deal not to have lost those men. But I would have done nothing differently.'

'I see,' White said, nodding.

'Perhaps now you can tell me truthfully what it is I have been brought back to England to do.'

And with that, the Immaculate Major went to find tea. And White did tell Finlay.

Two

'WE WERE not actually invited into the Underground stations,' Babcock said. 'But I don't suppose there were enough rifles left in London to stop us once we decided to invite ourselves.' He frowned at the top of his step-ladder and twisted his screwdriver between dextrous hands. 'If you give it proper thought, mind, there probably were enough rifles.'

'But nobody wanted to fire them,' Finlay said. He was seated on his cot, shining the buttons on his new tunic with Brasso. His uniform belt lay stretched out on the cot beside the tunic, its buckle dull with polish that he would shortly buff to a brilliant sheen with the cloth he was using on the brass, embossed buttons.

'It was not a matter of ethics,' Babcock said. 'It came down not to conscience, but to expediency.'

'Bad for morale, you mean. Londoner mowing down fellow Londoner.'

'They didn't want to waste the ammunition,' Babcock said, climbing down to the floor. 'They couldn't afford to squander the bullets on a handful of militant civilians.'

Finlay stopped polishing.

'You said there were hundreds of you.'

'Thousands, Finlay. There were thousands of us.' Babcock examined his work from the bottom of the step-ladder, sinking the length of his screwdriver into a narrow sheath riveted along the leg of his overalls. 'It was a scene reminiscent of the storming of the Winter Palace.'

'You were there too, were you?'

'No,' Babcock said. 'But the wife and I saw Mr Eisenstein's filmic interpretation of the event at the Locarno in Walthamstowe. Anyway, that should do you.'

Finlay looked up. Babcock had replaced the bulbs and shades and in so doing had changed the character and effect of the lighting in Finlay's quarters. He was going to have to study architects' plans of buildings that time and change of use had made intricate, obscure and sometimes labyrinthine in their complexity. The lights that had turned his bloodied shaving water violet would make the blueprints of buildings unreadable. So he had done as Grey suggested and telephoned Babcock, using the number Grey had given him, and had asked for a draftsman's table to study from and improved lighting to study by.

'Not asking for much, are you?' Babcock had said.

'Can you arrange it for me?'

'Of course I can. Captain – Mr Grey – says you're to have anything you want.'

Finlay had wondered about Grey's status, about his rank. 'Then what's the problem?'

'No problem,' Babcock said. 'The capital is being bombed into oblivion. And you request more amenable lighting. And exotic furniture. What could possibly be the problem?'

White's background briefing had been succinct. Some of it Finlay had learned since his return to England from the newspapers. But most of the detail was entirely new to him. All of it was confirmation of what he had seen already on the streets. The air raids proper had begun a month before, at around four o'clock on the afternoon of September 7, when more than two hundred German bombers launched an assault on the docks at West Ham and Bermondsey. Bombs strayed as far away from the target as Victoria Street. But Stepney, Poplar, Bow, Shoreditch and Whitechapel bore the brunt. The bombardment continued for more than twelve hours and left almost five hundred people dead. The bombers, one hundred and seventy of them, returned the following night. They concentrated their attack on the same areas as before and this time killed four hundred people. Dawn brought no respite. On September 9 the Luftwaffe despatched two hundred bombers to attack by day. Almost the same number of enemy aircraft delivered the night assault. Another three hundred and seventy Londoners died.

'And the following night, they came back and gutted St Katherine's Dock,' White said. 'The warehouses surrounding the dock were full of inflammable material. Paraffin wax, mostly.'

Finlay listened and imagined. Wax ran molten across the quays and into the docks, flooding into the water where it set on the surface of the Thames in a black and brittle sheet reflecting flames rising two hundred feet from the burning quayside buildings.

'Since then it has been pretty unrelenting,' White said. 'You can imagine the nightly destruction to property a hundred and fifty bombers brings. We're averaging around three hundred deaths a night. In the aftermath of the raids, people come up from overcrowded shelters filthy, hungry and frightened. They are increasingly weary because the noise of the bombing makes sleep impossible. They return to homes, if their homes are still there, without windows, water, sewage provision or power. Gas and electricity have become very scarce. Nobody wants to run the risk of working through the night, so no bread is being baked. Opening the Underground up as air-raid shelters has helped morale a bit. So has what anti-aircraft fire we are able to provide. We can't hit anything, but our citizens apparently find the noise of retaliation reassuring.'

'When were the Underground platforms opened up?'

'Night after the first big bombardment. Liverpool Street was first and the rest followed.'

'Whose initiative?'

White coughed. 'Popular demand,' the Immaculate Major said.

'Is provision elsewhere so bad?'

White looked at the Major. It was the Major who spoke.

'The London County Council realized several years ago that in the event of another international conflict, London would be a target from the air. It is not just the greatest city in the world. London condenses a fifth of the population of the British Isles into an area of seven hundred and fifty square miles. That makes it a very economical target. An LCC delegation asked the Government to provide funding for deep shelters. The Government declined to provide the funds.'

Finlay thought of Colonel Baxter and his batteries of antique guns.

'What defences were the funds allocated to in place of deep shelters?' he asked the Major.

White turned to Finlay. 'Are you aware of something known as Deep Shelter Mentality?'

Finlay shook his head.

'Should the civilian population of a city be provided with deep shelters and then bombed, they will survive the bombing, but they will be aware of it and speculative about the scale of destruction. Panic breeds and the people in the shelters simply never re-emerge. Chaos ensues. Since a city cannot run itself, defeat becomes inevitable.'

'That's the theory?'

'The LCC predicted numerous potentialities,' the Major said. He had taken off his gloves. Finlay saw that the flesh of his hands was pink and the skin flaking off them on to the desk, on which they reposed, like dandruff from a badly afflicted scalp. 'Their worst projection was thousands dead each day after mass bombing raids. They planned to fill disused quarries with quicklime and turn them into mass graves. They planned to fill fleets of barges with the dead, tow their cargo of corpses out to sea and dump them in the Channel. Thankfully, it hasn't come to that.'

Finlay was silent for a moment.

'What has it come to?'

The Major tapped out a tattoo with the pink tips of his fingers.

'The Oval cricket ground is a vegetable allotment. We fire an average of thirty thousand shells to score a single hit against an enemy aircraft. The black-out is facilitating a crime wave unprecedented since policing in this country began. And you can't get nylons. Not for love nor money.'

'There was some unrest in the East End,' White said. 'Too many things were left to local government in the first fortnight of raids and the town halls didn't have the wherewithal to cope. We believe that West Ham was closest to insurrection.'

'Pockets of insurrection,' the Major said.

'Then Jerry did us a favour,' White said. 'The bombers turned their attention west of London Bridge. Mayfair took a fearful pounding. Our East End friends felt much better once the toffs were getting a taste of it. And then terrific luck. The Palace was hit, with the King and Queen in residence.' He opened a drawer and pushed a ten-by-eight-inch press photograph across the desk. It showed the Queen, pretty and plump, picking a dainty path through Palace rubble at the side of her gaunt husband.

'I would like to contact my mother,' Finlay said. 'Write to her, I mean. I want to let her know where I am so that she can write and tell my brother. I want to know from my mother how my brother is. And I want to be able to send my mother money.'

'We can let her know how you are,' White said. 'We cannot for the moment let her know where you are, or permit any kind of direct contact. Am I right in believing that your mother lives alone, a widow, in Liverpool?'

'Yes.'

'We will reassure her about you and ensure that she is comfortable. That much I promise you.'

There was a silence.

'I haven't seen a single fire hydrant on the streets,' Finlay said.

White straightened the blotter on his desk. The Major coughed.

'The good burghers of London deemed that the river would suffice,' White said.

'It won't. Fighting fires requires water under pressure. Out of reach of the river, it requires supplies of static water.'

'Static water?'

'Ponds, tanks. Where do you live, Mr White?'

'Town, you mean, or country?'

'He means town,' the Major said.

'I've a place in Cadogan Square.'

'Flat, or house?'

'House.'

'Then if I were you, I would flood my basement.'

'There is the sand,' the Major said. 'We have turned Hampstead Heath into the Grand Canyon in the excavation of sand. But I don't suppose, Chief Fire Officer, that sand will satisfy.'

'Sandbags are adequate for blast protection,' Finlay said. 'At least, they are if they're packed tightly enough. But the weight of sand prevents easy transportation and handling and it won't fight fire except by smothering, and to smother, it needs to be dropped from above.'

'Useless, then,' White said. 'Do you have any more questions?'

Finlay rolled the blueprints he had been given and inserted them into the cardboard tube they had provided him with. He turned to the Major. 'Where were you gassed?'

'Vimy Ridge,' the Major said, without looking up. Finlay nodded and turned to go.

'I think we've got that chap all wrong,' White said, after Finlay had exited the room and the door had closed on his absence.

'One thing, anyway,' the Major said, stretching his gloves taut over tender flesh. 'Pound to a penny the fellow knows about Gommecourt Wood.'

Finlay left the Ministry building for a false dusk accelerated by the absence of light from street lamps and passing traffic and by soot, mournful and heavy in the autumnal sky. Vestiges of sun burned with an orange afterglow on the buildings to his left as he walked along Whitehall. The green Whitehall roofs shed slipping fingers of ochre sunlight and lapsed into shadow and refuge as night augured the onset of darkness and the bombs. By the time Finlay reached Trafalgar Square, the spaces of the night city were no longer singly articulated, but blurred, bringing a weird claustrophobia as the blackness grew close to absolute. He sensed rather than saw the mad, imperial apostrophe of Nelson's Column, just as he sensed rather than distinctly heard footsteps behind him, like an echo of his own blind but deliberate progress towards the east, and home.

Finlay's journey along the Strand was slow and groping. The sensation of the night river, coursing to his right, suggested itself in a swift breath of cold air on his right cheek whenever the buildings were breached by the flattened spaces of bomb damage in gaps blacker than the dark penumbra of the buildings lining the empty avenue. When Finlay passed these, he was aware of their absence of mass. He walked, listening for the sound of approaching aeroplane engines, for the oncoming rumble of death, still aware of the footsteps echoing his.

Finlay had traversed the black chasm of Aldwych and was on Fleet Street when the cloud above him shifted and stars and a fragment of moon swept the skulking city in a brilliant silvery light. He turned, convinced that his pursuer would be caught, exposed as if by the flash from a camera bulb. But Finlay saw, instead of one figure, a dozen phantoms flitting this way and that. He saw a caped warden astride a bicycle, searching the sky; two men in buttoned overcoats and hats hurrying under the clock outside the Express building; a woman with yellow hair splayed garish across her shoulders, hair spilling from a netting scarf as she smoked with the cigarette cupped in her palm in a surreptitious doorway. Then cloud shrouded the sky and blindness crept over them all and he was alone again. And then he heard the vibrant drone of the approaching Junkers with their cargo of explosion and flame. He was hurrying along New Fetter Lane when the air-raid siren sounded. Then he heard the crump of bombs and saw flashes of crimson and yellow rise in the east. Wapping, he thought. The docks again. He was further here from the intended target than he would be at Liverpool Street. But he knew that his sepulchre there was safe. He needed to study the plans he carried by the light of Babcock's newly fitted lamps. There was a public shelter close to Fleet Street and Finlay could have taken refuge there. But the Immaculate Major had told him about the public shelters earlier in the day, when White had left the room briefly to take a telephone call. And knowing what he knew now about the public shelters, Finlay felt safer taking his chances on the streets.

They had given him responsibility for five buildings. His job was to make them as fire-proof as possible in the event of attack from the air. He had to try to proof them against the assault of incendiaries. He had to try to make them reluctant to ignite into flame if hit by explosives, or burn in series as flames spread from bomb damage to neighbouring buildings. Finlay's buildings were a disparate lot. They ranged in age and original use from the town house of a bishop built by Thomas Hawksmoor to a cathedral of cement and granite that rose in six-storey tribute to the modernists of the Chicago school. Proximity was the single unifying element. All were located in the City, within a rough triangle of thoroughfares extending from its northern base on Leadenhall Street to its southern apex where Bishopsgate and Houndsditch coincided.

It was a tiny acreage and uncomfortably close to the prime bomb targets of the Bank of England, St Paul's and the main-line railway terminus at Liverpool Street. But the density and narrowness of the streets through which they were reached had not changed since the rebuilding that followed the Great Fire. Lanes and alleyways, some the mere width of a cart, teemed and tumbled with portico, column, keystone, cobble and arch in a great conumdrum of brick and beam. Finlay estimated that it would take a concentration of bombs, delivered deliberately and over many consecutive nights, to lay waste to everything inside his triangle. A stray 800-pounder; a spiteful string of incendiaries; a payload dropped in panic on the way to blast St Paul's to smoke and ruin: these were much more his likely concerns.

Finlay had asked Babcock for cartridge paper and a set of pencils with a range of leads from hard to soft. He heard Babcock chuckle into the telephone receiver, and he was delivered five sheets of tracing paper and a propelling pencil apparently cadged from Grey. He brewed some of the coffee Babcock had provided on the gas ring in his cell. The coffee tasted of acorns and cistern water. He doubted the ration coupons Babcock had brought him would fetch anything better from the streets. So he elevated his draftsman's board and set to learning, one by one, the singular intricacies of the five buildings committed to his care. Soon he would visit them. But the conflict had brought about a stifling officiousness in civilians charged with war work, as he had discovered walking the streets of Bootle on his last home leave, picked on and lectured needlessly by a man transformed by ARP armband and black bicycle into a haranguing god. Such men would lurk in caretakers' uniforms, haunting the vestibule of each of Finlay's buildings, he was sure.

It was why he had polished the buttons on his tunic. It was why he now pinned the five tracings he had made to his walls. He wanted to know these buildings intimately before visiting them. He did not feel he had the time to debate demarcation with Home Front martinets before going about the business of making these buildings as safe as he was able to.

But when obstruction came, it did not present itself portly and belicose, wearing a tin helmet and a tobacco-stained moustache. Obstruction did not confront Finlay. It stole into his new life over the telephone and was delivered to him by Grey.

'Absalom House,' Grey said, insinuated into Finlay's still slumbering brain. He looked at the luminous hands of the wristwatch on his nightstand. His mind's eye conjured a tall edifice, slender, flanked by a blank office façade and a Gothic Revival bank.

He coughed. 'Camomile Street,' he said. He was searching for the face of his watch, but could see only Absalom House, its polished black brick stretching upwards. He could hear Grey breathing into the telephone. Finlay wondered whether this wasn't a dream.

'Finlay?'

His eyes finally found and made sense of the glowing pattern of his watch dial. It was a quarter to six. 'Has Absalom House been hit?'

'No,' Grey said. 'There is a compliance issue. The skylight?'

'Atrium,' Finlay said. He sank back on to his single pillow with the telephone receiver cradled and his wristwatch in his fist. 'The building has a domed summit of glass.'

'Whatever. You need to get there and you need to find a different way from the one you suggested of making the building fire-proof. There's a not entirely disgusting café in the basement of a church on Fournier Street. North side of Spitalfields. Meet me there in half an hour and I'll buy you a spot of breakfast and we'll discuss the matter.'

Silence.

'Finlay?'

Finlay was thinking. 'There is no other way,' he said.

Grey chuckled. 'Invent one then, there's a good chap.' The connection was broken by what sounded like a hiss.

He got to Absalom House at nine-fifteen. He had breakfasted on boiled ham and bread and tea in the Spitalfields crypt with Grey. For Grey's table there had even been the extravagance of butter on the bread. Afterwards the barriers around an unexploded parachute bomb on Bishopsgate had impeded his progress back to Broad Street and another look at the plans of Absalom House. But he had still had over an hour to work out a way of minimizing the risk posed by the atrium.

'Be gentle,' Grey had said, spreading his lips to blow steam from the surface of his tea.

'Why?'

But Grey had merely winked and sipped and then smiled and asked about the progress in general that Finlay was making in his tasks.

At 9.30 a.m. Finlay was shuttered into the lift at Absalom House and taken up to the fifth floor. The lift did not extend to the sixth. The atrium was reached by a set of stone steps across the floor from where the lift stopped. The steps extended to a heavy door scrolled in some soft and decorative metal that time and perhaps damp had filigreed in its deep depressions with green. The door was not locked. Finlay had been asked to wait in the atrium. The door swung easily despite its weight, balanced perfectly on four steel hinges set in a massive stone architrave. Finlay examined the locking mechanism. He was seeing the door for the second time and was again impressed by its construction. The door was not only elaborate. It was immensely strong. The soft metal would absorb blast vibration and would not burn. Locked, it would form a formidable barrier against the spread of fire from above or from below.

Finlay walked across the glass-vaulted room. The floor was tiled in marble and the walls were constructed from large blocks of polished Portland stone. The big glass sections above his head were more than four inches thick. He knew because he had measured them. They were framed in bronze. He knew that a dome was one of the most rigid geometric structures known to architecture. He knew that glass was strong. He knew that the strength of glass was brittle and that bronze was a soft metal with little resistance to heat. But it was none of this that most directly bothered him. He looked out up at the sky. Five aeroplanes wearing camouflage paint flew eastwards in a delta formation a few hundred feet above his head. Finlay recognized them as Hurricanes. It occurred to him with a start that they were flying in silence.

'Soundproof,' said a voice behind him.

She was standing with feet set slightly apart and her weight spread evenly between them. She wore a belted, calf-length skirt. The skirt was narrow and her stance pulled its satin fabric taut so that light from the sky silvered its smooth surface. Light played too on the ivory blouse, buttoned with pearls and worn under a tailored jacket draped across her shoulders. She stood with one arm across her body, her hand cupped to support the elbow of her other arm. A cigarette burned between the fingers of her free hand a few inches from her mouth. She waved for Finlay to sit, and smoke spiralled upward.

Her gesture made him realize that he had been standing to attention. He looked around. She had indicated two leather and metal chairs beside a low wooden table. He took his cap from under his arm and placed it on the table and sat. She sat too. Sitting straight, the angle of her chair to his would have put her head in half profile. She twisted to face him and smiled.

'Are you A-two, or one-B, I wonder.'

She was not English. Her accent was close to perfect, in that it was accentless. Her mouth was sculpted. She pulled heavily on her cigarette and exhaled, watching him.

'Well?'

'I don't think I understand the question.'

'You have to be one or the other. Men who wear a uniform and don't fight always fall into one or the other category.' She pulled hard again on her cigarette and smiled at him through smoke. Her eyes were grey. Rings of iridescent blue marked the border between the grey of her eyes and the white. Finlay wondered how the white could remain so absolute under the assault of strong tobacco.

'Let me give you an example,' she said, standing. She gestured at the glass bowl inverted above their heads. 'Firstly, you should have all that curtained off,' she said. 'And B, you've no business anyway being up here at night.'

Her voice carried the lower-middle-class stamp of petty authority.

Already, to Finlay, it was horribly familiar.

'Or,' she said, 'A, a soundproof room makes a mockery of the air-raid warning system. And two,' she touched the tip of her second finger for emphasis, 'if you strike a match under that skylight, madam, you might as well be sending Jerry an invitation to tea.'

She dropped her spent cigarette and ground it out on the marble with her hands on her hips and a challenge in her expression.

Finlay smiled. A part of him was amused. But it was a small part in the fatigue he fought, and he thought her wilful battle pitifully little in the scheme of things.

'You should curtain off the glass,' he said. 'I don't give a tuppenny fuck about the soundproofing. But you should curtain off the glass, or secure black canvas over the dome, which would be the best precaution.'

He rose to leave, passed her without looking.

'Black canvas,' she said.

Finlay stopped but did not turn. 'Secured with hawsers rather than rope. But make sure that the hawsers are painted black, matt black, along with any brass eyelets, if the canvas has them.'

'Matt black,' she said.

He reached the door.

'You are angry because you polished your buttons for me and I made fun of you,' she said.

Finlay turned and looked at her. 'No,' he said, shaking his head. Her hair was heavy and loose and in this light silvery, like her skirt. 'I am angry because you're the most beautiful woman I have ever seen. And you made fun of me.'

The door whooshed in his wake, snug as it settled in its granite berth.

He walked through the monochrome and quiet of the City

back to Broad Street and descended the spiral steps to where they had him live. He unbuckled his belt and took off his tunic, laying it carefully across the bed. He walked across to his wall chart of Absalom House. He had listed the precautions requested. And taken.

Every inch of wood panelling, varnished and therefore volatile, had been stripped from its walls. The old drapes, swagged and decorous, had been swapped for fire blankets stitched together and dyed in a bad approximation of what they replaced. All the windows had been taped and wire mesh stretched across the insides of the larger ones. Every room on every floor had been provided with zinc pails of dry sand and spades to spread it with. The petrol generator that provided the building's independent power supply had been uprooted and dumped, replaced by one that ran on diesel oil. The presence of the generator meant that the basement of Absalom House could not be flooded with a supply of static water; but Finlay's triangle was in easy reach of tenders from the Moorgate and Shoreditch fire stations. Fire-resistant paint had been slapped in several heavy coats over the hardwood doors in the building. The doors had been reinforced with steel and oxygen-starving draft excluders attached to them once the building's carpets had been stripped. Gas had fuelled the small cooking range in the staff kitchen as well as some of the lighting at Absalom House. But the gas supply had been disconnected. Now the lights ran on electricity from the generator, and they had candles. And they pressured tiny Primus stoves into miserly life when they wanted to heat their tea, their acorn coffee, or their thin tins of soup.

'A compliance issue,' Finlay said to nobody. He looked at the tunic and cap on the bed, wondering if there wasn't some comic opera quality to the crest on the cap, the brightly embellished epaulettes stitched to the shoulders of the tunic.

He hung his dress uniform, worn for the Absalom appointment at Grey's insistence, and washed away as best he could with whale soap and cold water the patina of grime even the short walk from Camomile Street had left on his hands and face and neck. Grey, via Babcock, had brought him a suit of civilian clothes together with good shoes in his size and an overcoat. The only previous occasion he had worn these, he had been so roundly abused in a bus queue that he had walked through pouring rain to his destination. Today, however, Finlay felt that he might welcome a row.

He reached under the cot for the kit bag containing his personal bits and pieces. He took out a towel, a pair of plimsolls, a jock strap, shorts, an undershirt and a heavy sweater. He zipped these items into a canvas grip. There was a gymnasium he sometimes used behind the Strand. At least, it had been there before the war. If it was no longer there, he would find another gymnasium. He had some energy to expend and hungered for hard physical effort.

Finlay found his gymnasium intact, open, empty. He went through his old routines on the rings and the horse and the parallel bars until the muscles and tendons in his arms and shoulders were rigid with effort. Then he did floorwork until he reached exhaustion, mouth burning with lactic acid, abdominal muscles unable to raise his shoulders off the mat. He sweated for half an hour in the steam room and then paid five shillings for a masseur with the arms of a stevedore to rub alcohol and embrocation deep into his body.

'Been a long time, Jack,' the masseur said.

Finlay could not remember the last time anyone had called him by his Christian name.

'Been overseas, Harry,' Finlay said.

'Somewhere sunny, from your colour. Anywhere nice?'

'Egypt.'

The masseur walked over to the sink to rinse the rubbing alcohol from his hands. 'Served overseas myself, in the 'fourteen–eighteen,' he said.

That's what they must be calling it in the conversational occupations, now, Finlay thought. Since they can hardly any longer call it the Great War.

'Mesopotamia,' Harry said. 'A dirty lot, the Turks.' He lifted his sweater, still facing the sink. A livid purple scar gouged a crescent from the base of his spine to his ribcage.

Finlay had twisted on the massage table to look. 'Shrapnel?'

'Trench morter,' Harry said. 'You seen any action yet?'

'Not much,' Finlay said. 'Few skirmishes against the Italians. Tit for tat, really.'

Harry turned, towelling his hands. 'When do you go back?'

'I don't.'

The masseur could not mask a look of bewilderment. 'Injured?' he said.

Finlay smiled, wondering what kind of war wound it was could be concealed from a masseur's searching fingers. 'Incapacitated,' he said. He climbed off the table.

He ate a meagre lunch of potato and cabbage and what the menu claimed was haddock in a café behind the Strand, washing it down with two pale cups of tea. He paid and then walked along Whitehall and crossed Parliament Square for the Embankment, to his left Big Ben, all four sets of hands and four faces of the great clock miraculously unblemished. It was silenced now, of course, but telling the correct time, its mechanism intact. Finlay walked past the ravaged Abbey and the House of Commons and sat on one of the benches facing the river in the Victoria Tower Gardens. They had taken the statues from the gardens. The river was low and Finlay could barely hear the water lapping against the sand and small stones and gathered debris of a diminishing tide. Directly opposite where he sat, he could see St Thomas's, the hospital building scarred, holed, battered by the deliberate onslaught of bombs. There should have been something sad about those red brick edifices, Finlay thought; something pathetic in the Tuscan affectation of the architecture, in the dismayed fate of all that well-meaning Victorian money. But there wasn't. The hospital spoke to him only of the same weary indifference to its misfortune he had seen on the faces of Londoners.

He thought of the woman at Absalom House, picking a stray shred of tobacco from her lip with painted fingernails.

Finlay wished, with a heartfelt longing, to be back in the desert, coaxing Baxter's obsolete guns into delivering death to an enemy tangible, reachable, there to be engaged and bloodied and defeated without compromise. He did not doubt the importance of this war or the winning of it. Sitting there, with the smell of embrocation, a smell like horse liniment, rising in his nostrils when his skin stirred under his civilian clothes, Finlay felt despondency overwhelm him like a sickness. It wasn't fair. It just wasn't fucking fair. He had thought the two years spent in Borstal for a church fire he did not set an injustice. But the anger he had felt in adolescence was nothing to the desolation he felt now at being taken out of the waging of the war.

Finlay's eyes strayed to the right of the hospital, to Lambeth Palace, which had been hit, and to Lambeth Bridge, which had not. Beyond the bridge, on its southern side, was the fire station where he had trained. He wondered would the pub behind the station still be intact. He might benefit in the isolation he felt now from walking through the door of The Windmill and seeing familiar faces from a happier past. Certainly, he thought, he might benefit from a drink.

The beer was thin and brackish. Finlay abandoned his pint on the bar after two sips and ordered a double whisky. The whisky barely registered as amber and tasted watered. He drank it at a swallow and went back to his pint. Then he scented something at once forgotten and familiar, and turned. Someone had lit a pipe filled with a pungent and singular tobacco blend in the corner of the pub to Finlay's rear. The smell insinuated memories a decade old into his mind. He could not see who it was who had lit the pipe. He could see only a table-top, gusts of smoke, a set of dominoes and a pair of hands occupied by a solitary game. But he knew who it was, so he went over and sat without invitation in the vacant seat opposite the man.

'Albert Cooper,' Finlay said.

Cooper looked up through the folds of smoke in which his pipe had enveloped his features.

'Well, well,' he said. 'Jack Finlay. Didn't think to see you again, Jack. Thought you'd be dead by now. I'd have bet money you'd have toppled off a ladder a long time ago.'

Finlay looked at Cooper, at the grizzle of hair framing the face and the brass-buckled belt and the thick serge trousers tucked into boots.

'Albert. What the fuck are you doing in that uniform?'

'Playing dominoes,' Cooper said. 'Smoking a pipe. Minding

34

my own. But since you're here, Jack, you can treat an old comrade to a pint.'

'I'm serious, Albert,' Finlay said. 'You retired in 'thirty-seven. The date's inscribed on the back of the watch we bought you.'

Something receded in Albert Cooper's expression. He took his pipe away from his mouth and lines firmed in his face. 'Buy me that pint, son,' he said. 'Let old Uncle Albert tell you all about his retirement.'

Finlay went back to the bar and ordered. Late afternoon was making its melancholy transition into early evening in the pub and The Windmill was all but empty. Finlay could pick his spot at the bar without jostling to be served. So he chose a place from which he could study Albert Cooper in the big mirror framed high along the length of the bar while he waited for the barmaid to draw their two pints. Albert had let his pipe go out and was no longer concealed by its smoke. Like a lot of men, he had aged more rapidly in retirement. His nose and cheeks were a latticework of broken veins that from a distance made him look countrified and ruddy. But close to, he looked weathered and worn by too much life and an appetite for drink. He was a big man and there was still strength in his short neck and massive shoulders. But there was a stiffness to his movements even as he shuffled dominoes and when he relit his pipe there was a tremor in the hand that held the match. He looked towards where Finlay stood and Finlay looked quickly away from the mirror, making a show of searching his pockets for coins to pay the woman behind the bar for their beer.

Cooper lifted his fresh pint high as if to scrutinize its quality. The tilt of his head exposed the top of the scarring on his chest inflicted by the molten latex that had fallen like a monsoon of fire as they fought the flames at Pimlico Rubber. He lowered his glass and held it out. The scar disappeared again. The hand holding his drink was steady. Finlay chinked glasses with him.

'Cheers,' Cooper said.

'Cheers.'

'Here's to old times.'

And Finlay felt guilty for spying on his one-time colleague and friend in the mirror above the bar. 'Old times,' he said. Both men sipped and there was a silence between them.

'You look like the dog that lost its dick,' Cooper said eventually. 'Can't just be the beer.'

'Why aren't you retired any more?'

Cooper sat back against his seat, his pipe, even his pint, momentarily forgotten.

'I was born around here, Jack. Raised not five minutes' walk from here, in Fitzalan Street.'

The old fire fighter paused. Finlay remembered Cooper as a witty man, fluent in humour, seldom lost for a sharp line or a well-chosen word of repartee. Perhaps it was the unaccustomed seriousness of what he wanted to say that was making him inarticulate now.

'They've dug trenches in Archbishop's Park. Only they're not calling them trenches. They're calling them bomb shelters. No revetting. No roofing. No drainage. Already a foot deep in water. What state are these bomb shelters going to be in come the winter?'

Finlay sipped beer.

'Bomb shelters. For the women and the kids. Fucking comedians running the country.'

Finlay could think of nothing to say.

'It's a mess, all of it,' Cooper said. He remembered his beer and emptied half a pint in a couple of gulps. 'I'm back, Jack, because I'm too old to fight. But I'm not too bloody old to fight fire.'

His fists were clenched and massive on the table-top. His knuckles were white in rings around the bone the size of pennies and veins throbbed in the backs of his hands. It occurred to Finlay that Albert Cooper in this condition would have failed his routine medical on blood pressure alone. The rules must not so much have been relaxed as discarded.

'Do you think we can win this war?'

Cooper breathed for a while, recovering himself, before answering.

'You've been overseas, Jack. Nobody gets a colour like yours on the sands at Blackpool. When did you get back?'

'Eleven days ago.'

'Well then, you don't need me to tell you how bad things are. Norway, Belgium, Holland, France.' He shrugged. 'We're all that's left on the list.'

Heat crawled along the flesh inside Finlay's clothes and made him shiver, like someone trying to shed a leech. 'So you think we're going to lose?'

Albert Cooper leaned forward over his own empty glass and traced a circle with his finger in the scum settling on the surface of the pint Finlay sat neglecting. 'We can't lose,' he said. 'Not to Hitler. We lose to him, son, we've had it.'

The two men were saying their goodbyes on Old Paradise Street when the dusk was split by the sound of the air-raid siren and the rumble of Junkers amplified its way along the river. What happened next Finlay put down, in his own recollection, later, to drink. But it had been a long day and it might have been the result of a culmination of things. Whatever, he should have turned and walked to the shelter of the Lambeth Palace Crypt, or to the trenches in Archbishop's Park. Instead, he gripped Cooper's heavy arm and screamed against the siren in his ear.

'I'm still in the service, Albert. Get me kitted out. Please. You know I can help.'

If Cooper hesitated, it was only for a beat. Then he nodded and the two men sprinted across the fire-station yard and into whatever the night would deliver them.

The skin of Grey's face was tight with rage. He paced the linoleum in front of the single armchair in which Finlay sat. The Immaculate Major stood against the door. Finlay picked horsehair from a hole in the arm of the chair. Grey paced. The Major stared into disdainful space.

'You stink of smoke,' Grey said to Finlay. 'Your clothes are still smouldering, for God's sake.'

Finlay sat forward and laughed softly into his hands.

'He's broken,' the Major said to Grey. 'Absolutely broken. The chap is of no use to us at all.'

'Nonsense,' Grey said, wheeling on the Major. 'The man is perfectly all right. He needs a bath and then a few hours of sleep.

After that he will require a vigorous debriefing. And then he will be as good as new.'

Finlay was rocking back and forth in his chair with his head in his hands. It was unclear whether he was laughing or crying. And then a thin dribble of black snot escaped from between his fingers and the sight of it made his sobbing suddenly audible.

'He's gone to pieces,' the Major said. 'The fellow is an absolute waste of time.'

'He is fine,' Grey said, quietly. 'Mr Finlay is indulging in a show of grief. That's all.'

Grey pulled something from his overcoat pocket. It was evenly shaped, like a pebble, and wrapped in greaseproof paper. He walked across to Finlay and dropped it into Finlay's lap. 'Here,' he said. 'That's a bar of Palmolive soap requisitioned from the Royal Automobile Club. Take it, Finlay. And for pity's sake, use it.'

Three

THE FIRE had been beyond containing by the time the tenders reached the school. Because the Lambeth station was on the river, there was always abundant water in their tanks and the water pressure looked impressive enough in the play of hoses on the burning building. But the incendiaries had gone through the roof and detonated on the ground floor, spreading across parquet floors and igniting brittle classroom furniture. Flame blossomed about the panelled corridors and devoured tarpaper partitions. Flames licked and curled around the school roof and lolled in yellow and orange tongues through the shattered glass of the upper-storey windows. Wardens tried to usher onlookers back to safety through the gate in the high wall surrounding the playground. Fire auxiliaries winced against the heat in their shabby tunics and tin hats, waiting to be told what to do. Seeing their faces in the fierce illumination and stark shadows cast by the burning building, Finlay realized with a deflating suddenness that Albert Cooper did not command a man under fifty.

Cooper was holding an old man hard by the lapels of his coat and shouting and then listening intently to what the man had to say. Finlay saw that Cooper's men were trying the twin strategy of dousing the building and attacking the seat of the fire. The play of the hoses was precise but futile. They seemed well drilled and disciplined men. But their task tonight was hopeless. He ran across to Cooper. Cooper cupped his hands over Finlay's ear to counter the roar of fire and the bombardment, which had now moved on to tumble death over Vauxhall, Battersea and beyond.

'He says there were kids in there rehearsing their nativity play,' Cooper said.

Finlay looked incredulous. 'How many?'

'A dozen of them.'

Finlay turned to where the old man had been standing but he had gone, merged once more with the milling crowd of silhouettes braving bombs to watch the spectacle of the school visited by destruction.

Inches apart, Finlay and Cooper had to huddle and scream to be heard.

'Who is your most experienced man?'

'I am,' Cooper said.

'Then I'll go,' Finlay said.

Cooper looked around quickly. His crews were doing all they could. 'We'll both go,' he said.

Finlay fetched two fire blankets from the nearest tender and took the axe from his belt and used its wetted edge to hack an eighteen-inch slit at the centre of each of the blankets. Both men removed their oilskin waders. Cooper ordered the water pressure reduced on one of his hoses and then fiddled with the aperture of its nozzle. They needed to be doused, not knocked unconscious by the power of the jet. He gave the hose back to a fire fighter, who played it over both of them. Thoroughly soaked, they put on their makeshift ponchos, Finlay gasping at the sudden coldness of the water in the heat blast from the burning school. The fire fighter aiming the adjusted hose doused them again. Cooper gave a hand signal and the man nodded, running back to his tender to increase the water pressure once more. He would play the hose in an arcing deluge over both men until they were inside the building.

Cooper and Finlay were fire fighters familiar enough with the layout typical of South London's late-Victorian schools. The rehearsal would be held in the assembly hall. They would reach the hall through a side entrance put there as a fire precaution. They would get to it through a cloakroom with walls Finlay prayed to a God he did not believe in would be tiled, as they sometimes were, and not panelled in a parched inferno of cheap timber.

Cooper swung his axe and the door shuddered and crumpled inward. The two men flattened themselves to either side of the opening to avoid the explosive, oxygen-searching outreach of flame. Then they were in, running blind through the burning benches and empty coat hooks of the cloakroom and through its swing door, into the hissing floor wax, the blistered walls, the hungry, feeding flames devouring the hall.

They knew instantly that they would anyway have been too late. But there were no bodies burning in the hall. Cooper and Finlay turned to look at one another and the ceiling seemed to sigh above them. And then it fell, engulfing them. Finlay lay on his back. His back was burning on the blistered floor and he spat hot embers from his mouth and used the back of his hand to prevent embers from blinding him. He tried to twist and found he could do so. He lay under lathe and plaster, winded, scorched, alive. Struggling to his feet, he turned and saw Cooper. Cooper's head was unrecognizable, only the brilliantine crackle of sparse hair on a livid spread of matter to signal that this had ever been the skull of a man. Finlay fled. He had reached the outer door and felt the breath of the night and seen rainbow arcs of falling water when a smouldering vision abducted his mind.

In the corner of the cloakroom, through the smoke: gabardine. A scrap of blue gabardine and, above it, something a deader yellow than flames, like a scarf. He pulled one, long, fugitive breath of air out of the night and turned back, stumbling, his hands in front of his face, to the far corner of the cloakroom. It wasn't a scarf. Her hair was yellow on the collar of her school raincoat. She seemed to be sleeping and Finlay picked her up and held her bundled to his chest and begged his faithless God to let her be living still. His hands blistered, his hair on fire, Finlay wheeled about and bulled, bellowing, for the door.

There were far more cracks in the panes of glass than there had been when Finlay had last been summoned. The lengths of brown sticky tape did not appear to be equal to the task of keeping the panes intact. Fissures and hairlines provided a whole new sub-stratum of blast damage.

'They're trying to flatten the Abbey,' White said from behind the steeple of his fingers, reading Finlay's thoughts. 'And they've made an educated guess as to where Winston sleeps.'

'If someone hasn't told them,' Grey said. Today, Grey and the Major sat flanking White. They reminded Finlay of the promotion board he had faced when his rank had been Chief Fire Officer (Acting). His eyes drifted again to the windows. A barrage balloon had shed its moorings and was canted in the sky at an angle that made it look more than ever like a cartoon cigar. It was raining outside and enough of the atmosphere seeped through the cracks in the window panes to make the room feel damp. Finlay ached from his unaccustomed gymnasium work of two days ago. He ached too from the bruises collected at the fire on Kennington Road. His hair had been cropped close to his skull to get rid of the singeing. A patch of gauze covered his blistered cheek and both his hands were salved and bandaged.

'How do you feel?' White said.

'Never better.'

'She died,' Grey said. 'The little girl? Already stiffening when you got her body out.'

Finlay took this in. 'Where did the rehearsal story come from?'

'The bombing appears to breed rumour,' Grey said. 'There's a weighted corpse at the bottom of every water-filled bomb crater. A captured German spy. Ask anyone. Though nobody will own up to having seen him put there.'

'Truth,' White said. 'First casualty of war.'

'Don't take it personally,' the Major said. 'I was motoring back from Biggin Hill one day and my own driver told me that the Arsenal football stadium had been flattened. Transpired he got the information from a Tottenham Hotspur supporter.'

'Winston says that there were twenty thousand Nazi sympathizers in this country at the outbreak of war,' White said. 'Some harmful lies are no doubt told deliberately. But rumour festers in a situation such as this. We have to live with that.'

'Or, like Albert Cooper, die with it,' Grey said. 'What in heaven's name did you think you were about?'

'Are you aware that Babcock is a Communist?' Finlay said.

Grey and the Major stretched forward and looked at each other around White. Then Grey snorted with laughter.

'Nonsense. Babcock is a dyed-in-the-wool anarcho-syndicalist. He told me so himself.'

'None of you is sane,' Finlay said.

Grey looked serious. 'I have known Babcock since the autumn of nineteen-fifteen, Chief Fire Officer, and I would trust him with my life. Frequently have, in fact.'

'He thinks we have lost this war.'

'We are certainly losing this bloody war,' White said.

'Babcock is entitled to some leeway,' Grey said. 'He lost his boy last year when the *Glorious* was sunk. Robert was eighteen. And my godson.' He cleared his throat. 'None of which answers the question. What in hell did you think you were doing at that school?'

Finlay didn't say anything. Then he said, 'Can any of you gentlemen tell me why there are children still in London?'

'Chap wants a lecture in dispersal theory,' the Major said. 'Shall I do the honours?'

White turned his eyes towards the ceiling.

'Evacuation was always recognized as the safest and best way of avoiding child casualties,' the Major said. 'But no government could risk the mandatory removal of children from their parents. When war broke out, we suggested and facilitated the evacuation programme and achieved close to ninety per cent compliance. But then we waited for over eleven months for Jerry to start bombing London. Indignant parents, thinking they'd been misled and missing their children, began to bring them home. By the time the air raids started, almost all of them had returned.'

'Dispersal does continue,' White said. 'But there are those who insist on taking their chances.'

'Fatalism,' Grey said. 'A disturbing tendency.'

Finlay looked at him.

'Why?'

'Because fatalists don't win wars,' White said.

'I'd like to ask you a question, Chief Fire Officer, the Major said. 'Why did you make a pass at Rebecca Lange?'

Finlay was bewildered for a moment. 'I wasn't aware of her name.'

'You didn't ask her name.'

'She didn't offer it.'

'You didn't introduce yourself.'

'She has a way of sidestepping introductions.'

'You made a pass at her. Why?'

'It wasn't as simple as that,' Finlay said.

White picked up the receiver of one of his desk telephones and ordered tea. He replaced the receiver and, like the two men flanking him, stared at Finlay.

'It wasn't me who sent a foul-mouthed detail of prison convicts to carry out half the work I wanted done at Absalom House and a truculent bunch of conchies to do the rest,' Finlay said.

'The contents of Absalom House are sensitive,' White said. 'We felt that security was unlikely to be breached by Quaker pacifists or the residents of Wormwood Scrubs. And the work was supervised by a very good chap from the Royal Engineers.'

'Anyway, it wasn't them she took exception to,' Grey said. 'It was you.'

'Her and her fucking atrium,' Finlay said.

There was a knock on the door and a tea trolley was wheeled in.

'I'll be mother,' Grey said.

'Doesn't anyone know what that little girl was doing in the school?'

'Emily Green,' the Major said. 'Eight years old. Her father is aboard a merchant vessel avoiding U-boats somewhere in the North Atlantic. Her mother was doing an overtime shift in the machine-tool shop over which she presides as foreman in Camberwell. They manufacture gunsights. Emily was nervous of the family's Anderson shelter. Didn't like being down there alone. School was apparently where she felt safest.'

Finlay lowered his head into his bandaged hands and groaned.

'Let's get back to Rebecca Lange. She is the daughter of Frederick Lange, the architect?' White said.

Finlay looked blank.

'The atrium is the distinguishing feature of his only British building.'

'He can always build another one somewhere they aren't dropping bombs,' Finlay said.

'As he hasn't been sighted since boarding a train in Berlin in nineteen-thirty-eight, that's unlikely,' White said.

Finlay shrugged. White sipped tea. Grey stared. The Immaculate Major coughed. 'What is it you want, Chief Fire Officer?' he said.

'To fight the scum you lot call Jerry. To kill Germans and anyone who helps them. To stop them. To end it.'

'The work we have asked you to help us with will achieve that far more effectively than anything you could do as a gunnery sergeant,' White said.

Finlay reached for the tray on the desk and his tea, which was cold.

'I regret that we can't tell you more about the value of your task. I have to ask you to trust us.'

Finlay sipped cold Ministry tea.

'What do you want me to do?'

'You can start by apologizing to Miss Lange,' Grey said.

Finlay had walked through rain almost to Trafalgar Square when the car whooshed to a stop at the kerb beside him. The door was pushed open. 'Get in,' the Major said. 'I'll take you as far as Aldwych.'

'Emily Green did not die,' the Major said. They motored along the empty Strand. 'I can understand why Grey should tell you that she did, but she did not.'

Finlay said nothing.

They were at Aldwych. The car stopped at the junction with Southampton Row and Finlay climbed out.

The Major said, 'Do you understand why the man would deliberately choose to lie to you like that?'

Finlay smiled. 'Because of what happened to him. Because of what Captain Grey saw on a summer morning at a place called Gommecourt Wood.' He closed the car door carefully and walked the wet pavements of London to Liverpool Street.

Babcock had brought him a letter from Tom. It sat on his draftsman's table, which Babcock had lowered to the horizontal, along with tins of cocoa and condensed milk and half a bottle of Bell's whisky. He wondered why he had been given this peace offering. Then he remembered Babcock's boy and the fate of the

Glorious. Babcock, of course, would have recognized and identified Tom's as a service letter. Maybe he had read it. Maybe he had been told to read it and to inform Grey of its contents. Maybe Tom's letter had arrived yesterday, or the day before, and they had all read it, gathered around the big, leather inlaid table under the taped windows, Grey volunteering to be mother when the tea was fetched. Finlay poured a whisky and held it up to the light. Its buttery colour sat unadulterated in the glass.

'Here's to you, Albert Cooper,' he said, toasting the small mirror above his sink. 'And to old times.'

He took a sip. The whisky delivered fire to his belly. Then Finlay unbandaged his hands and washed them carefully with his bar of Palmolive soap. He rinsed and shook his hands dry rather than risk the friction of a towel on still-tender skin. He sat in his armchair with his Scotch to one side and thumbed open his brother's letter. The envelope appeared inviolate. The letter itself was written on flimsy, punctuated here and there by the thick strokes of a censor's pen that Finlay, knowing his brother and his brother's predicament, had little trouble reconstituting into words.

Dear Jack,

All is as well as it could be in circumstances that I can't pretend don't try myself and the rest of the lads. It is often said that we are all in this together. And that is nowhere truer than in the perculiar conditions in which my branch of the navy operates. All the same, it can get you down. So the sooner this is over, and we are all back enjoying Sunday roast with Mum again of a special weekend in Stanley Road, the better.

We play a lot of what the navigation officer calls cat and mouse. Though I have some trouble deciding sometimes which of these we are. I am learning morse code, with a view, in due course, to taking the radio operator's course (of course!)

I write to Mum regularly, but have no way of knowing if my letters get to her. I suppose the more I write, the better the chance that she will receive at least some of them. My letters to Mum are cheery, of course, but I do worry about her living so close to the docks. There is so much talk and rumour, among the crew, of air raids. Nobody can tell me if Liverpool is being bombed.

Hope things are not too prickly for you in the desert. Since you are likely to get home leave before I do, please give Mum a big kiss from her littler lad

I love you and miss you, Jack,

With all best wishes from your loving brother,

Tom.

Finlay had to fight the urge to weep after reading this. He felt the love he had for his brother overwhelming him in panic and despair. He struggled to rise above these impulses, knowing he had to, but at the same time was contemptuous of himself, for being able to do so. The innocence that he had not been gifted with, he had always celebrated through his brother, whose own innocence, through cunning and aggression, Finlay had been able to protect. He loved his brother, but knew he had used Tom as a surrogate for those qualities he had failed to come by in himself.

Now, his brother shivered in a tube of riveted steel under the Baltic Sea, beyond his help, or harbouring. Was it why he hated the enemy so?

Partly it was, he reasoned, sipping Babcock's Scotch. But he hated them too because of their bombing of this city, for their crude and relentless method of destroying his country and its way of being. And he hated the vile reasoning that fed their will for conquest.

Summoning physical courage had never been a difficulty for Finlay. It came to him in anger, or in indignation, conjured as easily as the will to stand and fight against unfavourable odds in a Friday-evening pub brawl, or during the dark part of the night in a Borstal dormitory. Thinking about what Grey had said, and the Major, and most particularly White, he wondered, though, if he had half the stuff they so relied on him now to provide.

He brushed his teeth in the small mirror above the sink. The pads of his fingers and thumb were tender with pressure against the toothbrush handle. But neither of his hands would require a bandage tomorrow. He peeled the dressing from his cheek. The blister had broken and fluid oozed from the raw flesh down his face. But that burn too would be much better by the morning. Jack Finlay had always been a quick healer. Given his occupation, his body was hardly scarred at all.

Four

JUST AFTER six o'clock the following morning, Finlay was
telephoned by the Watch Commander at the Moorgate station
and informed that a parachute bomb was swinging, unexploded,
from its silk canopy, which had snagged on the arm of a hoist
extending from the loading bay in the storage loft of a building in
Mitre Street under his care.

He visualized the building as he sprinted up the spiral of iron
steps to the street. Four floors. Brick construction, impacted on
both sides by much older buildings made from heavy sections of
quarried stone. He ran across Bishopsgate. There was a smell of
burn on the eastern breeze from the direction of Wapping and the
docks. Finlay ran along Camomile Street, Absalom House a
shiver of black to his right as he passed it. The Mitre Street
building had pitch on the roof, oak floors and joists of ancient,
bone-dry spruce. He had done what he could there, but had been
helpless to do anything about the library of parched reference
books and the arid forests of files that crowded every floor. He
had asked for the basement to be flooded. But he had also asked
for the hoist on which the bomb had snagged to be removed and
that had not been done. His building in Mitre Street would
desiccate under the impact of explosion and then burn to brick
dust and rubble in fierce indifference to the play of the Moorgate
station hoses. Finlay hurled along Bevis Marks, right into
Creechurch Lane and left into Mitre Street, where ARP warders
jostled warily with fire fighters and men dressed in the uniform of
the City of London Police in a wide semi-circle, under the

48

pendulum swing of the hanging bomb. Among those in attendance, Finlay recognized the Moorgate Watch Commander, Nevin.

'What do we do now?' Finlay asked him. 'Wait for the UXB boys?'

'You tell me,' Nevin said. 'No one will tell me why, but I'm told it's you that calls the tune.'

Finlay nodded. 'It is. But I've been on this job a fortnight. I thought I'd seek the benefit of home advantage, that's all.'

Nevin took his eyes away from the slowly turning bomb and looked at him.

'That's appreciated, Jack. The first thing to say is that we haven't a fucking clue what it is we're dealing with here. A conventional parachute bomb can weigh eight hundred pounds. That thing doesn't look like it carries more than seventy. My bet is it's an experimental piece of ordnance. Very volatile. Almost certainly a combination of HE and incendiary. If it goes off, I've got the two tenders you can see and a core team of six experienced men. There isn't a fire hydrant within a thousand yards.'

'The basement?'

'Dry.'

'Adjacent?'

'Dry.'

'Opposite?'

'Dry.'

'Shit.'

'It gets worse,' Nevin said. 'Bomb disposal have taken a terrible hiding during the night trying to defuse a cluster of delayed actions dropped around a fuel dump in Silvertown.' He nodded at their bomb. 'It means there's no chance of anyone except us dealing with this fucker.'

'Sum up our options.'

Nevin scratched his chin. Finlay could smell smoke drifting on the easterly from the night fires in Wapping, Rotherhithe, Shadwell, Bermondsey. He did not need Richard Nevin to tell him it had been a bad one. Soot particles drifted like black rags above their heads. A blackened sky stained the early morning into twilight. Above them, their bomb swayed.

'Our options are these,' Nevin said. 'We can try to trigger it ourselves with the play of a hose. We can ask for a couple of volunteers to try to bring it down and take it somewhere we can detonate it safely. Or we can bring it down and dump the sodding thing in the river. It could be a dud. But then, why waste the parachute silk? It could be booby-trapped. It could be a delayed action. In which case, we'd better get a move on.'

Finlay nodded. He knew that bombs were attached to parachutes to try to guarantee precision in hitting their target, not to deliver a nasty surprise. He unbuckled his belt and began to unbutton his tunic. 'Keys to the building?'

'Can't locate them,' Nevin said.

'Raise me an extension ladder,' Finlay said. 'Clear the ground. I'll bring it down.'

'No you fucking well won't.'

Nevin and Finlay turned. Grey stood behind them, a Burberry mackintosh belted over Paisley pyjamas, leather mules on his sockless feet. He had his hands thrust into his mackintosh pockets and his hair hung over his forehead, uncombed. He looked angry, unshaven and louche. 'I thought your priorities had been spelled out,' he said to Finlay.

'I've been given personal responsibility for the safety of this building.'

'You look after more than one building,' Grey said, lighting a cigarette. 'And you have a responsibility to stay alive.'

Nevin was looking hard at Grey. 'Who are you?'

Grey ignored him. 'You are in charge here,' he said to Finlay. 'Have the Watch Commander request two volunteers to bring that thing down.' He jabbed with the fingers holding his cigarette at the swaying bomb. 'A lot of lives depend on these premises staying intact and operational. See to it.'

Nevin gathered his half-dozen regular men and asked for volunteers. A sallow-faced fire fighter who looked to be aged in his mid-forties said that he would have a go. Then, after a hesitation, a younger man said that he would chance it, too.

Nevin brought his volunteers back to where Finlay stood. 'Ball and Sweeney,' he said.

Finlay looked at the older man. 'Do you have a family, Ball?'

Ball nodded. 'Two boys, both ground crew in the RAF. My youngest, Sally, has been evacuated to Wales. And the missus is at home in Hoxton, I trust making my dinner.'

Finlay looked at Nevin. Ball read the look.

'With respect, Chief Fire Officer, I can't exactly fight shy of explosives and expect to do my job.'

'This is a voluntary task.'

'And I've volunteered. When my number's up, it's up. Till then, I'm not losing sleep. After that, I won't have to.' Ball's sallow face broke into a grin that stretched the cheeks across their bones.

Finlay thought that whatever Mrs Ball was feeding her husband, it wasn't enough. He looked at Sweeney, who just looked sheepish in the glare of the senior officers' scrutiny. The two men shrugged off the harnesses carrying their sets of breathing apparatus and unbuttoned their tunics. This was a job that called for delicacy rather than the regulations manual and they would attempt to carry it out, on this twilit autumn morning, in their shirtsleeves.

'What say we smash down the street door, sir?' Ball said. 'We'd have a more stable platform for dealing with the bomb from the interior of the loading bay.'

'No,' Finlay said, 'we'll tackle it from outside.' He had asked for steel doors with deadbolts to be fitted, sealing every floor when the building was unoccupied. He did not know whether this had been done, or the recommendation ignored like his other requests. But even battering through the street door would cause unacceptable delay. And if the bomb were to go off, Finlay did not want it going off inside the building, where the damage would be most devastating.

As the men were about to go, Sweeney turned slyly back. 'You're Jack Finlay,' he said. 'My brother was on your crash crew when you boarded the *Empress*.'

Finlay groped back in time. 'Ted Sweeney,' he said. 'Couldn't ask for a more solid bloke. When you see him next, tell him all the best from an old comrade.'

Sweeney flushed like a boy and the two volunteers turned towards their task.

'Good luck, lads,' Finlay called after them.

Sweeney went up the ladder and shuffled on his backside along the lip of the loading bay to a position where he could try to cut or unravel the parachute from the arm of the hoist. Nevin's men had set up a safety cordon. From behind it, Nevin offered Finlay a cigarette. Finlay declined it with a shake of his head. Ball climbed the ladder as far as the level at which the bomb was suspended, twenty feet below the hoist and forty feet above the paving stones and cobbles of the street. The bomb was three and a half feet of polished, cylindrical steel with a swastika stencilled neatly in red on the gentle swell of its nose cone. If it goes off now, he'll be vapour, Finlay thought, watching Ball. They both will. Sweeney signalled with a soft whistle that the parachute was unsnagged and therefore he was taking the weight; and, like a skilled child constructing a cat's cradle, Ball gathered the six strings of sash cord securing the bomb to its canopy of silk and nodded to his colleague to let go. Silk drifted downwards. Carrying the bomb balanced on one shoulder, Sweeney descended the ladder. Nevin had been slightly off. From the way Sweeney moved, Finlay judged the weight of what he carried to be about eighty pounds. An inert weight of eighty pounds was not a huge amount for a trained and experienced fire fighter to have to bring down a ladder. But the knowledge that it could blow him to pieces might add somewhat to the burden.

Ball brought the bomb down to the street. Fire crew had fetched a stretcher from somewhere and, with the tenderness they would have accorded a wounded man, placed the bomb on the waiting stretcher and bore it away at a solemn pace.

'You've good men,' Finlay said to Nevin.

Nevin nodded and smoked. 'There's no call for any other sort just now,' he said.

Finlay turned to speak to Grey. He wanted to say something sardonic about Ball and about Ball being a fatalist and about what White had said about fatalism and it not winning wars. But Grey had gone.

'It's a simple enough mistake. In a man so born-yesterday naïve as you are,' Babcock said,

Finlay scraped Palmolive suds and bristle off his chin and shook his safety razor in the water in the sink. 'What is?'

'Mistaking greed for valour.'

Finlay took his chin between his fingers and steered his reflection this way and that. The burn on the skin over his cheekbone had healed to a shiny patch of pink. He would look presentable, which he would need to do. 'When was I guilty of that particular blunder?'

'Thinking your Moorgate volunteers were merely brave. Of course, you wouldn't know how hard it has become for women to find new clothes. So you wouldn't know the black-market price of parachute silk. You act with the sinlessness of the fanatic, in the sanctity of unshakeable faith. That's why you'll burn.'

Finlay dropped his razor with a plop and turned. Babcock sat on Finlay's cot, polishing Finlay's boots.

'Like one of those zealots sent to the stake in the Inquisition,' he said. 'I'm speaking metaphorically. I don't mean literally burn.'

'I should bloody well hope you don't,' Finlay said. 'Do you know I told Grey you were a Communist?'

'He wouldn't care. This is a country with a tradition of religious toleration and an honourable history of political dissent. We can't all share your rigid conviction about everything. It isn't British. Doubt. Prevarication. Fudge. These are part and parcel of our culture. If you think about it, you'd probably be a lot more comfortable fighting for the other side.'

'I'd feel a lot more comfortable fighting,' Finlay said. 'How did you meet Grey?'

'I was his batman.' He looked at the boot and the polishing brush in his hands. 'Talk about old habits dying hard.'

'Tell me about Gommecourt Wood.'

Babcock looked at Finlay for a long time with an expression

Finlay had not seen on his sharp, rodent face before. It was an expression more complex and ambivalent than Finlay would have thought that narrow set of features capable of.

'For a start, it wasn't Gommecourt Wood,' Babcock said. 'It was at a place called Serre, which lay between Gommecourt on our left and Beaumont Hamel to our right. There was a Serre Road. There was a settlement, a village, called Serre.'

'Past tense?'

'I don't know what they call it now, Chief Fire Officer Finlay. Or if it is still called what it was then, or if it even still exists. I do know that it cannot exist any more as it did then. Nothing does. But if you want to know about what happened to Captain Grey there, best ask him. I offered to polish your boots and press your dress uniform for your appointment at Absalom House. I never agreed to talk about Gommecourt Wood.'

Finlay had breakfasted with Nevin in the Moorgate station canteen and spent the rest of the day housekeeping at all his buildings but for the thin black pile in Camomile Street. Among a catalogue of tasks, he saw to it that the Mitre Street basement was flooded and two inches of powdery sand spread in close-packed bakers' trays across the joists under Mitre Street's pitch-heavy roof. He had got back tired and satisfied and was writing a letter to Tom when Grey telephoned, telling him to attend an appointment at Absalom House at six the following evening.

'I'd like a set of keys to all my buildings,' Finlay said into the receiver.

There was a silence.

'Grey?'

'Being a bit proprietorial, aren't we?' Grey said.

'I asked for the Mitre Street basement to be flooded. It wasn't done. I asked for steel doors with deadbolts to isolate the stairwell access to each floor. It wasn't done. Have you any notion as to how fast fire, unimpeded, travels upwards?'

'Skilled manpower and materials are in short supply at present,' Grey said. 'We take your recommendations very seriously. But things sometimes take time.'

'Perhaps in that case we should ask Herr Goering to give his pilots a few weeks' leave.'

'That's puerile, Finlay. Even by your standards.'

'I apologize.'

'Good. You need the practice.'

'But it would have been better if I had had a set of keys this morning. Surely you can see that?'

'Sorry Finlay, no can do. This is one of those frequent occasions where security concerns override practicality. If it were up to me, you would have five sets of keys cut within the hour. But it isn't, and so you won't.'

Finlay said nothing. He listened to Grey breathe. The quality of the connection was astounding.

'Good luck with Miss Lange tomorrow evening,' Grey said. He hung up.

Dusk, in collusive shadows, was claiming the corners of the atrium by the time Finlay pushed open its elaborate door and entered. Rebecca Lange sat in the chair she had occupied so fleetingly during their first encounter. In the starved light there was something monochromatic about her. Her painted lips looked black. She was wearing a charcoal suit with cloth-covered buttons and her legs, crossed at the knees, emerged from the skirt in stockings of black silk. A clatter of ebony bracelets slid down her arm when she rose to acknowledge Finlay's entrance. The arm they embellished was as pale as bone.

'Chief Fire Officer Jack Finlay,' he said.

'Rebecca Lange.'

She held out a hand and he shook it. Her flesh was surprisingly warm in the cool of the room and her detachment. 'It must be terrible for you, Chief Fire Officer. Having to go about denuded of all your brass and gilt.'

'Black-out precautions. I'm sure you'd enjoy a cigarette, Miss Lange.'

'Dying for one,' she said.

'You see? We all have to make sacrifices.'

She laughed. The stars were finding the sky and their light dabbed filaments of silver into the loose weight of her hair. He smelled her perfume and could tell that it was fresh and felt flattered, and foolish for feeling it, that she should have gone to the trouble of putting it on.

As the dark descended fully, the stars and an occasional sliver of moon were adequate to see by under the dome of glass. Rebecca Lange gestured to the chair set at an angle to hers and Finlay took off his cap and they sat.

'Do you find that chair comfortable?'

'It is exactly the same as the one you are sitting on.'

'That is not what I asked you.'

Finlay patted the leather flanks of the chair. 'It's fine.'

'It is a Barcelona chair,' she said. 'Does that mean anything to you?'

'That it was made in Barcelona?'

'What a literal mind you have.'

'Barcelona is a place I associate with bombs. Not furniture.'

'Quite a brutal haircut you've had since your last visit, Chief Fire Officer. It reminds me of the heads of those statues from imperial Rome. Except that you don't quite have the imperial nose.'

'My nose was broken a few years ago.'

'How was that?'

'A difference of opinion with someone intent on buggering me.'

'I take it he failed.'

'He succeeded in breaking my nose. Is your conversation always like this?'

'I find the English have a remoteness. It's very dreary. Sometimes it amuses me to try to overcome it.'

Finlay nodded. 'Like a child smashing the ice on a pond.'

'No, Chief Fire Officer. Not like a child at all.'

For a moment the room was silent and still. London was dumb beyond the vaulted glass of the Absalom dome. Finlay was sensitive to how much the darkness impinged upon them all. He was suddenly and desolately aware of the soft, pale, flaccid life that was the only kind of life that thrived in darkness. He fancied he heard the drone of impending aircraft. Then he remembered that the atrium was soundproof. He listened again. It was the thrum of piped water under pressure.

'Our plumbing hasn't been what it was since it was connected to the new boiler or generator or whatever it was you had us install,' said Rebecca Lange. 'One of your conscientious objectors did the work. I might say, not very conscientiously.'

Finlay did not reply.

'Perhaps he thought the task unnecessary.'

'As you did?'

She shrugged.

'For reasons I don't understand, you use a lot of power in this building. You were generating that power with an engine that ran on petrol. Petrol is very volatile and the fumes it produces even more so. In Absalom House, you stored your petrol supplies in metal drums. It does not take a huge increase in the ambient air temperature to turn a drum filled with petrol and petrol fumes into a bomb. The diesel engine is much safer and should be just as efficient.'

'Except that your conchie made such a shitty job of fitting it.'

Finlay was aware of the problem. Most of the men who combined ability with good will towards war work were wearing a combat uniform, or were already engaged on essential projects. His own work timetable had got bogged down for lack of available manpower and tasks grudgingly carried out often by men without the skills to complete them adequately. He had discussed his schedule in detail with Grey as soon as he had assessed the buildings in his charge and set out his requirements and they had been sanctioned. Finlay had planned to work predominantly through the days while he checked on the progress of his fire precautions and then, on their completion, switch to nights, on permanent standby through the duration of the night raids. But it had not worked that way. It had not worked because sowing chaos and confusion was one of the principal objectives of the raids.

'Jerry believes so utterly in order, he thinks that nothing enervates his enemy so much as random assault,' Grey had said to him. 'But we know that Jerry is not a random animal. These raids are planned. Targets are specific, charts plotted, missions logged and flightpaths painstakingly mapped.'

'How does that help us?'

'It doesn't. Not without high-level infiltration.'

'Which I take it we don't have.'

'We need something that will enable us to detect the massed bomb formations earlier.'

'Better eyesight?' Finlay said. 'Sharper hearing? Clairvoyance?'

But Grey had just smiled.

'What are you thinking?' Rebecca Lange asked him now.

'How nice it would be to go for a drink, Miss Lange. Just to stroll through the streets and find a pub and sit down and have a drink and a conversation.'

'The English don't have conversations. They have chats.'

'I'd like a conversation. And a drink.'

'If you are inviting me for those, you had better call me Rebecca and not Miss Lange.' She stood. 'What shall I call you?'

'Anything but Chief Fire Officer,' he said, standing. He was aware of the accelerated pulse of an artery pressing against his tunic collar. He put on his cap. 'Just Finlay would be comfortable.'

They stood there for a moment in the dark. He could feel her heat.

'I am very sorry, Rebecca, for my conduct during our prior meeting.'

'I am too, Finlay,' she said. 'I can on occasion be something of a bitch.'

She was able to conjure a taxi from somewhere. He did not ask her how. He wanted to settle into the swift slipstream of the woman's headlong momentum, not to hinder her impulsive progress with the sort of detail that had dogged his own every day since his unwilling delivery from the desert.

'Rathbone Place,' she told the driver.

Lightless, almost blind, the car hugged the dark kerb as they crawled along Gresham Street and then nosed along Aldersgate and groped towards Clerkenwell Road. A light rain had started to fall and the cab windows were open an inch on either side of its passengers to prevent their breath from steaming the glass. Passengers as well as driver shared the responsibility of trying to navigate safely the hazards of the blacked-out city. Stretches of the journey were visited by a darkness so absolute that the sounds, and more particularly the smells, seemed acute and pressing in the confined space in which they travelled. Finlay was shockingly aware of his proximity to Rebecca Lange. He could smell her scent, hear her breathing, taste the lingering sweetness of Virginia tobacco on her breath. Once, the silk of her leg brushed the uniform serge of his thigh, sending a jolt of unexpected sensation through him.

'Are we going to one of your regular haunts?'

'Ssh,' she said. 'I cannot think in English, blind.'

'I'm sorry.'

She found his arm and lightly squeezed his bicep. Then she squeezed it again, as if to check that the shape she had found through his sleeve really did have the familiar density of flesh. He felt her hand fall away.

There was a bitter smell through Finlay's inch of open window as their taxi fumbled along Theobalds Road. He recognized the odour of charred timbers from a fire put out by hoses. Burn and drench mingled in his nostrils with the smell of singed fabric and scorched paint. We must be passing a bomb site and its adjacent fire breaks, Finlay thought, feeling again the odd, vertiginous sensation he had felt passing a similar absence of mass on the Strand. It was forlorn and dizzying, as though a whole block, all its tumult and life, had been torn from there. He was forced in the profound darkness then to remind himself that buildings were just buildings and did not possess souls. The car trundled up New Oxford Street to the junction with Charing Cross Road. Throughout the journey, both passengers had been sitting in thrall to the sound of the air-raid siren. Everyone did everything by night sensitive to the siren's drear, despairing wail. So when they turned right off Oxford Street, into the dead-end of Rathbone Place and it had not come, Finlay wondered if Rebecca shared the same sense of exhilaration as he did at their freedom so far from the huddle and tedium of sheltering from bombs.

'Account,' she whispered to the driver after they had got out and closed the door. Finlay could just see the man nod as he put the cab back into gear and receded without payment into the surrounding darkness. Faintly, Finlay thought that he could hear piano music. He followed the click of Rebecca Lange's heels to a door. She pushed against the door, which opened on to a tiny vestibule. She closed the door behind them, adjusting its heavy black-out curtain. Then she pulled open a second door, opposite the first, and they went through it, emerging from their closeted space into the full sound and antic fury of a crowded London pub.

Crowded was not quite right, Finlay thought, as they found a small table and two chairs, easily enough, against a broad drape of black-out curtain on the far side of the bar from the entrance they had used. The bar itself was four deep with shouts and gesticulation, but the pub's hinterland, in contrast, was populated by small huddles and the odd lone drinker. Finlay went and fetched them each a drink. His first impression had been created, he realized, by the sheer flamboyance and disparity of the individuals who made up the throng at the bar. There was a woman there with a monocle screwed into one eye socket. She was smoking a cigarette through an amber holder the length and thickness of a crochet needle and wore her hair not much longer than a man would. He noticed that almost none of the men wore a tie. They reminded him a little of a group of Polish pilots he had seen on home leave in a pub in Crosby, the Poles regulars there while they learned to fly British fighters at the Freshfield aerodrome. Except that the Poles had worn their clothes better pressed and had been clean-shaven and buffed their shoes to a shiny brilliance before they ever left their barracks. A woman in a tight dress of orange leopardskin and a grey fur stole whistled from the bar at Rebecca Lange and then winked. The whistle made one or two heads turn and Finlay saw nods of acknowledgement and greeting which Rebecca responded to with a wave.

'What's the occasion?' he said as he sat.

Rebecca took a cigarette from a packet in her bag and tapped it on the table-top. He realized that she was waiting for him to light it for her.

'I'm sorry,' he said. 'I don't carry matches.'

She took a gold lighter from her bag and lit the cigarette herself and blew out smoke. 'Occasion?'

'Event. Celebration.'

'I don't know what you're talking about.'

'There are as many women here as men.'

'Yes?'

'This is a public house.'

She looked at him through eyes narrowed by smoke. Then she laughed, wagging a finger. 'I should have spotted the accent. The flat vowel sounds. Remiss of me. You are a northern boy, aren't you, Finlay? A provincial.'

Finlay felt himself stiffen and then made an effort to relax. Perhaps she was entitled to a joke at his expense. He leaned across the table, confidentially. 'Tell me. Did they ever catch that Jack the Ripper?'

She leaned towards him with a conspiratorial look on her face but was interrupted by a scrape of chair leg and the bulk of someone sagging into a seat next to hers and whatever it was she had intended to say stayed unspoken.

'Becks,' the man said. He was big-faced and florid and breathing heavily. There was beer, wet between the fullness of his short upper lip and his nose. Then Finlay saw that it was not beer, but sweat. Aware of Finlay's scrutiny, the man turned to him and gave him the slightest of nods, taking Finlay in for much longer than the duration of the nod.

'Becks,' the man said again. One syllable was enough to spell Dublin to Finlay.

'Darling,' Rebecca said. She squeezed the shoulder nearest her through the man's overcoat and a smile jabbed in his face. He took her cigarette packet out of her bag and picked up her lighter from the table, lit the cigarette and dropped the lighter into his pocket. Finlay put the heels of his hands against the table to rise but Rebecca covered one of them with hers as she tilted her head at him slightly and smiled. Finlay emptied his weight back into his chair. The man exhaled in Rebecca's direction.

'I don't think your pretty new pal likes me,' he said.

Rebecca said nothing. She squeezed Finlay's fingers. The thrill of her touch mingled in him with dissipating fury.

'Pretty boy would probably like to knock my teeth so far down my throat that I'll be chewing the rest of my life through my arsehole,' the Irishman said.

Finlay breathed and said nothing.

'Pretty lost his tongue?'

'I'm sure you'd rather suck than chew.'

'Stop it,' Rebecca said.

Finlay turned to her. 'Let's go somewhere else.'

'A Liverpool man.' the Dubliner said. 'Am I right in thinking you've an Orange Lodge in Liverpool?'

'Stop it, please,' Rebecca said.

Finlay looked at the Dubliner. 'Am I right in thinking that the first bomb exploded in this country in this war was an Irish bomb, planted by Republicans outside a Bayswater shop?'

The Dubliner stared and smoked. 'Whiteley's of Bayswater. Hardly a mere shop.' He picked up Finlay's glass and drained it. 'I'll be seeing you,' he said.

'I can't wait.'

The Dubliner rose to his feet and lumbered away.

Finlay reached into his pocket and pulled out a gold Dunhill lighter. He smiled and slid it back to its owner across the table.

'How on earth did you do that?'

'You need to go to the right school. Is that character really a friend of yours?'

'He is quite charming sober. And he's a wonderful writer. You should read him. Once there's paper for books again, he's bound to attract a major publisher.'

'They'll be publishing him posthumously if his manners don't improve.'

Rebecca laughed. 'What is an Orange Lodge?'

Finlay sighed. 'In nineteen-sixteen, my father was killed in France, fighting for this country. Three years later, his widow's mother was evicted from her home in a Tipperary village by a British army of occupation. It's quite possible men my father served with put her cottage to the torch. What's certain is that men risked their lives trying to bring my father back to our lines as he died in no-man's-land of his wounds. History is more complicated than that writer fellow thinks. Perhaps he ought to read more. What's the matter?'

Rebecca was looking at him with an expression of amazement. 'That's the first thing I've heard you say that wasn't connected with fire prevention,' she said.

Finlay laughed. He could not remember the last time he had laughed and doing so now felt like a kind of liberation. When he looked, Rebecca was smiling at him and he saw a release in the smile that had not been there before. Maybe tonight they would be spared the caterwaul of the air-raid siren. As he rose to fetch fresh drinks from the bar, he was surprised at how ardent was his wish for that release.

'There's still the matter of your atrium,' Finlay said.

'Ah. My atrium. I knew there would be a point, Chief Fire Officer, at which we would have to come back to that.'

The pads of his fingers searched for and found the geometric cuts in the crystal of his whisky tumbler. A feeble night light in an ocean of darkness suggested a tiny rectangle of gold in the motioning surface of his drink. Somewhere within himself, Finlay knew that he was trying to summon pain to his still tender hands to bring sobriety. He put the drink down on the low glass table separating him from Rebecca Lange.

'I ought to go.'

'Yes. You ought. I'd go further and say you ought to have gone.'

'You know – of course you know – your English is almost perfect.'

She laughed. Her laughter was heavy with tobacco and drink. 'Don't insult me with almost.'

'You smoke too much.'

'Everyone smokes too much. It's the Benzedrine. It's the times in which we live.'

'Your use of the word "provincial" gives you away. Gave you away tonight, at least.'

'It was last night.'

'"Provincial" is an adjective in England. Rarely a noun.'

For a time she said nothing. Then, 'That must have been a formidable school you attended, Finlay.'

They had left The Wheatsheaf and drifted between other north Soho pubs: The Fitzroy Tavern, The Marquis of Granby, The Black Horse. The same shabby, disparate, dandified mood prevailed in each of these places. It seemed to Finlay as though their clientele drank with an air of gloomy defiance, as though there was something heroic in getting properly drunk in the black-out's fugitive, miserly light, shuttered and still vulnerable at the defenceless heart of the city. Finlay did not find the mood contagious. His last, abbreviated evening in a pub had been with Albert Cooper in The Windmill, where Albert had told him thirsty fire fighters found the insipid beer and even the glasses they drank it from in short supply at the end of their shifts. So Finlay did not share what he assumed to be the prevailing conviction among the men in the pubs Rebecca took him to. He did not think wearing an open-neck shirt while you drank too much an act of gallantry or subversion. But he did, for the night, enjoy the company that Rebecca provided and the company she kept. He had not spent time before with such talkative, picturesque people and he appreciated their novelty.

Over their last drink, late, at a pub called The Highlander, Finlay asked Rebecca where it was she lived. He offered to walk her home and she accepted. There was enough starlight, through a skein of high cloud, for them to see by. Finlay was still educating his eyes to the absence of light and could make little but abstract geometries of the edgings of silver he saw on slate, marble, iron and stone. But Rebecca was expert at reading the dark and she guided them confidently to their destination.

Her home occupied the top floor of a four-storey block behind the British Museum. An enclosed stone staircase zigzagged up to her door. Ascending the steep steps, Finlay was reminded of Grey's assertion that these days all the significant people lived in holes in the ground. Rebecca locked the door behind them and then illumination crept with a hiss around the walls, defining the dimensions of the space they were in. Finlay turned and saw Rebecca adjusting a tap on the wall.

'Gas lanterns,' she said.

He looked around. The room seemed enormous after the black claustrophobia of the streets. His senses returned swiftly, but the space was still much bigger than the average sitting-room. Its furniture seemed to Finlay very much at one with the Barcelona chair. The floor was teak and scattered with rugs, and pictures, thick with pigment, portrayed a world wholly unfamiliar to him on her otherwise bare walls.

Rebecca went over to a gramophone player, hitched her skirt and sat on her haunches sifting through the piles of records scattered underneath it. The long and slender outline of her thigh curved hard against her skirt and her skirt hugged tightly across her hips. Her hair had fallen forward and as she shuffled through the record sleeves, all that Finlay could see of her face was the pale set of her jaw and her painted mouth, moving in silence as she read the titles to herself.

'What do you fancy?'

'Anything,' Finlay said. 'Really, anything at all.'

'If we ever become friends, I'll tell you about my schooldays,' Finlay said.

'I thought we were friends.'

'What do you do at Absalom House?'

'Voluntary work. Translation, basically. I'm afraid I can't really tell you any more than that.'

'It must be very important.'

'I wouldn't know,' she said. She stood and went over to the tall curtain shrouding her sitting-room from the night. She ran a hand across its ruched fabric. 'Please let's talk about something else.'

'All right,' Finlay said. 'Why are you so reluctant to hood your atrium?'

'My father's atrium,' Rebecca said. 'Why should I?'

'Light. From reflected fires, from detonations, from search-lights, tracer rounds, flak, flares, muzzle flashes, even from burning aircraft on the odd, fluke occasion that we manage to hit one. Glass covering darkness reflects light. And you have an entire dome of the stuff. The Germans would rather bomb what they can see. Anyone would. The roof of your atrium will glitter with reflected fire and their spotters will see it and they will target it and bomb it to oblivion.'

'I see,' Rebecca said, nodding. 'You want to put out my father's light.'

'Absalom House might survive the bombing if you do as I say. If you don't, your father's legacy to London architecture will be brick dust and rubble.'

There was a silence.

'What do you know about my father?'

'Only what Grey told me.'

'Who the hell is Grey?' Rebecca said.

Five

'YOU WERE supposed to apologize to her,' Grey said. 'Not fuck her.'

Grey was seated where White usually sat. The Immaculate Major was seated to his right. Before Grey, a collection of their vile biscuits occupied a thin green plate. Finlay looked up at the windows behind the two men. More tape had been applied to their panes. Mesh had been nailed across the exterior of the windows. There were fresher cracks in the glass than the cracks that had been fresh when last he had sat here. One of the big panes was so intricately fissured by blast damage that it looked more like a mosaic than a window. He could see enough through the others to observe that the errant barrage balloon had been retethered and supplemented in the air by others. They wore their camouflage clumsily against a sky that was unseasonably blue.

'I had an inkling that I was being followed,' Finlay said.

'An inkling,' the Major said. 'Chap had an inkling. And when precisely did this inkling occur?'

'After the first time I met White. Again when I left a gymnasium off the Strand. A third time when you dropped me off at Aldwych and I walked back from there in the rain to Liverpool Street. Footsteps following your own make a distinctive sound on wet pavements.'

Grey leaned forward and turned to the Major. 'We find our boy in unusually loquacious mood.'

'Sexual intercourse,' the Major said.

Grey seemed to consider this. He nodded and sat back in his chair.

'I did not sleep with her. Despite the chronic shortage of accommodation I keep reading about in what passes now for newspapers, Rebecca Lange lives in a large flat with plenty of space. It got very late and at her invitation I slept in her spare bedroom.'

'You are not being followed,' Grey said. 'Even if we had a very good reason for doing it, we simply do not have the resources. Babcock knocked to check on you, that's all. And when his knock went unacknowledged and he found the door to be locked, he took the relevant key from his keychain and discovered your absence.'

'Much as a gaoler might that of an absconded convict.'

'Dereliction of duty is a serious offence, Finlay.'

'I'm a civilian, Major. And I would have heard the air-raid warning from the fourth floor of a residential block in Coptic Street. I would have heard the siren even in the event of sexual intercourse. Does Babcock never sleep?'

Grey shifted in his chair.

'Babcock's wife has not dealt well with the death of their boy. Babcock will pretend that life goes on, that they queue just as they always did for the latest feature at the cinema. The reality is that Mrs Babcock resides in a sanatorium in Kent in what the doctors describe as a state of catatonia.'

'So Babcock has time on his hands.'

'He does,' the Major said. 'But not enough to go following firemen about.'

'Tell us your impression of Rebecca Lange,' Grey said. 'Leave nothing out.'

Knowing now why he had been summoned, Finlay felt able to relax. He lifted the cup from the saucer cradled in his lap and sipped his tea.

'There isn't much to tell,' he said.

Frederick Lange had headed his own prosperous architectural practice in Munich. His style, which his daughter described as modern eclectic, made him very popular. His buildings flattered his clients into thinking they embraced a set of aesthetic values symbolic of a profitable future, soon to be handsomely realized in a smoked glass and smooth stone edifice strengthened by shoulders of steel. His work did not threaten those who commissioned it with the prospect of public ridicule. It did not invite the risk of structural collapse. A building by Lange was typically an elegant and watertight construction delivered on schedule and within its allotted budget. Nobody would have said so, but he was successful, more than anything, because he was safe.

Richard Frentz had been a contemporary of Lange at the School of Architecture in Berlin. They had both studied as postgraduate students for a year in London, sharing a flat off Tottenham Court Road. Frentz was a brilliant student, a precocious talent intoxicated with ideas for grandiose public building projects fashioned from new materials which he would also develop for the purpose, heading a handpicked team of scientists and structural engineers. Eight years after their graduation, Lange was flourishing. And that was when Frentz, scraping a living drawing anonymous plans for any practice that would pay him piece rate for the work, knocked on the office door of his old student comrade and asked Frederick Lange for a job.

'He even had a job title dreamed up for his new position,' Rebecca told Finlay. 'He was to be called Chief Design Associate. When my father threw him out, he was crushed. But my father believed nobody could have taken him on after what happened in Düsseldorf. Between Düsseldorf and his turning up in Munich he must have lost a portion of his sanity, my father said. Because Düsseldorf guaranteed that Richard Frentz would never work as an architect again.'

His Düsseldorf project was the first over which Frentz had been given total control. It was an accommodation block for the city's police cadets. Frentz was briefed to make it as comfortable and enduring as possible. He decided that the best way to make the building strong was to cement the bonds between each rigid element of construction with a new type of adhesive he had developed himself. The building was six months old and considered a great success when a discarded cigarette set fire to a wastepaper bin in a basement lavatory. The fire spread. And the adhesive Frentz had developed did not just burn with a tenacity the fire crews of Düsseldorf had never encountered before. Its toxic fumes killed one hundred and forty sleeping residents before a party of cadet revellers stumbled back there from a Bierkeller and finally raised the alarm.

'Frentz must have come to believe my father responsible in some way for his predicament,' Rebecca told Finlay. 'Probably it had something to do with their having been students together. Certainly it had something to do with my father refusing so adamantly to give him a job. I believe my father's success began to eat away at the man. An architect enjoys very public success. Frentz had been responsible for a very public tragedy.'

Early in nineteen-thirty-seven, a pamphlet appeared deriding the ideas that inspired the designs of Albert Speer, the architect picked personally by Hitler to give his Third Reich physical substance of suitable scale and majesty. The pamphlet, though published in France, was printed in German and widely distributed in Germany. It made nonsense of Nazi claims to an Aryan cultural heritage. It described Speer's blueprints for the Thousand Year Reich as an attempt to build a Babylonian Atlantis. In poking fun at his pet architect, the pamphlet derided the Führer himself. Rebecca Lange first heard the rumour that her father was the author of the pamphlet at a Berlin cocktail party in the autumn of 'thirty-seven. By then it had been banned. Her father was visited, by appointment, by an SS deputation in October. In December, he was requested to attend a further private interview. Shaken, he told his daughter later that both Goebbels and Speer had been present. He had been told that an old student colleague had identified him as the author of the pamphlet. Then he had been confronted with a manuscript copy, written word by painstaking word in his own hand.

'Like I said, Frentz was a precocious talent,' Rebecca told Finlay. 'A quite astonishing draftsman. I have no doubt he was the erstwhile colleague who informed on my father. Just as I have no doubt he was the architect of the forgery with which my father was confronted.'

Frederick Lange boarded a train in Munich in January of 1938. It was the last time anybody ever admitted to having seen him alive.

'My father was talented enough to know that he was not of the first rank,' Rebecca said. 'But he was a good man and a wonderful father. He was enormously proud of his London building because it fulfilled a dream born during the time he spent here. The Absalom dome is both a conceit and a tribute. He was honoured to be offered a building so close to Wren's great cathedral. The summit of Absalom was designed and built in homage to Wren's surpassing dome.'

Finlay said nothing. Then he said, 'Do you know what became of Frentz?'

'I believe he works in the offices of Albert Speer,' Rebecca said.

'What about Düsseldorf?'

'Düsseldorf was nineteen-twenty-eight. It was Weimar Germany. Apparently what happened then is of no importance. There is a new order in Germany now. Had nobody told you?'

'What do you make of her, Finlay?' This from the Major.

Finlay shrugged. 'You'll have to be more specific.'

'Do you think, for example, that she represents a security risk?'

'I don't know why you would think me qualified to answer that question. She was evasive about her work. She keeps pretty bedraggled company. She seems to have a good reason for hating the people who run her country.'

'What would you do with her?'

'She's a German, when all's said and done,' Finlay said. 'I'd lock her up for the duration. Intern her. We didn't get bombed in London last night, but I'll bet somebody copped it, somewhere. There'll be grief and destruction somewhere in England this morning.'

'Chatham,' Grey said.

'Well, then,' Finlay said.

'So you'd lock her up,' Grey said.

'I would.'

'But then, if you had your way, we'd be lynching captured air crew,' Grey said. At this the Major, who had been studying his gloves, glanced up sharply.

'I didn't say I'd string them from lampposts. I just said I'm surprised it hasn't been done.'

'Yes, well,' Grey said. 'The British are a tolerant people. Fair play and all that. And crippled aircraft usually attempt to crash-land in rural areas, where lampposts are in understandably short supply.'

Finlay didn't say anything. Then he said, 'I know you people think I'm some kind of lout, but I'm not. I just don't think that fair play will beat this enemy. That's all.'

The Major said, 'Do you find Rebecca Lange repulsive?'

'Not at all. I said that I didn't sleep with her. I didn't say I wouldn't like to.'

Grey and the Major looked at each other. The Major coughed. It was Grey who spoke.

'You're quite sure, Finlay, that we can't change your mind about a biscuit?'

Finlay had taken, when he had the time, to eating his midday meal at the Moorgate canteen. He missed the comradeship of the desert and the pals he had made there. In skirmishing with the Italians in the first year of the war he had struck up new friendships and lost none of his new friends to combat. The Italians had been lightly armoured, unambitious territorially. They had practised for the war with their invasion of Abyssinia and their routing of a hopelessly ill-equipped Abyssinian army. Colonel Baxter, even in command of antique guns, was a different order of opponent. For one thing, he was a Scot. He engaged his enemy with an intensity so ferocious it seemed to Finlay sometimes to border on glee. But he was a professional soldier too, as punctilious in the care of his men as he was in the cosseting of his ancient ordnance.

Finlay did not find easy friendships at the Moorgate station, as he had in Egypt. His rank and his reputation prevented it. He would never again in the fire service be merely one of the boys and had long accepted that. But he did find company there. If the men were a bit deferential, at least they were men in the same profession who faced similar dangers and spoke, as Finlay did, the language of fire, and who shared his understanding of the always fraught and sometimes lethal struggle to contain and defeat it. And there was Nevin. They did not share rank, but this was Nevin's ground and they were pragmatic and isolated enough as service veterans to ignore that fact when in one another's company. Finlay liked Nevin. He liked him for the quiet, obdurate way in which he marshalled his men and nightly fought the huge, anarchic, capering flames brought to his ground by the bombs. There had been nothing like it. In history, let alone in the history of their proud and defiant service, there had been nothing like it. But the men coped and Finlay admired the manner in which Richard Nevin led them.

'I don't remember food being this colour before the war,' Nevin said. 'Do you?'

Finlay looked at the object impaled on the end of Nevin's fork. It was fishy, fibrous, covered in a substance the colour and consistency of wallpaper paste. Or sperm, Finlay thought. It could easily be jism. Nevin popped the object into his mouth and began to chew, thoughtfully, the heavy stubble blue on his masticating jaw in the electric cafeteria light.

Finlay knew that Nevin didn't like him much. But then he didn't care all that much for himself. Company was company and beggars could not be choosers.

'How are things shaping?'

Nevin swallowed and winced.

'Minke,' he said. 'Mange, more like. If whales had been meant to be eaten, they'd have come in tins with keys on the top. Like corned beef. Or sardines.'

'It doesn't look too appetizing.'

'It tastes like what my wife has been saying no to ever since I uttered those two fatal words at the altar,' Nevin said.

'How do you know what that tastes like?'

'If I remember rightly, you told me,' Nevin said, with a grin. His teeth were pearly and viscous with the sauce. Finlay thought him entitled to the dig. Nevin had lost friends at Pimlico Rubber.

'You were right to gamble on the sausage and mash,' Nevin said.

Finlay looked at his plate. The potatoes formed a blighted pile that slopped over the blackened breadcrumb and fat of his lone sausage. He picked up the pepper pot and heaved pepper over the mess on his plate in a patina of gunmetal dust.

'Things are bad,' Nevin said, shifting his plate away and

resting his elbows on the table, the blue dimple of his chin swelled by its two supporting thumbs. 'We were heroes at the outset, Finlay. Evacuation, gas masks, predictions of mass bombing. The fire service were heroes then, our crews lauded wherever they went. Jerry was very clever, holding off the way he did. In the autumn of 'thirty-nine we were brave boys. By summer just gone, we were shirkers and conchies and fit only for public abuse. Which, by the way, is largely what we still come in for. And all because nothing happened.'

'Tell that to the Navy,' Finlay said.

Nevin belched and looked at him. The pressure of his thumbs did something cherubic to Nevin's chin. Finlay could see soot sunk beneath the surface of the skin around his eyes and felt sorry for the carelessness of his last remark.

'Why did you join up?'

'To do my bit.'

Nevin nodded. 'Lost that bit of dash you had, didn't you, after Pimlico.'

'No,' Finlay said. 'I didn't. I wanted to fight the enemy. It was a war. I volunteered. Is there something wrong with that?'

Nevin sat back in his chair and folded his arms across his chest.

Finlay realized how little it was he actually knew about the Moorgate watch commander. How old was Richard Nevin? Had Nevin fought in what they were now calling the 'fourteen–eighteen?

'I've lost twenty men in the past fortnight, Finlay,' he whispered; they did not have the canteen to themselves. 'Close to fifty in the last six weeks. I'm talking here about regular men. Blokes I trained myself. Men you'd walk through hell with. Men who'd follow you there.'

Finlay said nothing. His food congealed under its coating of ash. He could feel the heat of Nevin's indignation.

'The auxiliaries are good men, don't mistake me. They have the right idea and an abundance of heart and some of them are quick learners. But I'm losing men I can't replace. And the bombing is getting worse. And in the end, I haven't a fucking clue what it is I'm supposed to do.'

Finlay said nothing. He did not know what to say.

'You are a fly-boy, Finlay, always have been,' Nevin said. 'I've seen more common sense come out of my arsehole than I saw the other day when Jerry draped that bit of underwear in Mitre Street. Asking for the telescopic rig! I've heard about your talent on a ladder.'

Finlay said nothing.

'Going to sort it out yourself. Who are you? The cavalry? Errol fucking Flynn?'

Finlay said nothing. Nevin breathed what smelled like angry sperm across their table.

'I'll go,' Finlay said, rising.

'Stay.' Nevin whispered. He gathered his bowed head in the sanctity of his hands and spoke through the grill of his fingers. 'Please stay, Jack. If you go, I've no other fucker to talk to. Stay a bit?'

'I'll stay,' Finlay said, folding his reluctant body back into the discomfort of his seat.

Finlay was dozing on his cot when he heard the double rap of Babcock's urgent knock. He had eaten treacle tart for pudding with Nevin that both men agreed, in sufficient quantity, would have made a more than adequate road surface. He had walked the pudding off on the journey to the gym behind the Strand and had exercised there hard, with a picture of Rebecca Lange painted on his mind as he limbered and heaved over the gymnastics apparatus and the mat. Spent from his gym work, sore and satisfied from the massage that followed it, he had walked to Camomile Street and been surprised, despite himself, to see an enormous roll of tarpaulin being winched slowly, inch by inch, by a civilian works crew up the face of Absalom House. The black fabric cracked with tar paint in the grip of the hawsers binding it. A crowd gathered, mostly brokers in top hats and frock coats shiny at the elbow, to observe this spectacle through a thin drizzle of October rain.

Babcock entered the room without waiting for an invitation to follow his knock and Finlay saw from his urgency that something was very much up. He got off the cot and started to pull on his boots.

'North Sea Coastguard reports a substantial number of aircraft flying in strict formation on a bearing for London.'

'What about our fighters?'

'They're flying with an escort of more than fifty fighters. Fighter bombers too. Sounds like most of the bloody Luftwaffe is airborne. Looks like being the biggest raid yet. They'll be over their target in about twenty minutes.'

And their target is us, Finlay thought. He looked at his watch. In twenty minutes it would be dark.

'You know the drill, Chief Fire Officer,' Babcock said.

He did. He was supposed to stay in his cell until Babcock summoned him or the telephone rang. He was instructed to remain on alert. He thought about the tarp he had seen being winched upward in Camomile Street. Winched through a thin rain. Had the tarp been secured? Had the rain strengthened to make the Absalom dome slippery and treacherous, the job impossible? Rain would embrace the city in blankets of damp brick and leaf-choked runnels, clogged gutters, dripping eaves. But even a deluge would not easily douse fire ignited in the dry heart of a building, deep beneath its pierced roof, fire burning scattered, jelloid, fierce against wood-panelled wall, across polished floorboards, in among the brittle debris of broken furnishings, amok in the paper ruin of archives and files. As he sat in his tunic and boots and speculated on the dumb chaos to come, hundreds of feet above him, Finlay felt sweat gather at his hairline and trickle down into his eyebrows. He felt a trill of panic and looked at the two air feeds emerging from the ceiling as if to ensure that they were still there. He well knew how fire could rob the air of oxygen. The worry of being entombed by tons of rubble was newer to him, but part of the same debilitating cycle of anxiety he found visited him now that he was forced to wait rather than to respond instantly to crisis.

Finlay had seen this debilitation again and again on the faces of people in the streets. He had mistaken the pinched exhaustion into which it pulled their features for the look of capitulation. He had mistaken their weary appreciation of what resistance was going to cost for resignation and even for defeat. It occurred to him now, deaf to the rumble of aircraft delivering their random spillage of death, that Londoners were a long way from defeat. It was knowing the strength and obduracy of their own resistance that made them so wretchedly grim. They were in it for the long haul. They might very well die. Probably they would be obliged to grieve. Many had died and more still were grieving already. Suffering was their certainty, made absolute by the certain knowledge that they were not going to surrender.

By birth a Liverpudlian, Finlay had a Liverpudlian's ambivalence about the capital. But deep beneath the pavements they trod, deaf to the air-raid siren's ugly ululation, admiration seeped into his soul, now, for the stubborn natives of this city, as he sweated under his tunic and waited for the coming of his call. His realization made Finlay wish that he were commanding a fire crew in Silvertown or Rotherhithe, where the bombs aimed against the docks so often dropped instead into the cramped terraces adjacent to their yards and quaysides and warehouses. He could do genuine good there. He could deploy men and machinery to save lives and, where lives weren't threatened, to salvage stored and bonded stockpiles of precious rations.

He waited for his call. He sweated inside his tunic. He tried and failed to hear the remotest hint of the carnage filling his imagination from above. He fixed his eyes on the clumsy black reality of the telephone on the night table beside the cot on which he sat. With a sudden wrench of his torso he reached and pulled the receiver free of its cradle and pressed it against the side of his face. No dialling tone. Silence. The implement was dead. Finlay heard silence and pictured that silence dumb and black in the pitch of his mind.

He took the reaching spiral of iron steps two and three at a time until the steps began to jounce and sing beneath his booted feet with the vibration of the bombs. He could feel the volume of the bombs vibrating through his clenched teeth. Then he could hear them. Then he could hear nothing else, not even his own urgent breathing or the clank of his climbing feet, the rumble and thunder of bombs – all cordite and powder and dust – drifting into his nostrils with the stench of fire and the smell of steam from playing hoses as he gained the bright, burning surface, gasping, awed.

To Finlay, it seemed the sky itself was on fire. Gobs dripped molten from the sky and flames licked across its width. Then a great gout of flame gushed, giving him perspective, and he saw that the glass roof of the station reflected the fire burning on the tracks and platforms and cavorting, crimson, through the shattered windows and doors of train carriages. Rows of entire trains blazed like so many logs in a festive grate. The station awning burned too, panes melting and glass raining through the hiss of playing hoses as the crews beneath were forced to cower and dodge. Heat, fierce, roaring heat, forced Finlay to look away from the station and he turned towards Bishopsgate and saw the buildings there, monolithic and strange, lit for a moment by bomb blast and then gone, an after-image and then an orange dimness etched by the station fire. Above, in the real sky, Finlay could hear the drone of massed engines and see the play of searchlights and the white, staccato brilliance of tracer shells stretched in lines across the night. Above all this, the night had cleared and he could make out stars in constellations smudged by the black bulk of shifting bombers.

Coming to himself, he looked over towards the darkness above the triangle of streets containing the buildings in his charge. Nothing there glowed. No sparks or embers climbed and drifted. He could not have heard the clamour of a fire crew, but he strained to hear it anyway. As far as he was able to tell, the sound of the bombers was receding towards targets to the south-west; to the power station at Battersea and the great conglomeration of rails and rolling stock at Clapham Junction. He felt a tap on the shoulder and turned to see Nevin. Or rather he saw Nevin's eyes, the rest of Nevin's face soot black under his helmet in the orange firelight.

'Evening, Errol.'

'Fuck me,' Finlay said. 'Al Jolson.'

'They've hit every main-line station,' Nevin said. 'Every single one.'

'What can I do?'

Nevin smeared soot around his face to no noticeable effect with the back of one hand. The hand shook and in the firelight Finlay could see that the Moorgate man's eyes were veined with fatigue.

'Wouldn't Noel Coward object?'

'Noel who?'

'Your pal in the Paisley pyjamas.'

'Very good,' Finlay said. 'Very funny.'

'Most of the rolling stock is a write-off,' Nevin said, suddenly serious, nodding towards the burning railway station. 'One civilian nightwatchman dead. Two railwaymen dead. Three fire crew dead.'

'From?'

'Two from Mile End. One of mine. Sweeney.'

'Water mains?'

'It'd be a hell of a way to go, wouldn't it? Drowning under a blanket on an Underground platform.'

'You'd have plenty of company.'

'We can't keep getting away with it. But the answer is no. No mains ruptured. Not tonight.'

'What happened to Sweeney?'

Nevin looked down at the road over his folded arms and spat.

'You're familiar with sprinkler systems?'

'With the theory.'

'Yank bullion company owns a building behind the station. Equipped with sprinklers. Usual bogus fucking rumour about trapped personnel. I designate four men. Sweeney goes in at the head. Sprinklers activate. Only the tank that supplies the sprinklers is directly over the seat of the fire.'

'Jesus Christ.'

'He smelled like boiled ham by the time we got him out,' Nevin said. 'Boiled ham is what he looked like, too. Though I don't suppose I'll be telling that to his nearest and dearest.'

'Is there nothing I can do?'

Nevin looked at him and his eyes narrowed in his soot black face.

'We're pretty near to November the fifth,' he said. 'Maybe next time you could bring along a box of sparklers and some treacle toffee. My lads would appreciate that.'

Six

I T WAS seven o'clock in the morning by the time Finlay descended the spiral of iron steps to the cell in which he was quartered and where he was supposed to wait for the call to sound from his dead telephone. His descent was weary. He felt in every bone and sinew the exhaustion of spent adrenalin followed by dull routine performed in conditions that contrived to be mundane while carrying, always, the potential for death. In a sense, in his occupation, it had always been thus. The blackened walls and torn roofs of burned buildings always held the poised threat of collapse. Unearthing cellars and exploring basements in the search for trapped survivors had always been deeply uneasy work. But Finlay found that the unexploded bombs, the duds and incendiaries and the mines, sleeping and volatile, required a new level of wariness. The bomb risk did not just pervade, it threatened at moments to overwhelm the teams of tired fire fighters in spasms of hysteria and fast, deep currents of panic. Despite Nevin's levity, Finlay had stayed. He had spent the night clearing debris in danger of disintegration, and damping down. His arms ached from the effort of training the brass nozzle of a water-swollen hose over the smouldering innards of buildings and dowsing the skeletal glow and spark of Liverpool Street Station's train wreckage. His head ached from the stink of burning rubber and his eyes wept in protest at the greasy billow of its smoke.

Towards the dawn he had walked along Bishopsgate towards Houndsditch and taken a look at each of the five buildings in his care. They had been so close to the violence visited on the fabric of the city the previous night. But each of his buildings still stood. Each occupied its given position in still and massive indifference to the havoc only a few hundred yards away. They aim their bombs very well, Finlay thought. His head thumped dully with the brilliance of last night's explosions and his throat was raw with a cindertrack thirst. But the thought came to him with gloomy clarity. The enemy were getting better with every raid at their blind navigation of the night metropolis. They were aiming their bombs very well indeed.

'My God, look at you,' Grey said.

'A sight for sore eyes and no mistake,' Babcock said, 'Lummy.'

'That bar of Palmolive gone already?' Grey lay stretched the length of Finlay's cot with one hand on the pillow behind his head and the other holding a cigarette poised in front of his face. He appeared to be looking at the end of the cigarette, as if studying the rate at which it burned. Finlay saw that there were at least twenty cigarette butts in a zinc ashtray placed on the night table beside his redundant telephone. Tobacco smoke blurred the light in the upper reaches of the room and Finlay was aware of its taste, thin and sour on top of all the other things he had recently been obliged to inhale. Grey wore a white shirt and a loosened tie and suit trousers held up by braces. His feet were crossed and his trouser crease ran smooth from his thigh to the tip of his topmost shoe.

'Hope you don't mind if I smoke,' he said.

Babcock sat in the armchair, polishing Finlay's shoes. A shoe covered one of his hands, he held a cloth in the other, and Finlay thought he had never seen such a shine on the toecap of a shoe as he saw now. Grey's shoes were suede, which it occurred to him was odd, in a military man, but perhaps not so odd in a pansy. Finlay saw that Grey's suit coat had been hung by a hanger on a hook. Behind it, on a separate hanger, hung the suit they had given him, what he could see of it looking freshly pressed and brushed.

'What's going on?'

'Take that tunic off and scrub up, why don't you, while

Babcock here gets some of the rough off it,' Grey said. 'Babcock's a wizard with a brush, aren't you, Babcock?'

'What's going on?' Finlay said again.

'You and I are going for a spot of breakfast.'

Finlay rubbed the flat of his hand over his shorn hair. 'Feels more like dinner-time to me.'

'You don't want breakfast?'

'What I'd like is a pint of beer.'

'Capital,' Grey said. There was a hard glitter in his eyes that Finlay did not like. Grey rose from the bed and shrugged his coat from its hanger. 'Don't I know just the place.'

A drizzle was dousing, with gentle relentlessness, those smouldering remnants the fire fighters had failed to, when the two men gained the streets. Rain damped the smell of night destruction and did something to sweeten the bitter air. But the grey light brought by the rain inflicted a sodden atmosphere of wet depression and turned defeat from a foreboding into something Finlay felt he could almost touch.

'I know,' Grey said, breathing deeply, perhaps in an effort at exorcising nicotine and tar from tainted lungs. 'And it will get worse, believe me, before it starts to get better.'

Finlay did not think the remark worthy of reply. Nor did he think the insight that had prompted it remarkable. Trudging the wet, uneven pavements towards Wapping and the river, he had the strong sense that London was its own universe and his sentiments universal; shared unspoken by the huddles of slowly drenching men he saw toiling to restore what was no longer; engaged, all of them, in attempting to revive a thing they reluctantly knew to be already dead.

'It is always like this,' Grey said. 'Custom and habit are made concrete in the places we build to work and live among. The destruction seems at odds with what ought to be. A shift in the natural order. An obscenity, almost, because it so flouts the fragility of what we think are our solid foundations. A thing like this violates us. It confounds our faith.'

'Like Gommecourt Wood?'

Grey did not break stride. He sniffed savagely at the air and then hawked from corrupted lungs and spat towards the gutter.

'It was at Gommecourt Wood you lost your faith,' Finlay persisted.

Grey turned to him. His eyes were green and anger glittered in them despite the absence of light.

'It wasn't Gommecourt Wood, Chief Fire Officer, though Gommecourt was close enough. And it wasn't faith I lost. It was hope.'

They walked. Finlay tried to remember what London had smelled like before the war. Smoke had always been a strong part of it, of course. Smoke had embraced the city, snug almost, from the fires that heated people's homes, the coal furnaces that fired much of its industry, its oil-burning boilers and the mountains of coke that kept the heating pipes of its schools singing with warmth through desolate winters. There had been braziers to warm the working men on every building site and the smell of chestnuts was always present in the autumn, cracking with heat at the heart of braziers mounted on the chestnut sellers' West End stalls. Smoke from a million cigarettes had mingled nightly in the West End of the city with the more subtle, sweeter scent of perfume. In pockets of the city there had been the bitter smells of poverty and damp, and in the listlessness of summer sometimes the Thames would smell like the sewer the Victorians had allowed it to become in their proud and bustling civic midst. The city had smelled of horses, of course, and horse shit, in Petticoat Lane and Clerkenwell and Lower Marsh and Essex Road and all the other places where there were workshops and market stalls and the choking flux of trade and manufacture. Fleet Street and the Strand and Piccadilly had smelled of the burnt oil and petrol vapour of the motor car and the bus. Ozone had showered sometimes in a sour, singeing odour from the electric cables that guided London's tram cars over track and cobble. The fogs had mingled all of these smells into what Finlay thought of now as a comfort blanket of warmth and recognition under which the city had snuggled; sightless, safe, cosy in a dim reverie of secure celebration of its unchanging manner and custom and status in the world. The smell of London had been the smell of ritual, of celebration, of enterprise and sometimes of sleep. London had smelled of life; a life, for the most part, successfully lived. That smell, of course, was gone.

They came across a tea wagon on a corner in Cable Street. Two women were tending the wagon. Both wore their yellow hair in a garish flush extending across their shoulders from a scarf tied over the top of the head. Finlay had thought this fashion strange, almost tribal, when first he had seen it, worn by a woman skulking in an Aldwych doorway sneaking a cigarette during the black-out. It was ubiquitous, he had since realized. But he still thought it strange. The women tending the tea wagon wore bright lipstick in crimson, waxy smiles that smudged their teeth. Steam escaped upwards from the pressure valve on the big copper urn mounted on their wagon and when they poured tea into a mug from a tap at the base of the urn it smelled wonderful in the ash and damp of the morning.

Finlay sensed that Grey was tempted to stop. They slowed and he looked at the people queuing for tea. Most of them were old. They had mouths crimped around toothless gums and the eye sockets were too deep in their pinched, bony faces for Finlay easily to read their expressions. They waited in a motionless shuffle for their moment at the urn and their portion of its black, sugarless beverage.

'Wonderful stuff, tea,' Grey said, and Finlay thought to himself. 'Amazing what men can accomplish on a humble mug of tea. Even on the promise of tea.'

'My father was there,' Finlay said, surprised at himself for saying it. The two men had stopped walking. 'My father was at the front. In France.'

'I know he was,' Grey said. 'Your father fell among the many brave Irish, men and boys, who fell at Beaumont Hamel. He is buried at Thiepval and I believe you have visited the grave twice, with your mother and your brother Tom, the first time in 'thirty and then again in 'thirty-six.'

'The second visit was in 'thirty-five,' Finlay said. 'My mother is a student of politics, as I'm sure you also know, and she saw the war coming. We went in 'thirty-five, because she said she didn't know when we'd be able to go again.'

'We are arranging for you to see your mother,' Grey said. They were walking again, Grey as always setting the pace of their progress. 'For practical purposes, you cannot leave London. For the purposes of this visit, you can spend a day somewhere on the Kent coast. It's only a day return on the railway. But in the circumstances, it's the best we can offer.'

'I'm grateful.'

They walked a while in silence. Abruptly, Grey let out a bark of laughter.

'What?'

'I was just thinking. About tea. Men will do almost anything for tea, Finlay. But what men will do for a ration of rum is the devil's own business.'

The Prospect of Whitby looked exactly the same. Probably it wore more dust, more detritus, in its old folds of brick and wood than it had before the conflict. And the river, low and still at its back, was a black puddle sunk under vaunting wharfs. The damage to the broken line of warehouse buildings on the far bank seemed no greater or less to Finlay than it had the last time he had been here. He felt that he should have been able to take comfort in the pub, standing mullioned, four-square and staunch. Or if not in the pub, then in the river and its vast, rhythmic indifference to the passage of time and the machinations of men. His mind sought permanence, but failed to find its buttressing strength. He had entirely lost his appetite and entered the pub feeling only a dark thirst for beer.

'Would you really intern her?'

Grey had pushed away his breakfast things and propped his elbows on the table. His chin rested on one thumb and a cigarette burned between his fingers. Finlay looked beyond him, out of the window at the barque, stranded, he thought now, rather than berthed, at its mooring there. The big sail, half-heartedly gathered in, sagged under its weight of soot. The rigging and the deck were black. The question had arrived without preamble. It hadn't needed any. She was, after all, a large part of what they had in common.

'Well? Would you?'

'Maybe I said that for effect.'

'That's not helpful,' Grey said. 'Saying things for effect.'

'You lot do it all the time.'

'Her mother is Polish,' Grey said.

'A countess, I suppose.'

'No. But a wealthy and vociferous patriot.'

Finlay didn't say anything. He drank more beer. It was his second pint and was going down with a dark, easy insistence. His belly was empty, but the beer was filling it.

'Her mother lives in Chicago,' Grey said, 'a city whose population includes a great many residents of Polish origin. Some of them, and these are her friends, remember, hold considerable political sway. All of them are angry and indignant about what has happened to their homeland. We're in a bit of a fix. We need all the American help we can get. You can see why gaoling Sophia Lange's daughter might prove counter-productive.'

Finlay didn't say anything. He was wondering at what point, in Grey's mind, a bit of a fix got bad enough to merit serious words.

'Do you really think that she's a security risk?'

'Like I said before, I am not qualified to judge.'

Grey picked a stray tobacco fragment from between his lower teeth. Finlay looked over Grey's shoulder, thinking, it's a funeral ship. That's what it is.

'Are you planning to see her again?'

'Yes,' Finlay said. 'Since you don't intend to intern her in the meantime, I'm going out for a drink with her tomorrow night.'

Grey said nothing. He frowned and looked at his wristwatch.

'When do I get to see my mum?'

'Early next week. Will you sleep with Rebecca Lange?'

'If I can. I like women.'

'Yes. Well. She's certainly one of those.' Grey looked over Finlay's shoulder into the gloomy body of the bar and widened his eyes in the slightest of acknowledgements. Finlay turned and saw a figure standing in the at-ease posture in a double-buttoned camel coat, almost a silhouette in a sudden mote of sunlight cast through one of the window panels at his back. It occurred to Finlay then that Grey's driver, whom he had seen previously only at the wheel of Grey's Bentley, had the build and carriage of a prize-fighter. He turned to look again at Grey, whose green eyes flamed and flickered in the beam of sudden brightness.

Grey said, 'Do you remember much about your father?'

'Not much. A little. I was four when he went away to fight and six when he was killed, so I don't remember much.'

'It must be a tall order to be the son of a hero.'

'They were all heroes,' Finlay said. 'You of all people should know that.'

'They didn't all win medals. I've read the citation, Finlay. Your father was a hero all right.'

Finlay said nothing. He could sense the bulk and menace of the figure in the shifting motes of pub light to his rear. He could smell the yellow insistence of the powdered egg scrambled on Grey's discarded breakfast plate, mingling with the odour of dead cigarettes in his ashtray.

'You must have been raised by women.'

'My mum. My aunts. Like most of my pals. It seemed for a while there weren't many men left in the world.'

There was a silence, then. Flushed with beer and fatigue, Finlay felt vaguely irritated at the pointless direction in which Grey had steered their conversation. The smell from the table was nauseating and the looming figure at his back made him nervous and more irritated for feeling the nervousness.

'What were you angry about this morning, Captain Grey?'

For an instant, Finlay thought that Grey intended to strike him, so brightly did the light of fury dance in his expression. Instead he rose, ground out his cigarette, grabbed his overcoat from the back of his chair and put on his hat with a stiffening pull at the brim.

'You can fuck Rebecca Lange to kingdom come, for all I care, Chief Fire Officer. But there are two things that you do not do. Under no circumstances do you leave your post at full alert. And never, ever, do you address me by military rank. Am I clear?'

'The telephone went dead,' Finlay said, thinking as he said them that the words sounded forlorn, even pathetic.

'I know it did,' Grey said, speaking in his own furious aftertow as he made his way towards the door. 'Even though I'm damned if we've been able to find out why.'

Finlay walked back to Liverpool Street, where fire fighters were still damping down and the air was acrid with the spent malice of the previous evening's bombs. He descended to his cell and scrubbed with the sliver of soap that was all that was left of his precious bar of Palmolive. The hot water and the scent of the soap dissipated the stale smoke still clinging to the room after Grey's night vigil. After scrubbing, Finlay towelled himself dry and then took to his cot and slept. When he woke, the luminous dial of his watch told him that it was after five in the afternoon. He felt refreshed and ravenous. Above, the light would already be fading and the sun descending in terminal decline. Finlay groped for and found the switch to the lamp on his bedside table.

'Blinder, Babcock,' he said.

A plate of sandwiches had been placed under a napkin on the table along with a Thermos flask and a small jug of milk. Finlay unscrewed the Thermos and poured some of its contents into the cap. It was coffee; hot, sweet and blessedly authentic. He poured milk into the brew and gulped greedily. He took the napkin off the sandwiches and bit into one. The bread was crusty, fresh, thick fritters of fried sausage meat slathered with brown sauce between its doorstep slices.

'Oh, Babcock, you marvel,' Finlay said around a mouthful of pulped food. He lay back on the bed and belched and chewed in the beige light of his lamp as the coffee thudded through him, bringing fresh alertness to his rested brain and body. He ate all the sandwiches and drank the Thermos dry. Then he brushed his teeth and flattened his hair with wet fingers. His hair was growing out in tufts and needed to be properly cut. He dressed, thinking about his breakfast with Grey. He could make no sense of it. Either it was an attempt at conviviality from an unconvivial man, or it had been pointless. Deciding it had been pointless, he opted to dismiss it from his mind. There had been something unpleasant about the episode that made it temptingly easy for Finlay to dismiss. They were letting him see his mum. He would retain that detail alone as the long and the short of it.

He did not think there would be a raid that night. It was what the Germans wanted people in London to think, he knew. The aftermath of a big raid left people too exhausted, in their imaginations, to anticipate a raid of the same magnitude and intensity coming upon them again so soon. Some part of the collective mind pleaded for the decorum of a respectful gap between such awful visitations. And some other part of the collective mind was generally lulled or seduced into providing it. Then, when the raid came, and there was no gap, and the following raid was even more awful than what had preceded it, a kind of bewildered, disappointed outrage was inflicted above and beyond the pain and sense of loss and desolation people expected to have to endure. It was this that had old men shaking clenched fists and mumbling toothless curses at the sky. It was this that caused the outbreaks of sobbing that spread with epidemic speed in the shelters and would not be stopped.

But tonight, Finlay did not think that there would be a raid. His intuition told him this and his intuition was something Finlay had learned to trust. He decided he would pass a quiet night by looking at the plans of the five buildings in his charge. He was curious as to the nature of the work that went on within their walls. He thought that the blueprints might offer some clue, some defining pattern that would make the nature of their function apparent and the mystery of their secret purpose plain.

A half-finished letter to his brother lay on his draftsman's table. Finlay remembered full well that he was not allowed to post a letter to his brother. He intended to give it to his mother and have her communicate in her own words the sense of what it was he was most anxious to say to Tom. Now, he gathered the incomplete pages and placed them between the pages of a book he returned to its shelf, anonymous among the other volumes.

When first in his possession, he had taped each of the blueprints to his walls. But that had been to familiarize himself with their precise layouts with only one consideration on his mind. That sole consideration had been fire. He thought of his buildings in terms of risk, of prospective rate of spread, of intensity, of capacity to fight, of salvage and, of course, of escape. The actual function of the building had never been a consideration; not even when he had inventoried in his mind the inflammable character of their known contents. Thus a library might teach, but it would definitely burn, and it was the burning only that Finlay had concerned himself with. He had ordered the summary dumping of the petrol generator that provided independent power to Absalom House only because the spare cans stored as its fuel reserve were so volatile a risk. He had never asked himself why a building of modest size required such a generator. He had not had the time for speculation beyond the immediacy of his tasks. But he had that now. He had rolled the plans and bound them in a bundle with a ribbon. Now he fetched them and untied the ribbon bow and unfurled the first of them, raising the tilt of the desk and anchoring the plan flat with strips from a roll of masking tape Babcock had brought him when he had delivered him the desk. It was the smallest of his buildings, the priest's house designed by Nicholas Hawksmoor and built at the end of the seventeenth century in St Helen's Place.

It was three hours before Finlay twisted his wrist and glanced at his watch in a gesture of capitulation that told him the time was just after ten. His neck ached and forcing his eyes to focus closely brought a dull rumble of pain to his skull. He was thirsty. And he was as clueless as to the nature of what went on in his quintet of City buildings as he had been when he had first sat down. He stood and stretched and went over to the sink and ran the tap and then gulped water. The pumped air and the artificial light that dried the air made him always thirsty when he spent any amount of time down here. He paused with his backside rested against the sink and wiped his mouth absently with the heel of his hand. He went over to the bookshelf and ran a finger along the spines until he located what he wanted. Finlay pulled free and then unfolded a large map of metropolitan London. He draped the map across his raised table and located the area he was looking for. Then he marked five dots on the map with a pencil and stood back and looked at them. And he folded his arms across his chest and laughed out loud as a knock tattooed against his door.

'Come in,' Finlay said, gathering and folding the map back in on itself.

It was Babcock. His visitor paused at an odd angle in the doorway for a moment and Finlay could not make sense of his posture. Then he saw that Babcock carried a beer crate under one arm, supporting its weight on his hip. The odd posture was to compensate. 'Thought you might like to wet your whistle, Mr Finlay,' he said. 'The wife's gone away for a few days, which is just as well because what they're showing at the Walthamstow Odeon this week represents a criminal absence of entertainment. Anyway, wondered if you were . . .'

'At a loose end?' Finlay said. 'I am, Babcock. It didn't look as though the Krauts were coming out to play tonight. And so I set myself a project to while away the time and keep mischief at bay. But my project seems to have scuppered itself.'

'What project would that be, Mr Finlay?'

Finlay looked at the man in the doorway, with his cargo of brown ale and his terminal case of solitude, and pondered briefly how much to confide in him.

'Did you know, Babcock, that the sites of those buildings I am obliged to keep free from fire form, on the map, the exact geometric points of a pentagram?'

'Occultism has never been my strength, Mr Finlay. Neither has strength, come to that, so do you mind if I put this crate on the floor?'

Finlay sat on the cot and Babcock in the armchair and Finlay drank and let his eyes recover from the fatigue of their earlier work as Babcock rabbited about the most recent events in wireless programming and motion pictures. The brown ale tasted faintly of the rubber seal around its stone bottle-stopper. The taste and the aroma took Finlay, as he half listened, back to his boyhood, when with his mates he would gather scrap metal they called slummy and sell it for pennies and buy beer at Hulse's corner store and say it was for the dads old Hulse knew damn well few of them had. From Hulse's it was a short step in his memory to St Theresa's, where they would take off their shoes and skate in their socks on the waxed floor of the sacristy, waiting in their cassocks and cottas to serve the evening Benediction when Father Carol finally prised himself free of the whisky bottle in the priest's house next to the church. Tommy Osbaldeston would ring the Angelus, and his feet would rise a foot off the floor with the peal of the bell and answering pull of the bell rope. And sometimes Anthony Ball, who was the best footballer Finlay had ever seen, would pick the lock to the sacristy safe and they would eat the unconsecrated hosts and drink sweet altar wine from bottles with a Vatican seal, giggling at the blasphemous enormity of their secret crime.

Finlay was journeying through memory, riding the long loop of association, dimly aware of what Grey had recently said about being brought up by women and wondering what that signified to a man like Grey, when the alert fragment of his mind registered Babcock pronouncing a word he had heard once before, only recently.

'What did you say?'

Babcock looked at him and Finlay could see from Babcock's expression that he had been in no way obliged to listen to Babcock's long monologue on Elstree and Broadcasting House and Hollywood. On the contrary, in fact.

'That word. What was that word you just said?'

Babcock pondered. There had been so many. 'Selznik?' he said. 'Budget? Gable? March through Georgia?'

'It began with a B. It wasn't budget.'

'Borehamwood. Brains Trust. Bandwagon. Bette Davis. Bogart.'

'It sounded foreign.'

'Benzedrine.'

Finlay snapped his fingers. 'What is Benzedrine?'

'A pick-me-up,' Babcock said. 'They're all on it.'

'Who are?'

'Selznik and the rest. All the movie people. You can buy it there over the counter. At what they call a drugstore, which is the American for chemist's shop. Drives 'em all bonkers, apparently.'

'It's the Benzedrine,' she had said. 'It's the times in which we live.'

Finlay looked at Babcock, who sat with his hands linked in his lap and an open bottle at his feet, beside the faded orange wood of the crate containing their empties as well as the brown-ale bottles yet to be opened. Babcock was wearing his frayed and faded blue overalls over a shirt with no collar. The soles of his boots were concertina'd with countless resolings and their uppers, though polished, were cratered and gouged into black moonscapes.

'Where did you get the money for the beer, Babcock? If you don't mind me asking. You strike me as too skint for the black market.'

'To which I'm anyway ideologically opposed.'

'As well as too skint for.'

'You're a cynic, Mr Finlay.'

'It's the times in which we live.'

'There is such a thing as the milk of human kindness,' Babcock said.

'I'm sure.'

'And then there is my brother-in-law, who works as a kitchen porter at the Dorchester. You know the Dorchester?'

'Only by reputation. As a place unlikely to shift a lot of brown ale.'

'Has to cater to a wide spectrum of tastes, a place like the Dorchester,' Babcock said. He nodded to himself. 'Very much a favourite rendezvous with Captain Grey, the Dorchester.' He looked at Finlay as if satisfied that this confirmed a sort of royal seal of approval on the old hotel.

'Is he a Captain? Grey?'

'Lord, no,' Babcock said. 'He's very much more important than that. These days, I mean. But he was Captain Grey to me, back in the old days, which as you know I have no intention of discussing with you at this or any other time.'

Both men drank for a while in silence. Finlay felt completely at ease in the silence, in the company of the other man, a circumstance he thought odd, but not so odd as to break the spell of his relaxation and the relative comfort he was taking in the moment. It was funny, when he thought about it. And the humour of the situation slowly insinuated a smile on his face. So long as he didn't try to get Babcock to recollect the summer slaughter of Gommecourt Wood, everything would be all right. It would be all right just so long as he didn't mention Babcock's boy and the aircraft carrier, *Glorious*, which had carried Babcock's nineteen-year-old boy to his sea grave. As long as he did not mention Babcock's wife and address the subject of her grief and derangement; or recollect poor Cooper and the brilliantine crackle of burning hair on poor Cooper's crushed skull; or speculate on the death agony of Sweeney with his flesh boiled; or the danger to his own brother, Tom, sheltered by a thin skin of steel and rivets at the bottom of the Baltic; or Nevin, coming to pieces behind the rictus of his minstrel grin; as long as he thought about and mentioned none of these things, just so long as he maintained the happy fiction of the waging of a painless war, then everything would be just tickety-boo, and wouldn't that be just the ticket? Christ, Finlay thought. No wonder the cinemas were full. No wonder baying crowds were mobbing the theatre and concert halls.

'When you grin like that, it makes you look a bit simple,' Babcock said.

'Who are they, Babcock?' Finlay said. 'Who are we working for?'

'The Ministry,' Babcock said, bored, as if by rote.

Both men swallowed beer in silence. 'Who are they?' Finlay asked. 'Who are they really?'

Babcock sighed and and looked at his beer through the dark glass of his bottle. 'Describe Hitler to me, Finlay.'

'Deadly serious,' Finlay said. 'Ambitious. Clever. Mad.'

'Anything else?'

'A bully. A murderer.'

Babcock nodded. 'How much do you know about politics?'

'Bugger all.'

'In the nineteen-thirties, only one senior British politician shared your opinion of Hitler. At least, only one senior politician was prepared to voice such an opinion publicly. That man was Winston Churchill. And his belligerence cost him his ministerial career. His was a view shared, however, by several senior army officers. And those army officers, some of them very senior indeed, communicated.'

Finlay drank and pondered the abyss yawning under his feet.

'White, Grey, the people working for and with them, were absolutely right about what would happen if Hitler were appeased,' Babcock said. 'But that's not entirely the point. Dissenting army officers do not get together and discuss

94

strategies opposed to the policies of their elected leaders. Not in a democracy. Not in peacetime. That's the point.'

Finlay was not used to conversations like this. But he thought he got Babcock's drift.

'Why weren't Grey and the rest sacked? Come to that, why weren't they court-martialled?'

'Maybe because dissent is a long way short of mutiny. Maybe for lack of hard evidence. Probably, in my view, because Chamberlain wouldn't have had the stomach for a purge of the armed forces.' Babcock sipped beer and smiled to himself. 'Or come to that, the mandate. Peculiar time, the 'thirties.'

'Churchill was a soldier,' Finlay said. 'He swore a solemn oath to serve king and country. And I should think he has the stomach for anything.'

'No doubt,' Babcock said. 'But he also wants to win this war.'

Finlay said, 'What do you know about my buildings?'

Babcock sipped beer and swallowed with exaggerated relish. He was enjoying himself.

'What am I supposed to know?'

'Absalom House, for instance. What do you know about Absalom?'

'Built by a dilettante architect for a greedy entrepreneur who got his come-uppance in the crash of 'twenty-nine. Threw himself off that glass dome, he did. It was years before they entirely got rid of the stain he left on the pavement. After that, the Government leased it from the Official Receiver. And I have as much idea of what goes on there nowadays as you do. Less, probably, since you've been inside the place.'

'Why do you say Lange was a dilettante?'

'Because he was.'

'He was good enough to complete postgraduate studies in London.'

'Yes. But in engineering.'

'How do you know that?'

'I work in engineering, Mr Finlay. In case you'd forgotten, that's my trade. I help maintain the London Underground.'

'I thought you worked for Grey.'

'That's voluntary.'

'I see,' Finlay said. 'It seems to me there's a lot that's voluntary.'

'Backbone of the war effort,' Babcock said. 'Secret warriors, Mr Churchill called us. Something like that, anyway. Some line of throwaway rhetoric.' He reached down and replaced his empty bottle in the crate beside his chair and then felt around until his fingers found the stopper of one that was unopened. All the time his eyes were on Finlay. Obliged into honesty by drink, his expression was by this time openly crafty. 'Lange's profession was architecture. But engineering was his passion. Most of the profit from those fashionable commissions was spent on his pet project.'

'Which was?'

'Some kind of energy source. He got interested in energy when he designed the turbine house for a dam in the Austrian Alps. But it wasn't energy derived from water pressure that interested him. It was something completely unexplored. He was working on it with a physicist he met during his year in London.'

'An English physicist?'

Babcock shook his head. 'Another German. Chap from Düsseldorf.'

'Richard Frentz,' Finlay said.

Babcock laughed and wagged a finger at him. 'You need watching, you do, Chief Fire Officer, and no mistake. You pretend to be a bit foggy. But you know more than you let on.'

Seven

FINLAY SAW his mother before she saw him. They had given him the number of a guest house at an address called Wavecrest at the Seasalter end of Whitstable beach. He had expected an exhaustive briefing from the Immaculate Major, or a feral-eyed warning from Grey. At the very least, he had thought he would get the chance to inspect the increasingly fraught Ministry windows and watch White practise semaphore with his eyebrows. But they had sent the ticket and directions and one line of instruction, via Babcock. The instruction had been to wear his civilian suit.

Walking towards the bench where his mother sat, he was glad he had worn the overcoat they had given him, too. Wind whipped off the sea in white smudges on the peaks of undulating green and screamed around his ears and stung his scalp with salt cold under its covering of shorn hair. His mother sat facing the sea and he could see her hair, thick and grey, undulate like a living thing responding to the strength of each separate gust. He could tell by the shape of her shoulders that her hands were shoved deep into her pockets for warmth. She was not a tall woman and her feet just reached the ground under where she sat on the bench. She had on a pair of imitation-leather ankle boots that were familiar to him. He knew that they zipped up the front and were lined with fake rabbit fur. He could see the arthritic swelling of her ankles from a hundred feet away, despite the boots. He recognized her coat, as well. It was a wool coat with a fox-fur collar Tom had bought for her from Peter Jones on his first home leave.

Still about twenty yards away from his mother, Finlay had to stop to try to compose himself. He loved her very much and felt he had been such a dreadful disappointment to her. Seeing her there, in the freezing blast off the capering sea, she seemed tiny and vulnerable. All the pain he had brought to those he loved most seemed to consolidate in that small, seated figure with her back to him. Then she cocked her head, though she could not have heard him in that withering wind, and he knew that she had sensed her son, become suddenly aware of his presence and proximity. And so he closed the distance between them in a few strides and sat beside her and gathered her in his arms and hugged her, in the gathering gale, for a long time before saying anything at all.

They walked first away from the open. The lanes of Whitstable were old and their timber cottages had been built with proper regard for the exposure of the town to a winter wind that travelled, unimpeded by land mass, all the way from arctic Russia. So the lanes were narrow and dense and their shelter a sudden relief after the exposure to the open sea. They walked slowly because of Margaret Finlay's arthritis. They gained the high street, which was dismal. Canvas awnings flapped and shuddered over dark shops devoid of anything in the way of goods anyone would want to eat or wear. Glass gave on to black space and displays of ration calculations done in crayon on the cardboard of flattened boxes and taped to the inside of the panes. The high street was almost deserted. Gulls wheeled, screaming, and a pub sign batted back and forth in a steel frame depending from a sort of gibbet. In the distance, carried by the wind, Finlay could hear the insistent anger of fighter engines from a squadron patrolling the coast.

They found a tea-shop and Finlay bought two cups of tea and a rock cake for his mother. The tea-shop was warm and quiet, wallpapered like somebody's sitting-room, but welcoming after the buffeting of the street. Three ovals of compressed coal slack burned quietly in the grate. They were the only customers and they took a table beside the fire.

'What were you doing there, mum, you'd catch your death,' Finlay said.

'The room they put me in is very nice,' she said. 'But I don't like to be cooped up in a strange room. I had to get out. You know I've never minded the cold.'

Only the damp, Finlay said to himself.

'Only the damp,' his mother said. She sipped tea and smiled at her son. She put a hand over his on the table. 'Why don't you tell me what's up?'

And so, of course, he told her everything.

When he had finished, they sat silent for a time. Finlay fetched them a second cup of tea and his mother broke pieces from her rock cake and dipped them in her tea and ate them.

'Babcock is wrong, you know,' she said, quietly. 'We have not lost this war. But men like White and Grey and your Major will not be the winning of it.'

'They seem so soft, mum. Effete, almost. I hate the way they all call the enemy Jerry. They don't seem men capable of waging war. They're not cut from Colonel Baxter's cloth, that's for sure.'

'You should read the newspapers, son.'

'I do read them. What there is of them.'

'Really read them, between the lines, I mean. There's a pattern, a general reluctance to engage the enemy with any conviction. Whole divisions are capitulating without a fight.'

Margaret Finlay's voice was little more than a whisper now. The woman who had served them had retreated to a back room. But sound travelled. And seditious talk travelled further. 'It isn't the men, it's the senior officers,' she said. 'And it isn't that they don't know how to fight, it is that all the appetite they had for a fight was bled out of them twenty-odd years ago in France and Flanders. The men who were subalterns in the trenches then are full colonels and even generals now, a lot of them. They haven't the heart for a repetition of what they went through then. They just have not got it in them to put men through what they endured themselves.'

'Baxter has.'

Margaret Finlay shook her head. 'I'm sure your Colonel Baxter is a brave and cantankerous soldier. Scots usually are. But he's an artillery man. He did not have to drop into German trenches and fight with a bayonet, wading through mud and slaughter as your father did at Mons and Neuve Chapelle. He was not obliged, like your Captain Grey, to try to lead men through Gommecourt Wood.'

'It wasn't Gommecourt,' Finlay said, remembering. 'It was a place called Serre.'

His mother played with the fragments of her bun on the tablecloth, fingers stiff with swollen joints. She looked directly at her son. 'Serre was worse. Serre was the Pals Battalions. At Serre, Captain Grey would have been leading boys to their deaths. Sweet, brave boys from Bradford and Barnsley and Durham who perished all at once on a summer morning.'

They left the tea-shop and walked back towards the shore. They found a wooden shelter built around a bench behind the sea wall, in the lee of the Whitstable Oyster Sheds, a looming permanence of wood and steel and corrugated iron that rose from the pebbled slope of the beach on the near side of the town's small harbour. Their seat faced the town. From where they sat, they could hear the boom of water forced between the wooden groynes of the beach. Water surged and dissipated under protest, wave upon hissing wave as it sank, high up the beach, into the shingle. There was spray and salt in the cold, vigorous air. From where they sat, Finlay could look down on the town, on its huddle of shellfishers' cottages, its labyrinthine lanes, on two pubs tucked against the sea wall and constructed, it seemed, from the spare timbers of ships. He saw a child in yellow oilskins running a stick along a gutter fouled with beach debris. Under the back porch of one of the cottages, a man in a tight wool sweater sat repairing a fishing net with a clumsy wooden needle. Further up the beach, three figures, huddled and rushing like fugitives, entered the door of one of the pubs. Finlay screwed up his eyes and could just make out the name, The Neptune, written in signwriter's script on the pub's wood-planked facing wall. Above the words, a bearded figure with a trident rose florid from painted waves. Finlay stood so that he could follow the sweep of his vision, blocked by their shelter, beyond the pub, out over the water. He took a step to the right, into the exposure of the wind, and narrowed his eyes against the grit and salt spray scouring off the shingle. The sea was turbulent, composed of huge green folds laced with white intricacies of foam, the folds so big in their slow, rhythmic undulations that Finlay had to steady himself against the pitch and yaw of false motion brought on by watching them. The tide was up, the water high on the shore, but in those brief intervals between advancing waves, when the sea receded, Finlay could just make out some structure built by men beyond the beach. Four or five times he snatched sight of it, before making sense of its flat, boarded deck and staunch supporting pillars of wood and spindly, topmost rungs of iron ladder. It was a diving platform. It was a thing built not for defence, or observation, or naval training, as he had first supposed, but for recreation. Whitstable endured the violence of a late October sea, its small fleet of fishing smacks sheltered no doubt in its harbour, beyond the oyster sheds and the breakwater, hidden in their sanctuary from storms. Thirty miles to the west were the Medway towns of Rochester and Chatham, pounded nightly by the bombs. The same distance to the south-east, across the Kent peninsula, Folkestone and Dover faced occupied France, and who knew what massed and looming threat of invasion. Finlay looked out over the sea as the swell diminished and the diving platform came grey, gaunt, dripping into view. He wondered would the next happy gang of swimmers to climb its ladder in summer play be English, or German.

'There's more than one England,' Margaret Finlay said.

Her son sat back down.

'I was just thinking that.'

'You couldn't but,' she said. 'I've never been to Kent before. But I've never seen so many aeroplanes in my life.'

'What's Liverpool like now?'

'Much the same, really. It's hard. Harder for anyone with kin aboard a ship. And that's a lot of us. Some have had their younger kids evacuated to Wales. So the streets are quieter. There's talk about bombing. But of course there's been no bombs. You can almost always get some kind of food, living near the docks. And the pubs are packed, most afternoons and every night, because the war's brought wages.'

'What's the atmosphere like?'

Jack Finlay's mother looked at her son. 'What do you mean?'

'The attitude.'

'To the war?'

He shifted on the bench. 'I suppose to the war.'

She thought about this. 'Well the last one was a patriotic war. At least, it was until nineteen-sixteen. After that, after the losses that summer, it became a war of revenge. This one's different because nobody wanted it. There's no flag-waving. Anyway, you know what Bootle is like. There's nights in Bootle you'd think you were in Dublin.'

Finlay nodded.

'But the feeling generally seems to be that this is a war that needs to be fought and has to be won.'

Finlay nodded again. His mind was back in Liverpool, in the house in Stanley Road, in the parlour, where his father's medals lay on the polished sideboard under desiccated light from the net curtain over the window, there with his brass cap-badge, his bronze belt-buckle, his grinning picture in a leather frame. 'What do you think, mum?'

She took his hand. 'Hitler is an evil man. Fascism is an evil creed. But I don't want to lose a son. And when I hear Winston Churchill on the wireless, Churchill, the hero of Gallipoli, pontificating on the wireless, I want to vomit.'

Finlay squeezed his mother's hand. Her eyes were wet.

'The seances have started again,' she said. 'All those poor mothers of sons sunk in the convoys. So we've got all that again.' She sniffed and laughed. 'I've started going to St Theresa's of a night and lighting candles. Even me.'

'There's no harm in lighting candles,' Finlay said.

'I just want you and Tommy to come through it and come home,' his mother said. 'I've had enough taken away from me.'

'Come on,' Finlay said. He stood.

'Where are we going?'

'We're going to the pub.'

'I don't drink during the day, Johnny. Neither should you.'

'It's a one-off, mum. A special occasion. Come and have a couple of port and brandies. Maybe one of the oyster catchers will sing us a sea-shanty.'

'God forbid.' Margaret Finlay stood. She winced at the weight of her afflicted ankles and then, with a smile, erased the pain from her face. 'I'll come to the pub with you on one condition.'

'Anything.'

'You tell me truthfully how you came by that black eye.'

'I've already told you,' Finlay said. 'I slipped holding a power hose and the nozzle kicked and hit me in the face.'

His mother tilted her head and looked up at him through her eyebrows. Her eyes were as bright as the sea in sunlight and brimmed with mischief. He laughed out loud and took her arm and some of her weight and they set off, slowly, in the shadow of the sea wall towards The Neptune.

He had picked her up at the door of her flat in Coptic Street at eight o'clock and they had groped their way, the night moonless and blind, through Bloomsbury and into Fitzrovia and The Wheatsheaf, where, through the tobacco smoke and loud babble of excitement and intoxication, he had his first opportunity to look at her face that evening in anything approaching light. The sour mist of countless cigarettes hung around a few feeble overhead globes.

This miserly illumination made the men in the pub appear mere shades and the women cadaverous. Then he looked at the face in front of him and it did not look like that at all. Rebecca Lange looked poised, her skin nourished, her face, bold-featured, lit as if from within. Finlay supposed that this was beauty. He did not think that it could be Benzedrine. She took off her headscarf and shook her hair and Finlay was relieved to see that it had not turned a bright yellow, as had the hair, it seemed to him, of almost every other woman he saw in London. Rebecca unbelted and unbuttoned her coat with a dip of her head and then raised her head again and pushed back her hair with a hand and looked at him and smiled.

'Get me a drink, Jack. I'm about to expire of thirst on the spot.'

He inhaled her breath, her perfume. She had not used his name before. He had asked her to call him Finlay. He felt the heavy bulge in his trousers of a trapped erection at the complete unexpectedness of this intimacy and was glad that his own coat remained buttoned. He felt an awkwardness he had not felt since adolescence as he progressed, with burning cheeks, to the bar. He did not worry too much about blushing. He was walking with his back to her and anyway was concentrating on walking normally. His dick felt so hard and constrained it was all Finlay could do not to limp.

She had found a table and taken off her coat and lit a cigarette by the time he returned with their drinks. As he sat, Finlay became aware that someone was playing a piano in the corner of the room. The piano was loud, the music some jazz tune with a lot of counterpoint that flirted with dissonance but kept meandering back to its strong, resonant theme. It was loud, but the pub was louder with conversation, laughter, screams of recognition, all competing. The tobacco smoke was as thick and bitter in the back of Finlay's throat as bile. He sipped beer. As though prompted, Rebecca sipped her whisky and soda. He leaned towards her and found he had to shout. 'Who are these people?'

She frowned and leaned forward. She was wearing a black dress with slender satin shoulder straps and a low neckline, and leaning over the table plumped her pale breasts against the fabric. 'Who do you think?'

'Homosexuals. Refugees. Writers like your Irishman.'

She tapped ash onto the floor. 'And the women?'

'Bohemians. Lesbians. Tarts.'

Rebecca narrowed her eyes and smoked. She reached for the ashtray and ground out her cigarette.

'Have a real look,' she said.

So Finlay did.

He was sober, and in the merciless light he looked at the people choosing to crowd The Wheatsheaf to its walls, its rafters, its heaving gills, on a Friday night. He looked hard and was shocked by what it was his eyes, rather than his expectations, led him to see.

Half a dozen of the men in front of the long bar wore fighter-pilot moustaches. A couple of them still had on their uniforms, ties askew, the sky-blue tunics bled to monochrome in the pervading absence of light. He saw a cavalry flash on the shoulder of a greatcoat. Three ratings were talking to a group of young women at the far end of the bar, adjacent to the lavatory. Finlay tried and failed to make out what ship they were from. Then a lavatory door swung open and they were joined by a fourth. He had emerged from the ladies, which his party considered to be a huge joke. Finlay turned to share his conclusion with Rebecca but by now she had turned away and so, instead, he studied her. And with the same objective scrutiny. She had twisted her head towards the bar, to her left, with her shoulders straight against the back of her chair. The pose made her long neck taut under the clean insistence of her jaw and Finlay's eyes were drawn up from her pale throat, across her cheeks, to the sudden budding of her full, ripe, shockingly crimson mouth. His eyes were moving to examine the one of hers visible when she turned back sharply to face him.

'Well?'

'Servicemen. Half the bloody war effort's here.'

'Yes. Exactly. Would you like to sleep with me tonight?'

'Of course.'

'Good. Light me.'

He lit her cigarette. She exhaled.

Finlay sat back in his chair. The pianist was playing some piece of trilling whimsy by Noel Coward or Ivor Novello. To Finlay, they were interchangeable. His coat lay over the back of his chair. Anticipation unfurled through him in a thrill of sensation that sang into his scalp and fingertips. At least he seemed now to have his tackle under control. 'Why are you smiling like that?'

'When first I saw you, Finlay, I thought you were queer.'

He could feel his own smile dry into idiocy.

'Why?'

She pouted. He thought it her first contrivance of the night and felt deflated by it, as though gut-punched.

'Don't you think it ironic that a man who looks like you do wants to put out fires?'

'I don't know what you're talking about.' He didn't.

Her eyes lifted suddenly. There was a commotion to Finlay's immediate right and her Irishman dumped a chair out of one of his big hands at their table and sat on it. He was sweating freely under an overcoat and was clearly drunk. Drunk, his eyes were challenging rather than furtive, drink contorting everything into a sneer between the damp curls on his forehead and the clump of his chin. Finlay could hear the voices of the pilot officers, grouped around the piano now; raucous verses, a chorus leaden with repetition. The Irishman belched rank, abattoir breath into his face. Finlay wondered, not for the first time, if the man had ever shared Rebecca's bed. If he still sometimes shared it.

'You again?'

Finlay said nothing.

'You're as persistent as a bad habit,' the Irishman said. 'But nowhere near so much fun.' He reached for Rebecca's whisky. But Finlay had seen the trick before and was too quick. He just pushed the drink a few inches across the table beyond the Irishman's reach. If he wanted it, he would have to lunge and lose his balance or stand and walk around the table, which would spoil the effect. The reaching hand stopped on the table and withdrew into a heavy fist.

'Let's take this outside,' its owner said to Finlay.

Finlay was on his feet and threading through the crowd for the door almost before the sentence had been completed, taking off and folding his tie, unstrapping his wristwatch, putting both into the same jacket pocket. As the pub door closed behind him he blinked and struggled to adjust to the faint, fugitive hints of light he knew must be there somewhere in the night. His shoes slithered over cobbles and he smiled invisibly, remembering what Baxter had always drilled into his men about choosing the ground for a fight. Well, too late for that.

He heard the swing of the pub door and sensed the advancing bulk of his adversary, breathing hard with drink and aggression. Finlay balanced his feet evenly eighteen inches apart, allowed his weight to slightly favour the front foot and his knees to bend a little. He extended his hands, dropped his shoulders, folded his hands into fists, extended the left slightly, and waited. Alert as he was, he couldn't help thinking to himself that this was going to be too easy to be as enjoyable as he wanted it to be. He felt the breath and glower of the Irishman come on in the dark and pivoted into a left-hook-cum-uppercut intended to land under the ribcage, force the man's breath out through his crumpled diaphragm and drop him to his knees. The punch landed. The Irishman's stomach had the weight and density of a sodden sandbag. Finlay's fist did not sink, it stopped, and pain blossomed bright in the darkness across his knuckles. He heard the shift of his opponent's feet and then felt his own cheek slither and graze along wet stone. He knew that he was not unconscious, because he could hear.

'If it wasn't so fucking dark, I'd give you a kicking, you cunt,' the Irishman said, whispered, still sounding breathless.

The next thing Finlay remembered was being helped out of a taxi.

'I can't carry you. You'll have to help me get you up the stairs,' Rebecca said. It sounded more foreign than Rebecca, but it was her, he knew. He came round properly on a sofa in the wide prairie of her sitting-room, to the soughing of gas lanterns on the walls, in the presence of pictures like windows on a world he had never known. She put a glass in his hand. It was brandy. He sipped and swallowed and then felt around his mouth. His teeth were intact and there was no pain from his jaw. Then he felt wetness on his cheek and realized that one of his eyes was entirely closed. It was weeping, tears independent of him, that squeezed their way through the swelling.

'He carries a knuckleduster,' Rebecca said. She had sat on the sofa beside him and was pressing a cold, wet cloth over the eye swollen shut. 'He fights a lot. Usually he wins.'

'You could have warned me.'

'I did try. It would have made no difference, would it?'

'It's like punching a medicine ball.'

'He works on building sites.'

'It shows.' Finlay sank back on the sofa. His head hurt. Brandy vapour was making him feel a falling, drifting sensation. Of itself it was not unpleasant. But he was uneasy about where it might take him. 'Can we talk about something else?'

'I don't think that right now we should talk about anything.' She was tugging off one of his shoes. Finlay sat up and reached for her. She put a hand in the centre of his chest and pushed him back against the sofa. Either he was weak, or she was strong. Perhaps both.

'I thought you said—'

Blackness blossomed in Finlay's head and the brandy fumes filled him with sudden nausea. He swallowed vomit and Rebecca took the glass from his trembling fingers.

'I asked would you like to sleep with me tonight. I did not promise that you would get to do so.'

Finlay had the cloth over both eyes. 'You seemed happy enough at the time with the answer I gave.'

Rebecca took a moment to reply. He sensed that she was weighing words foreign to her with care.

'We all wish to be wanted,' she said. 'It is a very human failing.'

Finlay didn't say anything. He had never thought of desire as a failing. A weakness, perhaps. And he remembered that lust was a sin. But a failing?

'You have a lump the size of a hen's egg where your head hit the cobble-stones when he knocked you down,' Rebecca said. 'In the one eye I could see, your pupil is dilated to the size of the iris. And the white is not white, it is red. You have a concussion. You need darkness. And rest.'

She laughed and framed his head between the outstretched fingers of gentle hands. She leaned into him and kissed his mouth, deliciously. Concussed or not, he wanted to inhale her. She broke the kiss. 'I'm not taking you to bed, Chief Fire Officer. Not tonight. Tonight I'm putting you there.'

'I know the bloke,' Babcock said.

'You know everything.' Finlay said.

Babcock was still grinning. He had looked in at eleven with a Thermos of coffee and two speculative mugs and now, fifteen minutes later, could still not contain his amusement at the yellow-and-purple swelling that disfigured Finlay's eye. Nor could he conceal his delight at how Finlay had come by his Technicolor mishap.

'If you'd said Kilburn or Camden Town, that would have been a different thing. There they have obstreperous Irishmen by the baker's dozen. But off Oxford Street? You're quite sure it was off Oxford Street?'

'The geography is pretty much the only thing I am sure about,' Finlay said. 'He decked me outside a pub called The Wheatsheaf in Rathbone Place.'

'Then it was him,' Babcock said. 'Big drunken fucker.'

'On the nail.'

'Carries a knuckleduster. When he's looking for an argument, he shoves a couple of telephone directories under his belt.'

'Does he? Crafty so-and-so.'

'And a knife. A skean-dhu he wears down his sock, like the kilties. Proper nasty piece of work.'

'I won't debate the point. I'm gratified for the information, Babcock.'

'I don't know why,' Babcock said, dolefully. 'He's another war you'll be obliged to walk away from. Once I tell Captain Grey.'

On the train on the way back to London from his visit to his mother in Whitstable, Finlay was preoccupied for a while by the strange scene that had taken place in The Neptune pub. He had been a party to it, central to it, because without the presence of himself and his mother, it would never have been enacted. But already it seemed remote from him, alien, like a film shot in a location he had never been to, featuring actors whose faces and mannerisms he found entirely unfamiliar.

They had been in the pub for an hour or so. His mother had sipped half-heartedly at a port and lemon and then with more enthusiasm at a second drink as they reminisced and she talked about Tom's plan to try for a university place on a Naval scholarship once the war had ended. The university plan was a new one on Finlay, but it did not surprise him; any more than had the seminary plan or the one involving medical school. Tom had always been the sort of boy who fulfilled parental ambition. Maybe he would even like university. Certainly he was bright and curious enough for knowledge to study for a degree.

A third drink anaesthetized his mother's arthritis enough for them to attempt a game of bar billiards at the vacant table at the rear of the pub, under a window the width of the wall, facing the sea. It was a local game and neither of them had played it before. The dimensions of the table, the size of the balls, the balance of the cues and the strange mushroom-shaped wooden obstacles to potting the ball were all new to Finlay and his mother and the sheer intrinsic daftness of the game struck them both at the same time so that their alternating shots wobbled with hilarity.

They were playing the decider of a best of three when the pub door opened and a police constable walked in, followed by an ARP warden and the woman both Finlay and his mother recognized as the proprietress of the little high-street tea-shop in which they had spent the first part of their day. The policeman was wearing a long, blue-black gabardine with two rows of buttons embossed with the crest of the Kent constabulary. Rain, or sea-spray, was spattered around the collar and shoulders of the gabardine. He was over six feet tall, looked to be in his mid-forties and carried a Lee Enfield rifle at port arms. He stood to the right of the pub door and looked out of the window above their heads. The warden, who was around fifty, had a Sten gun under one arm, hanging from a shoulder strap, his forefinger pressed against the trigger guard. The weapon was clumsy and looked home-made. He stood to the left of the door. The woman, who was not armed, whispered something to the policeman, who nodded without shifting his eyes from their neutral focus through the window on the place over the sea where the island of Sheppey would have been visible on a less turbulent day. Now that he thought about it, Finlay was aware once more of the crash of the sea on the shore, the collision of waves against the sheltering wall outside, the slap of shifting pebbles, wave-borne, colliding with granite. He looked over to the table that had been occupied by a trio of shrimp fishermen, the only other customers, on their arrival at the pub. Now there were two.

'Pound to a penny there's a bullet already in the breech of that copper's rifle,' Margaret Finlay whispered to her son. He ignored the remark. She dug him in the ribs with the heel of her billiard cue.

'Your shot,' she said.

Finlay took his shot. They finished their game. His mother sat and Finlay fetched them another drink each from the bar. The woman who had served them in the tea-shop had taken some knitting from a bag and she worked with a busy click of bone needles at a table near the door.

'They used to knit like she's doing in France during the Revolutionary Terror,' Margaret Finlay said. 'While they waited for another victim to be dragged up to the guillotine.'

Finlay said nothing.

'The toothless hags,' his mother said, and Finlay was forced to swallow a laugh.

The policeman and the warden flanked the door. Finlay glanced at the ARP man's weapon. He had no doubt that it had been knocked together with painstaking study of a Home Guard instruction booklet at a local forge well practised in the hooping of ale barrels, the fashioning of ornamental gates. The thing looked inept and terrifying. The man with his finger on its trigger guard looked afraid. Then the door opened and a middle-aged civilian walked in, wearing plaid socks, plus-fours and a waist-length jacket made of mackintosh material and fastened with a steel zipper instead of buttons up the front. He removed his cap and smiled generally, and in the hard light through the window off the sea, Finlay saw that the entire right side of his face had been subject to some surgical procedure, a reconstruction that left it plastic and smooth from jawbone to eye socket.

'Constable Rennie,' the man said, without looking. 'Mr Whittle. Mrs Halliday.'

'Brigadier,' the three of them said together, like a slightly ragged chorus.

'Would you care for a game of bar billiards, Brigadier?' Margaret Finlay said.

The Brigadier turned to her. His body suggested a sort of spontaneity, as if he were responding to the invitation with nothing more than nonchalant surprise. But the plastic made his face rigid and impossible to read. And his pale eyes were alert and cold. 'I don't believe I've had the pleasure,' he said.

'Margaret Finlay of Liverpool. And this is my eldest, John, who serves with the London Fire Brigade.'

The Brigadier didn't look at Finlay. He didn't take his eyes off the mother. 'I'm afraid bar billiards isn't my cup of tea at all, Mrs

Finlay,' he said. He said it with a finality that was followed by a silence. Even the knitting had stopped. Finlay looked at the ARP warden, whose finger was white at the knuckle over the Sten gun's trigger guard.

Margaret Finlay said, 'May I ask you where you got your wound?'

'Place called Beaucourt, Mrs Finlay. French town. Hamlet, really. I doubt you are familiar with the name or with the place.'

'In a manner of speaking, I am. My husband fell at Thiepval.'

The silence this time was shorter.

'Good God,' the Brigadier said. 'You are Colour Sergeant Patrick Finlay's widow. Constable Rennie?'

'Brigadier?'

The burr of the policeman's dialect spoke to Finlay of hops and cider apples and bigotry. His mother was right, he was sure. There was a bullet primed already in the rifle's breech.

'You have dragged me away from a perfectly good game of golf for nothing.'

'Can't be too careful, Brigadier.'

'I still think you ought to check their papers,' the woman from the tea-room said, her voice a peevish whine. She nodded at Margaret Finlay. 'That one was most disrespectful about Mr Churchill.'

'Yes, well. This is still a free country. We are fighting a war to keep it that way.'

'I think they're Fenians,' the woman persisted. 'I think you should ask to see their papers.'

Quietly, so that only her son, standing beside her, heard, Margaret Finlay said, 'It would be instructive to know on what authority.'

The Brigadier appeared to rise an inch in his shoes.

'Papers can be forged, Mrs Halliday. One thing you most definitely cannot counterfeit, however, is the regimental history of the Irish Guards.'

He replaced his cap and with his heels together, bowed shortly at Margaret Finlay.

'Madam,' he said.

Finlay saw that his shoes, brown brogues, were skirted with

freshly mowed grass which adhered to the damp leather. The Brigadier turned, the ARP man opened the door for him, and he was gone. The policeman put his rifle over his shoulder and the tea-shop woman got to her feet, stuffing her knitting into her big, wood-handled bag. They shuffled in an ungainly struggle of winter clothing and weaponry out of the door.

'Fetch me a large brandy, Johnnie. There's a good boy.'

'That mouth of yours will get you into trouble, mum,' Finlay said, sitting back down with their drinks. He said it quietly. The Neptune barman was one of those background functionaries almost defined by absence, like the referee in a boxing match. But the man was present, somewhere.

'He should have looked at our papers, though.'

'You said it yourself, mum. On what authority?'

Margaret Finlay sipped from her glass. She didn't say anything for a while, and then she smiled.

'The number of people from this town he employs. The size of the house he lives in and some of them earn a living helping maintain. The extent of his disfigurement. Locally at least, I'm sure the golfing brigadier doesn't want for authority. And he should have looked at our papers.'

'He should,' Finlay agreed.

'He was one of them, wasn't he?' his mother said. 'Like White. Like the Major, and your Mr Grey.'

Out of the train window, Finlay watched dusk descend over the Kent fields. The landscape offered stunted hedgerows, pasture and the occasional glitter of the sea, orange under the October glow of descending sun. The train rattled and cajoled its way towards London. Finlay sat alone in his carriage, feeling a vague sense that he should be pondering the mystery of Absalom House and the contradictions in the histories he had heard concerning its absent creator. It was not his business unless he chose to make it so. And if he did, it was still none of his business. His mind was occupied, anyway, not with her absent father, but with Rebecca Lange. His mother had observed in Whitstable that there was more than one England. Casting his mind back to that night in Bloomsbury, at the conclusion of a day spent in his mother's company, he felt that they were women who inhabited different worlds.

His concussion had denied him sleep. He had lain for a long time under goose feathers stitched into a sort of swollen, fleecy counterpane and the warmth of the bed had almost lulled him into unconsciousness. But lust and pain from his weeping eye contrived together to deny him rest and in the small hours he climbed from the warmth of his bed and wandered naked into her sitting-room and opened the curtains and watched silver beams carved by vigilant searchlights set a pattern of defiance in the night sky. After a while it was hard for Finlay to see the searchlights as anything but a sort of dumb, empty display of rhetoric and so he drew the heavy drapes and blinked against absolute darkness and then saw a flicker of light from under Rebecca's bedroom door.

With infinite care he opened the door. The light was cast by a single candle, its flame small but resolute on her bedside table. Finlay almost expected Rebecca to sense him and to waken and turn, indignant at his trespass. But she did not.

She was sleeping naked, on her stomach, her arms splayed to either side of her body, flushed gold in the light from the candle, ochre deepening into dark shadow at the nape of her neck, in the cleft of her spine and dividing the pale rise of flesh at the base of her back, where the bedclothes bunched and gathered. To Finlay the room smelled tawny with liquor and tobacco and pooled wax and the scent of Rebecca's recumbent flesh and the subtle, pervasive perfume she wore. His father had brought spices home from the docks sometimes and now Finlay recognized the base of Rebecca's perfume as cinnamon. He stood in the door-frame and breathed the breath of her bedroom in for a while. The still light of the candle seemed to embrace her as she slept, holding her at the centre of encroaching shadow and diminishing brightness, shaping her hair in coils and ribbons of darkness and light.

Finlay groaned and his head sank back into the greasy velveteen upholstery of his train compartment. His eyes opened and he blinked and brought a hand up to his brow. He could not have said how long it was he had stood at the threshold of her secrecy and watched Rebecca Lange. But he remembered now that the candle in her room was guttering when she stirred, dreaming God knows what dream, and spoke audibly, urgently, in sleep and in German. He had been fascinated rather than excited by her during his clandestine study. But when she spoke those words, the forbidden language sounded strange and savage coming from her lungs, through her throat, to her lips. And despite his concussion and the pain from his leaking eye and his voyeuristic guilt, he had felt then the strong tug of arousal. His only surrender to instinct, though, had been to blow the candle out.

The train was labouring through dim suburbs when the act of waking told Finlay that he must have fallen into fitful sleep. He rubbed his eyes and yawned. He could taste beer and brandy, stale on his breath. The incident in The Neptune came back to him. He wondered, then, for a moment, if the whole thing had not been engineered by Grey as some sort of lesson, or entertainment. But he dismissed the idea as the same sort of self-important notion that had persuaded him he was being followed on those occasions he had heard footsteps echoing his at Aldwych, and on the Strand.

It did not surprise him that the disfigured brigadier had heard of his father's exploits at Mons and Neuve Chapelle. Officers were often jealous when the gallantry of other ranks was recognized and given tangible reward. His father's name must have earned a sort of status, even notoriety, among those glory-hunters who had spent their leaves reading the military des-patches in the *London Gazette*; or studied at leisure, in later years, accounts of the war on the Western Front, from plush armchairs in their hand-tooled, calf-bound military histories. It could not be expected to occur to them that his mother had slept without a man in her bed since the age of thirty-two. They would know nothing of the enervating dread of awaiting the hammer of a bailiff's fist at their door. They would not have suffered the shameful heartbreak of having to send their children to school in shoes with cardboard soles. His mother was right. There was more than one England. And Finlay thought it had been a far easier thing to fight for in the abstract, in the desert, under the command of Baxter, the cantankerous Scot. The train clanked and wearied into some dark siding, trying to insinuate its way along a platform still intact at one of London's shattered railway stations. He had given his mother twenty pounds, pressed the money into her protesting palm and held the notes there as she hugged him goodbye. He had expected from that token gift the selfish consolation of feeling better about her. Twenty pounds would not buy absolution, but he had hoped it would bring respite. It hadn't, though. Finlay still felt, in his troubled soul, the bad man he had always suspected himself to be. The train stopped with a lurch of finality. He groped for his coat and the door handle. In darkness, he would have to find out where he was.

Eight

THEIR SUMMONS sat on the night table beside the telephone. He was to present himself the following morning at ten. There would be tea and biscuits and intricate new details in the mosaics wrought so elaborately in each of their vaunting windows by the percussive violence of bombs. They would talk in a code, as they always did, for which birth and education had provided them, whilst denying him, the key. They were at an advantage. But central to their whole narrow, comfortable, unshakeable view of themselves and their influential position in determining the nature of things was the God-given right and necessity of advantage.

It was not so much a code, when Finlay thought about it, as a map. Talking to them was like studying a relief map full of dense and complex contours shaped in irony and understatement and sometimes just in frank, emphatic, plum-vowelled, cornflower-blue-eyed lies. He was sure, for one thing, that Grey wasn't a civilian. He was bloody certain of it. Drunk on brown ale and fatigue, he had fallen wholesale in the moment for Babcock's collusive tale of mutinous goings-on among the generals. Sober, though, this seditious conspiracy unravelled itself in his mind. Babcock was a man, after all, proven to be untruthful even to himself. And while Finlay's mother had laboured Churchill's failings to him often enough, the accommodation of treachery seemed an unlikely addition to her angry catalogue. Babcock had been making mischief. He was jealous of Grey, still the scurrying batman seeking to chivvy and wheedle favour, resentment hardening in him at the indignity of each volunteered service and errand. In his suggestion of intrigue and cabals, he'd been merely foggying the picture, pulling Finlay's leg. But Babcock had been reliable, he felt certain now, about Grey's exalted rank.

Finlay remembered the word and the meaning of the word from learning catechism at Sunday School and the word was omnipresent and you didn't get to be as omnipresent as Grey after chucking in the army over a few hundred unexpected corpses from Burnley or Durham. The man was a poof, but Finlay didn't think him a sentimental poof. Grey was wearing civvies on the outside only. Inside, he was strictly Brass. He was Top Brass. Finlay was sure of it. He took another gulp from his glass. He was fucking sure of it. Jesus, Finlay said to himself. He was sounding like Babcock. At least, he was sounding like he imagined Babcock would sound as far as Finlay was, now, into the bottle of Johnny Walker Scotch with which Babcock, because it could have been no one else, had provided his quarters while he was visiting his mother in the wind-cursed, weary old war limbo of Whitstable.

'Whitstable,' Finlay said to nobody. He stretched his legs out from where he sprawled in his armchair. 'What a fucking shithole fucking dump.'

Hearing his own voice made him feel low. He despised himself, suddenly, overwhelmingly, for the mock-heroic of his own profane, blustering words. It wasn't Whitstable's fault. They had chosen Whitstable, probably, because you could get to the place by train and because the Luftwaffe were unlikely to launch a mass raid on a town chiefly significant for oyster beds. They had chosen it as a meeting place for him and his mother because Whitstable, to them, was amenable and safe. What really worried him, deep down, in a part of his mind that no amount of hard drink seemed able to infiltrate, was how little his mother had talked of his brother Tom.

Almost from his first conscious understanding of the inter-action between family, friends, neighbours – and this understanding had come to Finlay surprisingly late – he had been aware of the strong and widely shared supposition that his mother was 'gifted'. Gifted did not mean good at playing the piano, or sketching likenesses. Gifted, to everyone who had whispered the word in Finlay's proximity in Finlay's boyhood, had meant psychically adept. His mother had always denied it. She had never, to his knowledge, so much as studied the pattern of tea-leaves left at the bottom of an empty cup. She had never read a palm, never owned a tarot pack. But her mention of the seances had omitted, he knew, the relentless nagging and cajoling and imploring she would be facing now in the neighbourhood to hold a seance of her own. Throughout the entirety of the life he could remember having lived under his mother's roof, there had been oddities, enigmas, inexplicable events, atmospheres, coincidences, occasional thick, heavy forebodings. Individually he had ignored them all, in unspoken collusion with his brother, once his brother became old enough to acknowledge and be scared by them and happy to agree to ignore them too. But if you looked at these phenomena collectively, they amounted to a catalogue of the unexplained and inexplicable. Finlay remembered the time he had been awoken by the sound of singing in the kitchen and descended the stairs with Tom, and in the moonlight through the tiny kitchen window they had seen sitting at the kitchen table the spectre of their dead father, polishing his bayonet and blithely roaring some sentimental song. The shock had been in the detail. Finlay had been able to smell the black brew in his father's mess tin on the table, a mingling of hot, strong tea and stale bacon fat. He had smelled Brasso on the bayonet pommel and blade and the cold odour of steel under the polish. There was blood in the singing. Bright, coppery, it coloured the song as it bubbled from the fatal wound in his father's throat.

The song had been a lullaby and that's how Finlay had known, peeking through the door crack into the kitchen from the bottom of the stairs, that the apparition had not been real. It existed in his mind, where his father only ever sang lullabies to his infant boy. At the age of nine, when he saw this thing, it did not sit right with John Patrick Finlay that a man putting a shine on a killing weapon would croon a lullaby while he did so.

Then the apparition turned its head and smiled and winked at its watching sons.

Reason had been no comfort to Jack at the time or after. The ghost had frightened the life out of him and did so often, later, whenever he conjured it in the dark, tormenting himself, as children will.

In the here and now, Finlay shivered and gulped good whisky. Its flames answered the craving for escape from the chill settled inside his brain and belly. He had imagined that, of course. They both had. He and Tom had only imagined their father come back to sing in the kitchen in their house in Stanley Road. But Margaret Finlay, over the course of a singular day in Whitstable, had not mentioned her second son anything like enough to her first-born for comfort.

The train had terminated at Waterloo. In darkness, piled sandbags could not soften the sound echoing against marble, iron and glass in the great hall of railway space beyond the ticket collector. Finlay eased through knots and columns of men in greatcoats and packs, carrying rifles. He sensed rather than saw this mass of men and was glad it was too dark to see the disdain he felt his civilian clothes would provoke on their individual faces.

The smell of wet wool heated gently by paraffin stoves brought a strange comfort to him, a sort of nostalgia. It was similar to the smell after a match, as his father and his father's friends warmed themselves in a Bootle pub after a rainy afternoon spent watching the Reds from the Kop at Anfield. He could smell hair tonic and tobacco breath and coke embers and piston lubricant and leather and canvas webbing and gas-mask rubber and boot polish and occasional wafts of cologne signalling officers and the sour lack, everywhere, of hot water and soap. Amazing how important smell had become in the prevailing absence of light. Then his body tensed at the insistence of his brain, forcing him out of reverie. He had caught the train they had instructed him to catch. He was back, so he was back on duty. Alert to the sound of the sky, he walked to the entrance of the station, past the scrolled names of Southern Railway men who had fallen in what those who had survived it were now calling the 'fourteen–eighteen. He could not see, of course, the gold leaf etched into stone commemorating its long list of dead on the ornamental tablet as he passed underneath it. But he looked anyway.

The pavements were wet, but it was no longer raining. A

bright moon silvered the cold edges of cloud in a sky full of the brittle, cruel onset of winter. Finlay stopped at a tea wagon on Waterloo Road.

'What did you do in the war, Daddy?'

'I queued,' he thought to himself. He thought then of Albert Cooper. He was on Albert Cooper's ground. Not exactly, but near enough for the inexactitude of sentiment. His turn eventually came and he drank his tea alert to the gathering wail of the siren and the distant, foreboding throb of German engines. But neither actually sounded. It was quiet.

Finlay stopped walking half-way across Waterloo Bridge. From this vantage-point, in odd dabs and caresses of moonlight emerging from shifting cloud, you could convince yourself that London slumbered peaceful, and intact. In the distance to his left, moonlight filigreed the spires and fancies of the House of Commons and its fairy-tale clock tower. To his right, he could see almost as clearly as in daylight the dome of St Paul's. They had hit the cathedral twice. Neither bomb had exploded. The second had been an 800-pounder. Finlay knew that Richard Nevin had been a member of the fire crew that had winched the second bomb from the cathedral vaults. It had crashed through the front steps and travelled twenty-five feet through ancient masonry and sanctified space. They had tunnelled after it through gas mains, electrical cables and finally through the black, sucking mud into which the missile further descended when they tried to tether it. Christ alone knew how the thing had not detonated. Finlay rested his arms on cold stone and looked at the river. Under the exposed moon he could make out ropes of current towing urgent water forty feet below. It ran in braids and coils of tidal force that stippled the surface and forced water, white, caroming up the bridge buttresses.

Frederick Lange had seen energy harnessed by the hydro-electric turbines of a dam he had built on a glacial lake in the Austrian Alps. And this had inspired in him an interest in energy itself. But it must have been an abstract interest, because it had nothing to do with water turbines, Babcock said, or electricity. Now Frederick Lange was dead, or at least, had disappeared. His daughter was engaged in work that might be voluntary and that she described as translation, but was definitely secret. Either she deliberately lied about her father, or she had been misled about him. She carried out her clandestine work in a building of his design that was one of five Finlay had been tasked to protect, if he could, from the ravages of fire. And those buildings had nothing in common but for a certain geometric elegance, should you draw intersecting points between them on a map. He pictured in his mind the pentagram he had described in pencil on his own map. Maybe it was magic they were involved in after all. Hadn't Newton himself spent more time studying alchemy than astronomy? Finlay recalled reading something to that effect on the reverse side of a cigarette card, or in a comic book. His own scientific knowledge was pitiful, dismally limited to fire and how to put fires out. He knew the precise temperature at which almost everything that would support combustion would start to burn. He knew sufficient about water pressure to instigate and command the effective play of power hoses over a blaze. He never needed to hesitate over the choice between fighting fire with water or with foam. He knew about volatility and he understood as well as any man alive the way to fight a noxious, or a chemical, or an explosive fire. About the science of energy, he knew nothing. He looked at the water toiling beneath his feet and allowed his vacant mind to scan the plans of Absalom House. They were transparently anodine, blank with maddening mystery.

It must be a runic thing, he thought, resuming his journey. Absalom House was built on a ley line and gathered dormant energy from the stars, or from deep under the earth. Then of course there was the Absalom dome. A picture came into his head from a film he had seen, Victor Frankenstein, frazzle-haired and mad, channelling lightning from an electrical storm through a humming transformer and jolting life into his grotesque creation. Finlay was entertaining himself with more of this nonsense when he turned on to the Strand and was stiffened into motionlessness by the sound of a stricken aircraft. Then he saw it, sparks and white flames engulfing its huge shadow not sixty feet above his head as it juddered from the north, across the Strand, towards the river. It must have just come out of a stall,

Finlay realized, to have flown, burning, in silence. Its engines had re-engaged literally above him and he felt their volume judder through him as he registered the twin swastikas painted on to the underside of the wings and identified the stricken aircraft as a Heinkel bomber. Its undercarriage was half-down and rubber from its burning tyres descended and blazed a path of dripping fire that lit the road. Then with a groan the aeroplane had passed beyond view and there was a coughing lurch and its engines ceased. He saw something tumble, ablaze, cartwheeling over the road. The object came to a halt in a welter of sparks against the obdurate stone of a Strand building and he saw that it was a chair, leather and horsehair burning furiously, a steel frame giving the thing identifiable shape. Finlay heard something tear the sky in spasms and felt an intense joy at the metal, strafing sound. Our ground-to-air has brought this fucker down, he thought. Yes! And then, while he was constructing his next thought, he heard the smack and then the rumble and roar of impact as the bomber descended into collision. Some poor mother's son, more likely sons, entered his mind unwelcome, interloping, momentary, before he banished the speculation. Our ground-to-air brought that fucker down. We have not lost this war, he said to himself, skirting shards of metal as the chair debris skittered and contracted, in the angle of pavement and edifice, with unaccustomed cold. A part of him wanted to scrutinize the wreckage closely, better to appreciate the actual fabric of the enemy. But more of him wanted to travel on and Finlay was too acutely aware of just how rare in his life had become the luxury of personal choice, to linger.

'You really do want to go?'

It was a statement of fact, not a question.

'I do. Yes, sir. I do.'

It was White. It was White only. The windows had been repaired. More accurately, they had been replaced. The new ones were opaque and tough-looking. Maybe they were bomb-proof, Finlay thought, as Grey had insisted Winston was. Their new windows allowed a sort of second-hand, sufficient light, but no view. Finlay regretted the absence of their former, exalted vista.

He had enjoyed the expansive sky, its comedy of errant barrage balloons.

'Tea?'

'I'll have a cup if you're having one, sir.'

'Biscuit?'

'No, sir. Not unless a biscuit is obligatory.'

White sighed. He spread his hands across the unblemished blotter covering the centre of the desk. He pressed a button on his telephone and they sat in silence until, after a short interval, tea was brought. Tea was poured. Milk and sugar were proffered. Presently, both men sipped. White sighed again.

'What is it you miss, Chief Fire Officer?'

'Beg pardon, sir?'

'There's bull, I suppose,' White said. 'Buffing buttons and belt-buckle and cap-badge. Whitening belt-webbing. Spit and polishing of boots. Scouring your mess tin and cleaning and shining generally, for kit inspection. Keeping the breach of your rifle spotless, keening your bayonet blade.'

Finlay said nothing.

'Drill, then. Perhaps you are that rare martial perfectionist who craves the collective percussion of boots on a parade ground. Bayonet practice. Obstacle courses and cross-country runs.'

'No, sir.'

'Is it men? Do you revel in the company of men in the confines of a barracks hut? Do you find a fulfilment there?'

'No.'

'Pale buttocks. Vaseline. Acceptance and understanding, dark and manful. Do those words suggest to you a sort of bliss?'

Finlay did not know what to say.

'You need not be ashamed,' White said. 'Really, you needn't.'

Finlay said nothing. He sipped tea. White sat. Finlay had not yet seen him blink.

'You were in a gunnery unit, of course. I forgot. Forgive me. Where they teach you to love your gun, rather than to fuck your comrades. And did you, Finlay? Did you unrequitedly love your gun?'

'Our guns were rather old, sir. Somewhat unreliable. They were more in need of constant care than deserving of affection.'

There was a silence. White's anger was of a different order from that of the Immaculate Major, which Finlay now recalled, on an earlier occasion, confronting in this room. White's anger was altogether of a different magnitude.

'What, then?'

'I'm buggered if I know. sir.'

White brought his hands up off the blotter and pushed his fingers into his cheeks. 'Three days ago you tendered your written resignation from the Fire Service and reapplied to join a unit of the Royal Artillery.'

'Yes. Yes, sir.'

'After all we have told you. About your value to us.'

'Negligible, sir. With respect. I have done everything possible to those five buildings in terms of fire prevention and the retarding of fire. I have drilled the staff of each building. I have drilled the auxiliaries. I have lectured on the specifics to the Chief Officers of each and every Fire Station in the remotest proximity, in the direst emergency, to those buildings. I don't want to wait. I want to fight. I want to fight until this war is won and then when the enemy is defeated, if I survive the fighting, then I'm sure I'd be honoured to return to London and the Service.'

White looked at him. 'I understand there was some unpleasantness last night at a tea wagon not far from Waterloo Station.'

'How did you know about that?'

'We are not having you followed. That's only one of your many conceits. There was a Home Guard Captain at the scene and he made a report.'

'I was spat at in the queue,' Finlay said. 'Corporal from the Lancashire Fusiliers. Hawked and gobbed in my face.'

'And what did you do?'

'I didn't do anything. The Home Guard Captain pointed a pistol at my chest before I could do anything. I made it fairly plain, verbally, that I thought the Corporal should have stayed in Lancashire, sir. Specifically in an anatomical location. Then I took my hanky from my pocket and wiped phlegm off my face.'

White looked thoughtful. 'The chaps who cut coal suffer much the same sort of abuse,' he said. 'Miners are not provided with a lapel button such as those the merchant seamen on the convoys are given to wear. It's damned unfair on them.'

Finlay tried to imagine a chap mining coal.

'We could get you a lapel button, I suppose. Perhaps the wisest thing would be simply to keep you, for the duration, out of civilian clothes.'

'What happened last night happened after I tendered my resignation. With respect, sir, being spat at is nowhere near the point.'

White brought both hands down on to the desk-top with a thud that jerked Finlay to his feet at attention. His eyes fixed, for fear of looking at the inferno of White's furious face, on a framed chart behind White on the wall. It was a plan of a ship, one of the iron-clad merchant vessels of the previous century, described in section from its keel through each of its dividing decks to its superstructure. And then Finlay had it. Absalom House had a concealed floor. It was so fucking obvious! The disparity that had nagged away, without his consciously knowing it, between the height of its rooms and the exterior dimensions of the building allowed for a hidden floor. Finlay looked at the section of the old ship hung on the wall behind White's head and it all became abundantly clear. There was a floor in the building that did not appear on the Absalom blueprint; at which the lift did not stop, to which the turns of the stairwell did not correspond, in which God alone knew what went on. Unless Babcock knew, because Babcock seemed to know a lot about Frederick Lange. Unless Rebecca Lange knew, and had lied to him in a language foreign to her with the fluent conviction that could only come from long practice. White was roaring. Finlay recognized the ship on the wall. She was the *Great Eastern*. He was aware of the undistinguished, even pathetic, fate the vessel had met. But he thought that unlike Brunel's iron-hulled folly, doomed by ambitious design and preposterous tonnage, he was likely to weather this particular storm.

Finlay stood and concentrated his gaze on the plan of the ship on the wall; on riveted iron plates and immense boilers and steam turbines designed to churn those great bronze screws through ocean water. His eyes focused on bulkhead and funnel, on mast, sail, winch, girder, anchor and chain; on the vast intricacy of the floating city that comprised a great ship. His mind pondered the power that would be needed to urge motion, speed, direction, out of inertia. It was the lurch into life from idleness to propulsion. It was the lurch into life. Power. Energy. Absalom's hidden floor. White raged at the edge of Finlay's senses and Finlay pondered Brunel's flawed leviathan as his vile breakfast conspired with his nerves, rebelling against his stomach and forcing a series of sour belches from his throat.

He had breakfasted with Nevin.

'Your guess is as good as mine,' Nevin had said, bravado apparently intact, as Finlay slid his plate on to their table and sniffed at its charred contents.

'It may have been welsh rarebit, once,' Nevin said. 'But that was before last rites and cremation. I can probably find you an urn for anything you don't eat.'

Nevin did not look good. He was eating porridge. His hands were shaking so badly that it was difficult for him even to manipulate a spoon. Finlay thought that the porridge had been not so much chosen as necessitated by the need for the spoon. A knife and fork would have been beyond the tremors Nevin was failing to conceal. As if to prove the point, Nevin reached half-way to the salt cellar on the table-top between them and then pulled his hand back, as if he had changed his mind. Finlay picked up the salt and reached across and shook some over Nevin's bowl.

'Much obliged, Errol.' He gestured at his side plate. 'Maybe you could spread a bit of margarine on to that piece of toast and chuck it at me, the way the kids chuck sprats to the seals at London Zoo. I could probably catch it after a few practice tries.'

Nevin smiled, but the smile came out all wrong. It stretched his face into something ghastly, the smile of a clown from some morbid circus dream. Finlay sawed with the serrated edge of his knife at the culinary pyre on his plate. The knife was light in his fingers, its blade like counterfeit steel, dull-edged, inadequate to its task.

'Didn't they give you a bayonet in the army?' Nevin said.

'They did.'

'You should have hung on to it.'

Finlay put his knife and fork down on the table and picked up the charcoal-coloured construction from his plate, pulled it apart and bit into the smaller of the two resulting pieces. It was hard, resisting his bite. When he bit through it, it tasted like the dead, damp aftermath of fire.

Nevin watched with interest. 'You've your own teeth then,' he said.

'Why shouldn't I have?' Finlay said, chewing, wishing he wasn't.

'Scouser. Borstal boy. Just assumed you'd have had a full set by now. No offence.'

'None taken, I'm sure,' Finlay said. He swallowed, thinking the reflex rash, even dangerous, when he considered what it was that was now on its way through his system. 'I could tell you that I owe the present state of my pearlies to the fresh food I was able to steal as a thief and a Liverpudlian, which as you know are one and the same—'

Nevin nodded.

'—from the docks down the road. But it wouldn't be true. The truth is that, like every Hollywood star, I have invested a portion of my fortune in dentistry.'

Nevin dropped his spoon into the congealing mess of his porridge. 'I can't eat this. Not even a Jock could stomach this slop.'

'I thought you were a Jock.'

'Londoner. Born and bred.'

'Nevin's a Jock name.'

'So is Finlay,' Nevin said. 'If you think about it.'

Finlay got to his feet. 'More tea?'

'I don't mind if I do.'

Finlay walked over to the canteen counter and smiled at the woman standing closest to the tea urn and gestured with his fingers for two cups. She took a big metal pot off the counter and revived the stewed brew inside it with a blast of steam and boiling water from a tap on the urn. The woman wore her hair in a peroxide fan spread over her shoulders, hoisted up from the nape of her neck by a folded scarf secured by a knot on the top of her head. Finlay could not fathom the seemingly universal popularity of this style. He thought it looked unflattering at best and on its older wearers positively sinister. The great swathes of yellow hair looked dead and bleached the features. He took the two mugs she slid across the counter and thought that Nevin's would provide less refreshment than struggle, one more morning ordeal in the man's convulsing hand.

'We thought we had it tough. Do you remember?' Nevin said, staring at his untouched tea.

Finlay sipped. The brew was weak and scalding. 'We did. Sometimes.'

'Nah. Cake walk. All of it.' He reached for his mug and retracted his hand. 'No comparison.'

'Did you hear any reports of crashed aircraft last night?'

'Ours or theirs?'

'Theirs.'

'One. Heinkel. Came off second-best against a Hurricane over Gravesend. Lost its compass, lost its bearings. Came down over one of the Southwark wharves. The pilot was the only one of the crew to survive the dogfight, but he was badly wounded, apparently. They reckon he knew he'd bought it and was trying to bring the aircraft and its full payload of bombs down on top of Bankside power station.'

'Sweet Jesus.'

'Yes indeed,' Nevin said. By diverting himself with his story, he had successfully manoeuvred his mug into a position in front of his face, where it shook only slightly. His elbow was braced on the table. 'Your Jerry, Errol, is nothing if not single-minded.'

After hearing the last of the stricken bomber, Finlay had crossed the Strand and walked along Wellington Street. His route was as dark as the sky maintained it. He passed and saw nobody. He negotiated the labyrinth bordering Covent Garden by touch, by moon, by memory. He continued as the route, despite its straightness, became Bow Street and then Endell Street. He crossed St Giles High Street into Dyott Street and emerged on to New Oxford Street, turning left for Tottenham Court Road. He had turned into Rathbone Place and was actually engaged in the blind door elaboration of entering The Wheatsheaf pub before it occurred to his conscious mind that this had always been his destination. Finlay quickly realized that outside the incandescent orbit of Rebecca Lange, he could be easily anonymous in here. Nobody spat at the supposed cowardice suggested by his civilian clothes. Perhaps two thirds of the men in the pub, and almost all of the women, were dressed as people had dressed for a casual evening out before the war. There were uniforms, some of them, Finlay saw, denoting surprisingly high rank. And for a Monday night, almost all of the women and some of the civilian men wore the scruffy flamboyance Finlay had thought such a novelty on his first visit. Whatever his prejudices, whatever the depth of his instinctive contempt for anything that defied his preconceptions and so intimidated him, he had to admit that in their contrived, bedraggled way, they were a stylish lot. And better than that. Tonight their general effect was to enable him to hide in plain sight at the bar, where he sipped a surprisingly satisfying pint of bitter as he waited. Shaping his lips to the drink, he felt the stickiness of phlegm not properly cleaned off tightening the skin of his nose and cheeks. Never mind. Washing would wait. Washing was no longer the luxuriant pleasure it had been before the final sliver of Grey's abducted Palmolive bar had finally slipped into nothing between his fingers. Perhaps Babcock's brother-in-law had access to proper soap. Finlay would have to ask. Don't ask, you don't get, as his mother, who had never in her life asked for anything, was fond of saying.

Some Air Force men were singing around the piano. It was amazing how long they were allowed to wear their hair. The pilot officer seated at the piano had a cigarette clenched between his teeth and his hair flopped down over his forehead half-way to the keys. He wore no tie and the collar of his shirt was splayed out over his tunic lapels in the manner of someone basking in a summer deck-chair on Blackpool sands. He could play the piano all right though, Finlay thought. He looked about, but did not think he would see Rebecca Lange here tonight.

As she had dabbed his eye and cooled his head and undressed him on her sofa after rejecting his feeble Friday evening advance, he had tried to salvage something, tried to assure her that his interest lay in more than just a swift sexual conquest, by committing her to another date. She had agreed to this, but said not until the following Thursday, when she would meet him at seven at Absalom House. As she slept and he watched, it seemed to Finlay a yearning eternity until the following Thursday. Either the delay signalled a fatal lack of ardour, or she was engaged in something that would genuinely occupy her for the better part of a week. So when he went through her bag, as she slumbered on into the small hours, he had been relieved to discover there a return train ticket to Edinburgh.

He sipped good bitter and listened to the pilot officer at the piano play something full of choppy syncopation until his mates pressured him again into hammering chords anthemic, familiar; yet another of those tunes framed for the roar of their beery doggerel. They were drunk and Finlay envied them; not their intoxication, but what they must be feeling, as fighting men. Finlay was too intrigued by life to envy these men the risk they faced of dying. Nor did he envy them the manner of it. Fighter pilots most often perished in the bright agony of a burning cockpit. What he envied in these men was the intensity of life lived defiant and full, as death, patient and watchful, coveted them. He emptied his glass. He was ordering another when the Irishman walked into the pub.

Finlay took him in the lavatory. He waited the half-hour until the Irishman weaved his way from the raillery at the bar towards the gents and simply followed him. He paused in the Irishman's wake for a count of five and then swung open the door. The fellow was in full flow. He sounded like a dray horse pissing on cobbles. Smelled like it, too. All that was missing was the steam. He was whistling as he pissed. Finlay put the heel of his left hand at the base of the Irishman's skull and straightened his arm with a snap that propelled the man's face with a hollow thud into the iron cistern in front of him. Still holding the Irishman there, he landed two fast hooks with his right up into the man's kidneys. Fair play, Finlay thought, he's game, as the Irishman turned and tried to stiff-arm him with a sweeping blow. But Finlay was under it, sinking short, accurate lefts and rights into the

Dubliner's midriff. The man's body was obdurate with muscle, but Finlay wasn't hitting telephone directories. He took a step back and the Irishman dipped at the knees, his right hand reaching as he dropped. He was going for his kiltie blade. Finlay kicked as hard as he could and his right foot connected just under the Irishman's descending chin. He had time to wish he was wearing boots and not brogues before his man realized he had lost this fight and hit the privy floor where he lay in a foetal ball.

'There'll be a next time, cunt,' the Irishman said, from between the fingers curled around his face. The kick must have hurt him. His voice was slurred and foggy. 'She's got the clap, you know.'

Finlay dropped down, dead-legging him in the meat of his thigh with a knee. The Irishman groaned and then sighed.

Finlay got up and stood over him.

'Where did you hear that?'

'I was the one gave it to her.'

Finlay said nothing. He gave the man a kick.

'There'll be a next time.'

'Yeah. And next time I'll stick that knife in your sock up your arse.'

Finlay rinsed his face free of phlegm and sputum and settled in the armchair to Babcock's gift of Scotch. It had been a full day and it was still only ten o'clock. He sat there mindful of bombs, alert to the silent telephone, more than half-expecting Babcock to knock and claim the company his whisky had bought and paid for. But Babcock didn't knock and the time came, eventually, when Finlay knew that he would not, just as he knew that the siren would not sound, the telephone ring, the crump and shudder of bombs send him climbing on feet that would be drunken now, and uncertain, up the spiral of iron to the streets. The Germans were saving their carnage for another night. He hefted the weight, in the hand not occupied with his whisky glass, of the knuckleduster he had plucked from the Dubliner's pocket prior to straight-arming him, as the man pissed. It was heavy and smooth, fashioned from brass and buffed to a dull, workshop sheen. It was a quite beautiful object, seductive to the touch, if you were ignorant of its function. Finlay tried to imagine Grey wearing one of these over his fist, creeping through no-man's-land in dead of night, filthy with mud and the rank water of shell holes, boot polish smeared across his face as camouflage, leading a trench raid. But the image defeated him. He could connect an object like a knuckleduster with Grey only in some ironic context. As a paperweight on an antique desk, perhaps. He suspected dimly, drunkenly, that this prejudice worked to Grey's advantage. The knuckleduster slipped heavily from Finlay's fingers to the floor.

'Please let Tom be alive,' he said before descending into sleep. 'Please, please, let Tom be alive,' Finlay pleaded aloud. He must have been talking to himself. Jack Finlay did not believe in a God. And there was nobody in his cell with him to listen to his entreaty.

He carried his grip from the Ministry building along Whitehall, across Trafalgar Square, to the Strand. In the gym off the Strand he punished his body on the apparatus and the mat until his muscles were defeated and any summoning of strength brought in response only dry retches from his belly.

'You stink of drink, on top of everything else,' White had said, when the rage had finally subsided.

'I understand the men who fought in the 'fourteen–eighteen drank quite a bit,' Finlay said.

That made White blink.

'Rarely drew a sober breath,' he said. 'Personally speaking. But you are hardly in the trenches now.'

The pupils of White's eyes blossomed, black, in acknowledge-ment of his crass mistake, but Finlay did not want to let the thing go.

'I want to fight. All I want to do is fight. Evidently the job is easier this time around. I'd be more than happy to do it sober, sir.'

'Go away,' White said. 'For God's sake and the sake of your country, do what it is that you are best qualified to do. I cannot say that you will ever know the true value of the work in which you are engaged. Probably you will not. Such is the nature of modern war. But your work is not futile. Far from it. And you should have the humility to take comfort and even satisfaction in that.'

Finlay turned to go.

'Chief Fire Officer?'

'Sir?'

'I doubt we could have accomplished what we did entirely sober. I doubt we could have got through it, frankly. I greatly regret that your father did not live to tell you something of it. If he had, then you would know.'

'I regret it too, sir.'

Finlay saluted, a genuine salute, a salutation, not a goading provocation, and he left.

Nine

THE GERMANS hit Mitre Street that night. Bombs were dropped on two of Finlay's buildings, destroying them. Finlay arrived at the sites to look at craters lit by burning wood and drifts of paper debris, illuminating only vast strews of rubble. There were no bodies that Finlay could see. There were no fire crews, either, because the destruction had been sudden and complete and the fire crews were anyway engaged elsewhere. At Mitre Street, Finlay fingered flurries of floating ash away from his face and felt in his throat the familiar tightness inflicted by dust and destruction.

A half-hour after Mitre Street, a second wave of bombers hit a third of his buildings. This time, it was incendiaries rather than high explosives, and it gave him a fight to engage in. By now, auxiliaries had arrived and there were pumps to play pressured water over the flames. The auxiliaries were willing. But there was no seat to the fire for them to attack. And the water pressure from their hoses was not sufficient to deprive the jelloid, sporadic, scattering fires of oxygen. They hit the fires with their hose jets and the effect was only to spread them further; to have them spit and scatter, antagonized, through the parched and brittle innards of the building, now exposed, by blast, to burn. Through guttering windows, Finlay saw flames embrace panelled walls and devour smashed furniture and the lathe of torn ceilings and then the oak joists protruding from every floor like so many shattered, combustible bones. There was not much smoke. But as the blaze gathered impetus the heat grew searing, light-bending, blasting water from hoses to steam in mid-trajectory. Men surrounded the building, their tunics drenched and filthy with ash, drying in the blast of heat and then threatening to smoulder and burn when their wearers tried to edge towards the blaze. There were men, too, fighting the fire from the floors of adjacent buildings. It was safer to attack from there, out of the reach of falling debris and protected from the incendiary rounds fired in stippling, ricocheting bursts from the machine-guns of the Messerschmitt fighters that had flown as escort for the raiding bombers. The fire fighters on top of their turntable ladders were totally exposed. Finlay had two crews in the sky and hoses from buildings across the street trained on them to prevent the men atop the ladders from bursting into flames. Above the roar of reaching flame there were odd, sporadic pops of noise, like rifle shots, as volatile objects exploded in the heat and sent shrapnel fragments of white-hot debris zinging into the night. There was a loud report and a commotion among three men manning a hose a few feet to Finlay's right. They lurched for balance as one of them gurgled and fell and Finlay grabbed the ungoverned hose nozzle just as they lost all control of the jet. Order and aim re-established, he looked at the man on the ground, who was dead. Something was buried in his neck, half-severing his head. It was red, not with blood, but with paint. It looked like part of the cylindrical cone of a fire extinguisher. Finlay recognized it as one of two with which he had recommended they equip each floor. He felt his hands blistering on the hose nozzle and signalled to the men holding the hose with him to retreat. They shuffled back carefully over the corpse of their colleague. Shrapnel impact had removed the man's helmet and his hair was starting to smoulder. Finlay roared for a stretcher, eyes fixed on the still-strengthening blaze embracing the building in front of him, but no stretcher came. Long shots would not defeat the blaze, Finlay knew. But the heat was too intense for crews to get close enough really to attack the fire. Other buildings, all around them, were burning. There was a danger that the collapse of buildings would crush hoses, even branch hoses, under rubble. It was the worst fear of the men; to lose their weapon of water, surrounded, engulfed, by burning buildings; to be trapped, defenceless, by fire.

'Foam?' Finlay screamed at a leading fire fighter, who stumbled towards him out of careening heat.

'Foam?'

The man gasped and removed his helmet with fingers padded with blisters. He threw the helmet on the ground. If I spit on that thing, it will hiss, Finlay thought. But I will not hear the hiss for the roar of the fire we're fighting. Reluctantly, he beckoned men away from his building. For whatever reason, there was no foam. The cause was lost, the risk urgent. He could sense mortar diminishing in heat between blasted bricks. The whole edifice was about to come down. Its collapsing floors would push buckling walls out towards his crews and they would be buried under tons of descending stone. There was no point in losing brave men to a lost cause. But brave they were, or merely inexperienced, and they retreated with a creeping, tenacious reluctance. Then the building perished with a deafening crump and Finlay saw two crews simply vanish into the melding, red-white brilliance of raining masonry. Finlay steadied the men on his own hose and then skirted the periphery of the blaze, directing each retreating crew within range to aim their hoses at the places where the missing men had been. With the collapse of the building, the impetus of the blaze was diminishing and with it, the heat. Fire crews, first sensing and then feeling this, got closer in a tightening circle about the high, huge cone of volatile ruin where the building had been. But the missing crews were gone, swallowed by hissing bricks and girders still white with heat and black, skeletal beams.

'Lost,' Finlay said.

'Three down,' said a voice to his left. 'Two to go.'

Finlay turned. It was Grey.

'There's a basement,' Grey said. 'I mean, there was. Do you think there is still?'

'My mind's on six dead men. Incinerated. Crushed.'

'Of course it is,' Grey said. 'We should try not to let their deaths be in vain.'

The aeroplanes had gone. The raid was over. At least here, the fires were under control. Men were damping down now. But branches of hoses and perhaps some of the pumps as well had been crushed under the debris of other buildings and the jets of water were fitful and weak. Some of the mains had been hit and so not all of the pumps were being replenished. They were a long way from the inexhaustible water source of the river. Surrounding buildings still burned, taking the attention of the men, making them anxious and fearful of being trapped. Those that had not seen the deaths had by now heard about the casualties.

'Pull them out,' Grey said.

'My men stay until the fires are extinguished. It's our fucking job and we'll fucking well do it.'

Grey put a hand on Finlay's shoulder. The epaulette had been torn from his tunic there. Steam was rising from the sodden cloth. Grey squeezed and then patted. His voice was gentle. 'At best they will flood the basement. At worst, they will be trapped by the fires burning around us and needlessly die. Pull them out, Chief Fire Officer. Please.'

Finlay skirted the building for a second time, seeking out and giving each lead fire fighter the instruction to withdraw. The order spread, as welcome as pestilence through the chain of command. Dirty, dishevelled, dull with fatigue, the men receded in reluctant clusters from the scene, gathering hoses, dismantling ladders, regrouping around their big Dennis appliances, seeking tea. The men, regular and auxiliary, were well drilled and unshirking in their dedication. It was all they could do to obey an order they considered so fundamentally at odds with their duty. There was fight and determination in these men. They were a bedraggled, weary lot. They were also a very long way from defeated.

'Now what?'

Grey nodded at the rough pyramid of ruin in front of them. The pile glowed and smouldered and spat. Small avalanches tumbled here and there down the general mass as it cooled, reluctant, volatile. Finlay tried to remove from his mind the sight of men perishing under a deluge of scalding stone. He estimated that their unrecovered bodies lay under ten or twelve feet of debris. They lay under coping stones, sections of concrete floor and reinforcing girders as wide as his waist. It was the girders, steel, contracting now as they cooled, that made their pyre so dangerous a ruin. But the dead men were covered by several tons of it. At least they had not been burned alive.

Finlay looked Grey in the face for the first time. 'The basement is intact. That's why we're looking at a hill and not a field of debris. That much you know, however clueless you find it convenient to seem. The ground floor of this building, or the ceiling of its basement, because they're one and the same, is composed of twenty-seven inches of high-grade concrete strengthened by steel reinforcing rods with a one-and-a-half-inch diameter. Heat rises. But there will have been sufficient radiant heat to reach the rods.'

'And what? Melt them?'

'Nothing like. Just enough to put a bit of flexibility in the floor.' He nodded at the unquiet pyramid. 'That lot will have put a bit of curve on the basement ceiling. A bit of concave.'

'Will it hold?'

'I'm a fire fighter, Captain Grey. Ask a structural engineer.'

'Will it hold?'

Finlay looked and considered. 'Probably. Depends on how many cracks there are in the concrete and the weight above those cracks. And then there's the fact to consider that when those reinforcing rods cool, the metal will have turned to something more in the nature of iron than steel. And iron, Captain Grey, shares one of your own characteristics.'

Grey stroked his chin.

'Illuminate me.'

'Iron is brittle,' Finlay said. Grey lit a cigarette. The cigarette was lit with a lighter, with a flourish, in flagrant disregard of the black-out. Finlay would have been less shocked seeing somebody piss in front of the altar half-way through mass. Then it occurred to him that with pockets of fire burning throughout their entire, blasted vicinity, the glow of a cigarette tip was a less than significant thing.

'Can we get into the basement, Chief Fire Officer?'

'You might remember I wanted to fill it with a supply of standing water.'

'But you couldn't, could you, because I told you it was out of the question.'

'It might contain water now,' Finlay said. 'The depth of the basement is twenty-five feet. We've played an awful lot of water over the site.'

'Most of what I saw evaporated,' Grey said, drily.

'Some of the mains around here have ruptured in the bombing,' Finlay said. 'That's why the lads were struggling with water pressure. The water table is high in this part of the city anyway.'

'You're fencing with me, Chief Fire Officer. Unless you've got the wind up.'

'There's a storm drain runs under the basement. It's a fair size drain. And there's a fair chance it could have kept the basement from flooding. But there's no guarantee.'

Grey dragged hard on the last of his cigarette, wincing, his face cadaverous in the firefly brilliance of its extinction. He flicked the butt away. 'How do we find out?'

'We'll know pretty quickly,' Finlay said. He nodded at the pile. 'With that lot there, the storm drain is our only means of access.'

Grey would not leave the site and Finlay had to run as far back as Bishopsgate to locate an appliance equipped with what he needed. He collected two fire axes, two electric torches, a crowbar and a pair of boots, helmet and spare tunic for Grey. He was buggered, he thought, if he was going to let Grey go down there in civvies. It occurred to him then that buggered was not a wisely chosen word to use in this connection and he laughed, spirits raised at the prospect of the mad, perhaps even crucial adventure which was imminent. The crew of the appliance turned and looked at this barking apparition, teeth and eyes brilliantly white against the soot blackening his face, and they recognized his rank and were able to stop the incredulity and contempt from spilling into their weary faces. It would not have mattered. Finlay was at a pitch where he would no longer have noticed. He had a fire fighter help him back with the equipment for the sake of speed, the pair of them sprinting through still-smouldering chasms of brick, over hot rubble and furniture shards heaped high in the streets, like scree, through crunching, blackened glass, breathing always ash, soot; everywhere the dank, bile-bitter flavour of defeated fire. Grey pulled on the rubber boots and buttoned the tunic without comment. He buckled his belt and fastened the chinstrap of his steel helmet and then stood there with the fire axe held between both hands at port arms, the way an infantryman might carry a rifle into combat. Attired in the tunic, belt and helmet, in the glow of heat and the light of diminishing flames, he did not look very much like a fire fighter. He looked more than ever like a soldier, one awaiting the word of command that would take him unflinching into action. Finlay appraised Grey, full of confusion about him. He had never before so respected and despised a man. He had not thought so contradictory a combination of feelings possible.

'This way,' he said. To his own ears, his voice sounded flat, devoid of its usual inflection. Grey's remark about having the wind up had stung. Finlay knew that what they were about to do was very dangerous. But he did not want Grey to hear in his words a hint of the trepidation he felt. He was exhilarated at the thought of doing something important. His experience and his training urged him to be cautious. Experience had demonstrated to him the sometimes lethal distinction between vanity and courage. He was about to take a man undrilled, unconditioned and entirely ignorant of the most basic procedures into a place of potentially lethal hazard. He knew it was a stupid thing to do. At that decisive moment, there were many opposing imperatives in the mind of John Patrick Finlay. But he was a man for whom, in an emergency, action had always presided over thought. He started off towards a manhole from which he knew he could reach the basement storm drain of his bombed building. This was always assuming, of course, that the manhole in mind was not covered by a ton of newly delivered rubble. Finlay started off. Grey, like the dutiful soldier he was, fell in behind.

The water was no more than ankle deep in the stink and quiet of the storm drain. Moisture dripped down the curvatures of its moss-covered brick like a busy rumour of the catastrophe above. Finlay held his torch at waist height and pointed the beam a few feet ahead of where they were going. There were no rats. The dank and furtive slither of rats had always been a feature of his past excursions under London's streets. Their absence was at once welcome and strange. He could hear Grey splash after him, guided by his light. He had told Grey to save the battery of his own torch. It was quieter than Finlay had thought it would be. The density of the brick above them made it silent to the chaos of the streets. The quiet had a dense, subterranean quality. Finlay fought his claustrophobia as he always had to fight it, with measured breaths and images of space and light in his mind and at the back of his mind, with the anchor of responsibility tethering the high flights of panic. He thought briefly, and with self-reproach, of his brother, trapped in a tube of steel and rivets under a turbid sea. He listened for the steady splash of Grey's rubber boots through the runnel of filth. And he heard them. And he heard Grey's panting breath. His consumption of cigarettes had inflicted poor wind on the Captain. It was a habit Finlay assumed he had taken up in the trenches. The cigarette ration had been more generous than the food. They had all chain-smoked. Except his dad. After the armistice, Jimmy Breslin, his father's best mate in the battalion, had come to their house and spent an hour in the kitchen talking to Finlay's mum. When Jimmy went, he left a scattered snowfall of stinking dimps on the kitchen floor. As if at random an image of Rebecca Lange, slumbering in the dawn light, invaded Finlay's mind. Finlay had never smoked.

'How do you know which way to go? I'm lost already.'

'There are two ways of telling.' Finlay gestured at the water in his torch beam. Curls of weightless ash floated towards them, past their ankles. 'The current is one indication. Storm drains are designed to empty outwards.'

'Obviously,' said Grey, chiding himself. 'What's the other sign?'

'Heat. We're walking towards a heat source. A bloody great mountain of hot rubble. Can't you feel it getting hotter?'

In the glimmer of reflected light from the torch beam, Finlay saw Grey nod and unfasten the collar button of his tunic.

An iron grille protected the branch tunnel that Finlay estimated would access their basement. It was secured by heavy steel staples sunk into cement. Finlay examined the obstacle and then offered his torch to Grey and asked him to play the beam steady on it. He took his fire axe from his belt and swung the blunt of the head upward, using the power of his hips and then his shoulders in a savage blow that struck sparks and sang with metal protest around the tunnel walls. After the third blow aimed at the same spot, the bar of the grille under Finlay's assault snapped.

'Brittle. Just like you said.'

'Not that fucking brittle,' Finlay said. He grinned and spat on his hands and went back to work. After ten minutes of loud violence he had smashed his way through four more of the bars. Then both men worked together to lever off the grille with a crowbar.

The branch tunnel they had accessed was no more than three feet high and they were obliged to crawl along it through a thick sludge of sodden ash. After about forty feet, they came to another obstacle, this time a set of bars, set vertically, like those that confine a convict behind the window of a prison cell. Finlay examined these in the torchlight. By now, the heat and damp were tropical in their intensity and both men were sweating heavily with effort under the clumsiness of protective clothing and equipment.

'Looks pretty formidable,' Grey said.

'Could be worse,' Finlay said. 'If those bars were set into concrete we'd be well and truly fucked.'

'What a marvellous thought. To be well and truly fucked,' Grey said.

Despite himself, Finlay laughed. 'Here, I'm going to try to kick our way through these bars. They're only secured by screws cemented into the stone, so far as I can tell. They seem to be there mostly for effect, as a bit of decoration.'

'Cosmetic,' Grey said.

'You will have to brace me, Mr Grey. I can't get the purchase lying in this shit. I'll just slide about.'

Behind Finlay, Grey wedged himself sideways in the tunnel with the pressure of his feet and shoulders. And then with his back braced against Grey, Finlay lifted both feet and kicked hard at the bars. They shuddered and flaked with rust and falling brick dust. But they did not budge. In minutes Finlay's feet were sore, the heels tender and bruised. He cursed his rubber boots, wishing he could swap them for a pair soled and heeled in stiff and heavy leather.

'I don't think this is going to work,' Finlay said.

'Do we have a fallback plan?'

'Yes. We fall back.'

'Not possible, I'm afraid.' There was command in Grey's voice, sudden and unmistakable.

'You're not in charge down here,' Finlay said, angered. 'Turning back has nothing to do with having the wind up. There are no people here in need of rescue. And you don't carry out salvage ops in conditions like these.'

'This is not a salvage op.'

'I've seen the machines this building housed for myself. They look like the sort of contraptions kids feed with pennies in amusement arcades. How hard can it be to make more of them? You must have plans. Circuit diagrams. Technicians.'

Grey sweated and breathed through his mouth. 'It isn't the machines, Chief Fire Officer. It's the information one of them contains. The information is irreplaceable. And therefore priceless.'

'We're being bombed, for fuck's sake.'

'What's your point?'

'You should have copied the information. Duplicated it.'

'Do that and you immediately compromise security.'

'What's the nature of the information?'

'Please,' Grey said. 'Trust me on this.'

Just then there was a groan, melancholy and terrible, like the sigh of some great beast of the sea. Finlay and Grey looked at one another. 'That was the floor above the basement,' Finlay said. 'We don't have a lot of time, Captain.'

'Swap places,' Grey said. This was difficult in the cramped, wet space, and lack of time made them both urgent and clumsy when they needed to be deft. But they swapped around and Grey lashed and jack-knifed with his long piston legs against the bars. They gave with a sudden clang, an opening rent on one side, and Finlay felt the impact of recoil as Grey kicked even harder.

'You are stronger than you look,' Finlay said, as they crawled into the cellar.

'Just as well,' Grey said, trying and failing to brush brick dust and rust in the gloom from his sodden tunic with his fingers. He nodded to a corner of the cellar where something glowed. 'What we're after is over there, I believe. Best not hang about.'

The heat in the cellar was intense, like weight, or the pressure of being deep underwater. Heat forced air from their lungs and sang in their ears and made movement a slow wade through something denser than air. Above them, in protesting girders under tons of rubble, the beast noise rumbled again. Burned-out electricity cables gave the air an acrid, ozone stench. Other smells assaulted them; a cocktail of ether, tar, machine oil, steam from stagnant water and, everywhere, burn.

'Do we need to put on our respirators?'

Finlay shook his head. 'No time. Just don't light a cigarette. And we need to be very quick.'

'Right,' Grey said. He was panting for breath, his face slick and his eyes wild, pale, the pupils adrenalin pinpricks even in the darkness encroaching on their tiny cone of torchlight.

The basement was a hidden clutter of equipment. Finlay followed as Grey picked a path through the obstacles, barking a shin on something bolted to the floor and biting his lip with the suddenness of pain. The beast above gave another great, heaving groan. Fragments of ceiling fell with a wrench in a far corner and clattered heavily on machinery and stone.

'This is what we're after.'

Grey's torch was pointed at a smallish object, a bakelite housing bristling with valves and coloured cables and jack plugs. It looked to Finlay not unlike a wireless set with the back taken off, only more complicated. Instead of one frequency tuning dial, there were several dials set into it. Some of them were calibrated with arabic numerals and others with letters of the alphabet. One elliptical dial was marked with symbols entirely new to Finlay. The housing was charred on the top and heat had cracked it along one side. Up close, it smelled strongly of hot bakelite. The dials set into it glowed greenish and dull. It was sitting on a metal table. Finlay felt relieved it wasn't bolted down. Grey picked the apparatus up. It was no bigger, really, than a wireless set. And obviously it was no heavier. The beast above them moaned, sinking. Dying. Finlay fumbled on his belt for his torch.

'Get us out of here,' Grey said.

The Ministry's car was parked at the kerb when they emerged from the manhole, with the Immaculate Major seated in the rear and Grey's pet prize-fighter at the wheel. Grey opened the boot of the car and put his machine in there carefully, wrapping it in the swaddling of a tartan picnic blanket. He closed the boot and nodded to the pug at the wheel and the car slid away without them. The Major had not even looked at them.

'A drink, I think,' Grey said, 'When I get out of these borrowed clothes and into something a little less histrionic.' His eyes were still bright and empty with tension, but his voice was firm enough. Under them, the pavement shuddered and air escaped in a hot, foul, urgent exhalation out of the manhole from which they had just emerged. The two men looked at one another and though it was mad, inappropriate, they both laughed, weeping, convulsed by laughter.

They recovered Grey's clothes from the cab of the tender in which he had left them and walked through the streets in silence. Finlay felt fatigue under the dissipating tension in his body and brain, but knew that the dull insistence of alert thought would be slow to leave him in a fit state to rest properly. A drink would help, if Grey could locate one at such an early hour. Finlay thought that he probably could. He thought that Grey had been very cool under the ground, unless he had merely been ignorant of the extent of the danger. He was stronger than he looked. Finlay struggled to keep up with Grey, following him through the still-dark, rubble-pitted streets eastward. He had gashed his leg quite badly in that basement. The bone of his shin had been exposed, pale against the blood and torn flesh. One of the fire crew dabbed it with iodine and covered it with a field dressing while Grey changed his clothes. A steady throb of pain was starting to bother him, and he sensed that under the bandage the wound was still leaking blood. But it was better than being burned. And it was infinitely better than being buried under a thousand tons of implacable rubble. They got within sight of The Prospect of Whitby. They were walking on cobbles now, close to the river, the wharves silent, looming in the dark, a slight smell of pitch and cordite borne like breath on the incoming tide. Finlay thought about the docks; about all the things that could and would greedily burn, about the gathered cargoes, piled and roped, waiting to perish in a roaring riot of flame behind these slumbering walls. Paint, varnish, glue, tar, timber, petroleum, rubber, hemp, candle and paraffin wax. Everything packed in barrels and boxes and crates made of wood, their contents cosily bedded in straw or gun cotton. Jesus, how everything burned.

They reached the pub. Finlay was glad. His leg throbbed and he wanted very badly to sit down and sip cool, dark beer from a pint glass. He realized then, through his fatigue and with a start, that he was beginning not to mind the company of Grey. Beggars and choosers, he supposed. He still didn't know, though, how they were going to gain access to the pub, outside opening hours, without making a lot of noise and causing lights to be switched on. Then Grey fished in a pocket and in the light that ghosts off the river presaging the dawn, Finlay saw the dull flourish of a key.

'Blinder, Captain,' he whispered.

Grey did not react to the fourth mention that night of his forbidden rank. He just turned the key in the lock and they stole quietly, two men with soot-black faces and hair stinking of smoke, into the snug refuge beyond.

Grey pressed a bell under the counter of the bar in the tap room and in no time a man wearing a dressing-gown and the folded posture and crumple of sleep came down and poured them pints by the melancholy light of Finlay's service torch.

'I wish we could lengthen the battery life,' Finlay said, irritated, as the two men sat with their drinks and he switched off the thin beam.

Grey lit a cigarette and inhaled like a newborn at the nipple. 'It's one of the things we're working on,' he said, his eyes closed now, his focus on the nicotine reaching through his febrile frame.

For a while, Finlay let Grey smoke and contemplate and recover from their shared ordeal under the streets. He thought to ask the man why they could not simply have drawn their own drinks from the pumps on the bar without having to resurrect the pub's overworked proprietor. But that question, he knew, would merely have annoyed Grey. Auspice. Custom. Tradition. Ritual.

Rank. Such men as Grey were from a differently structured world.

'Tell me about Pimlico Rubber,' Grey said.

What the hell, Finlay thought, in weariness and a sort of capitulation. They know it all already. It's on my file. And so he fetched himself and Grey, without prompting, fresh pints from the now-deserted bar, and recounted his saddest litany of misapprehension, and death.

'He's like one of those Catholic confessors,' Babcock said. 'He'd get you to tell him anything in the end. And because you've told him, and because he is the great confessor, it really is the end. And you burn.'

'I wish you'd stop banging on about burning. It's morbid.'

'I mean metaphorically. As in to burn in the theological sense.'

'How does a Communist know so much about the history of religion?'

'Because the study of religion helped make me what I am,' Babcock said, triumphantly. And I'm not a Communist.'

Finlay sank back against his pillow.

'Now,' Babcock said. 'I'm going to have to clean this wound. What did you tell Mr Grey?'

'All about Pimlico Rubber.'

Babcock whistled. 'Lock, stock and barrel?'

'It was supposed to be an exchange of information.'

Babcock dabbed gently with the disinfectant. He was good at this. He had insistent, healing hands.

'And what did he tell you?'

'Not one single thing. I think I'd lost more blood than I realized. I passed out.'

'I can suture this wound. Or I can get you transport to a hospital and a surgeon and he can suture it instead. Organizing transportation will take time.'

Finlay thought about the giant pugilist who walked into pubs on silent feet and sat with patient malevolence behind the ticking engine of Grey's car.

'A surgeon, of course, will have more expertise than me. On the other hand, he'll likely have a bigger workload and poorer concentration, dealing with a non-life-threatening wound. That's because all the while his hospital will be a target for bombs, whereas down here, we're relatively safe.'

Finlay was barely following this.

'It's your choice, Chief Fire Officer.'

'You do it,' Finlay said.

'And you'll tell me about Pimlico Rubber?'

'I'll tell the world,' Finlay said, expansive on morphine and pain and tiredness.

Finlay dreamed about Tom. In the dream they were in Ireland. They had been taken by their mother for a holiday in Bray in County Wicklow. Tom, who was not yet two and was toddling, was wearing restraining reins. They were standing on the big pebbles at the top of the beach by the low sea wall. There was Wurlitzer music from one of the rides outside an amusement arcade on the opposite side of the coast road. The tune was 'Oh, Susanna'. The tune drifted in loudness, up and down on the strength of the breeze. It was early in May and chilly and Tom had on his blue duffle coat with the toggles and the chinstrap fastened. A blue cap with ear muffs was secured by a tie under his chin. He had on his wellington boots and was frowning and under the frown, his huge eyes, blue and serious, were staring intently at the sea. The sea broke in big, rhythmic waves and sang into the shingle. The breeze came off the sea and pervaded the air with salt. Their mother, younger, suppler in movement before the affliction of her arthritis, was squatting at Tom's side, unclipping his reins. 'Oh, Susanna' was jaunty in sudden warm sunlight between shifting oceans of cloud. And then the boys' Aunt Cath, their mother's slightly older sister in whose house they were staying, stepped over the sea wall with ice-cream cornets for each of them held between the bridged fingers of both of her hands.

Jack had taken the first sweet, frozen bite from his cone, had swallowed it and was experiencing an intense tingle of cold at what felt like the back of his right eye when he saw his mother point with her free hand and let out a sound stifled by ice-cream. He turned and saw Tom, tiny, arms outstretched, toddling for all he was worth down the shingle decline of the beach towards the breaking waves. His legs, those of a baby becoming a little boy, were pumping furiously inside his rubber boots as he hurtled on the very edge of balance towards his goal.

Jack was agile and quick. In seconds he was parallel with Tom. And so he was able to see the intense determination to reach the sea focused in the toddler's set mouth and immovable gaze. Tom continued, unaware of Jack. He was unaware of anything except his destination. But in the determination on his brother's face Jack could see past adventures denied; toddler exploits cruelly dashed and above all the will, this time, to succeed. In Jack's mind, in the rushed appreciation of the moment, there was something hugely impressive and at the same time hilariously funny about the antic race of the baby in his hampering duffle coat and rubber boots towards the sea, about the resolution cast in features shaped by such a short experience of the world. Tom continued helter-skelter towards the surging water, arms outstretched to either side of his tiny body for balance, tiny hands wobbling up and down at the ends of their plump wrists.

He was less than a foot from the furthest reach of the last, exhausted wave when Jack swung him up by his armpits and held him to his chest, his own back to the water, the baby still staring over Jack's shoulder, the reverie broken, but his eyes still on this latest, newest and most mysterious and exciting element to confront his emergent life. He lifted a finger and pointed.

'Sea,' Tom said.

Jack Finlay kissed his little brother on the cheek. The baby's skin was soft and cool in the chill of the wind. 'Oh, Susanna' was cheery and faint.

'Gack,' Tom said. 'Gack.' It was how he said his brother's name. He was still pointing.

'Sea,' he said. 'Sea!'

Jack Finlay awoke and appraised himself. His leg was a percussive, endurable throb. He tossed aside his blanket and hooked his hands behind his knee and lifted the injured limb and sniffed. His wound smelled only of antiseptic cream. The rest of him, he realized in the total absence of light, smelled of no doubt tiled and marbled areas of the Dorchester Hotel. Babcock must have negotiated soap and unguents and scents and bathed and barbered him while he slept.

Finlay groped for light and found it, taking no great comfort in these discoveries to do with health and hygiene. The dream had occurred in real time. The event had unfurled itself on the blank screen of his unconscious mind in the exact time it had taken to happen in the actuality of his history. The reality had been in colour, and Finlay had dreamed it in black and white, but he could take no comfort in this departure from reality. In his adulthood, Finlay had always dreamed in monochrome. For that, he blamed fire.

'Jesus Christ our Lord, don't let him die,' Finlay said. The words emerged loud in the dim, encroaching silence of his cell. He said them again. And he felt no shame in saying them. 'Oh, Susanna', like a happy lament, echoed around his gathering alertness, the tune jauntily haunting his waking mind.

Ten

FINLAY BREAKFASTED with Nevin, after a call from Grey summoning him to Whitehall; after packing his grip with his gym kit and posting a letter to his mum, dropping into the Moorgate station merely on the off-chance of some proper company.

Finlay arrived at Moorgate to find Nevin seated upright and asleep, alone at a table in the canteen. A breakfast of sorts congealed in front of him. There was a full cup of tea beside his breakfast plate, pale, a skein of condensed milk thickening on its surface. His elbows rested on the table-top and a cigarette burned between Nevin's fingers. The length of grey ash suggested he had dropped off soon after lighting it. Finlay was no expert on smoking, but judged Nevin's fingers to be three or four minutes away from a cigarette burn. Callused patches of ochre flesh to either side of the cigarette suggested it wouldn't be the first. The canteen was a weary hum of men trying to cheer and replenish themselves. It smelled of tea and tobacco and sweat and the sour polish with which someone daily buffed the floor. The low insistence of conversation was brightened surprisingly often by bursts of laughter.

A man he recognized as the B Watch lead fire officer slid into the chair beside Finlay's.

'We've found it's best to let him wake of his own accord, sir,' he said.

'Just so long as he doesn't do this in bed.'

'He doesn't go to bed, sir. He just catnaps. Like this.'

'Jesus.'

'He hasn't slept a night since it started, sir. Can I fetch you a mug of tea?'

'If you would.'

Finlay was half-way through his tea when Nevin came to. He actually took a drag of the cigarette burning his fingers before dropping it and grinding it out under his boot. His eyes registered the man opposite.

'Some of my auxiliaries are looting,' he said, quietly. 'I could understand it if they were taking goods from shops. But they'll take anything. Wallets. Watches. Rings. Caught one of them stealing coal. Another one taking a pair of boots from a corpse.'

Finlay took this in.

'Thing is, these are good men, otherwise. Brave as you like. Committed. Full of initiative.'

'I suppose you have to have a degree of initiative to pull the boots off a corpse,' Finlay said.

Nevin smiled. He looked terrible. 'I challenged one of them personally after seeing him pick something up and slip it in his tunic pocket. It was one of those silver bracelets children are given when they're christened.'

Finlay swallowed.

'Fellow seemed very put out I'd taken it up with him at all, Jack. Said it didn't seem the same as stealing when bomb blast had put it there. Seemed to think it was fair enough. Like finding a fiver in the pocket of a second-hand coat. Perk of the job, so to speak.'

'What did you do with him?'

Nevin said nothing. He blinked a couple of times. He seemed on the verge of dropping off again. His fingers tapped a tattoo on the table. 'Same fellow, previous week, smothered two incendiaries by hand in a schoolyard coke store. First one damaged his gauntlets so badly, he sorted out the second one by wrapping it in his tunic. What do you do?'

'What you can, I suppose.'

'Thing is,' Nevin said, 'there was blood still on the christening bracelet.'

Finlay couldn't think of anything appropriate to say.

'I was at Ypres in the 'fourteen–eighteen. On the Salient,'

Nevin said. 'And one morning I drew the ticket for a firing squad. There were two of them, roped to the wheel of a wagon with a sheared axle, a few hundred yards behind the line, in a depression in the ground so that the Bosch snipers couldn't kill them before we did. Deserters. Kids, to tell the truth, Jack. They'd shat themselves and the shit and the fear off them smelled something terrible. It had brought the birds. Crows, ugly fuckers, squarking and preening. I aimed over their heads. Both volleys.' Nevin jerked his head. 'The bloke who took the bracelet is sitting over there. He's the one they're laughing at. He has a real way about him with a joke.'

Finlay nodded and looked over at the man and reached for his mug of tea. His curiosity had been satisfied, at least, concerning Nevin and the 'fourteen–eighteen war.

Pimlico Rubber was five storeys of yellow-glazed brick that was cracking and pinging like shrapnel with the heat spreading outwards from the burning building by the time the fire crews got to it, shortly after dawn on a beautiful April morning. The ground and first-floor windows exhaled smoke in great billows of black that climbed skywards in a column so dense it looked solid, like a pillar fashioned to grotesque dimensions out of obsidian, or coal. Finlay was in the first tender on the scene and right behind it came the second and then the third, which carried Sub-Officer Dicky Gaines, possessor of a near-photographic memory and a man whose knowledge of the ground was generally held to be encyclopaedic. Together, Finlay and Gaines sought out the beat officer who had raised the alarm. Police Sergeant Paul Armitage had joined the force straight from the army in the winter of 1918 and served all of his time in the borough of Westminster. More tenders arrived, their bells shrill and insistent in the calm of the morning. The flames at the base of the building roared and spread heat. Finlay could feel the familiar prickle of menace as heat caused sweat to trickle under his shirt and tunic down the length of his spine. The flames were blackening the brick at the base of the building, smudging greasy daubs of black around the lower storeys, causing windows to implode and glaze to snick and shatter and fly from the storeys above. About them, well-drilled men set up radial branch holders; static hoses with a delivery of 600 gallons of water a minute and a throw of 100 feet through a nozzle only an inch and a half across. Their back pressure too formidable for men to hold them, these hoses were mounted on a brace, with men standing on its backplate and a forward strut clawing the ground to anchor them. As the radials began their assault on the blaze, Gaines and Armitage told Finlay what they knew about the burning building. And Armitage, vitally, offered his opinion as to the probable cause of the fire.

'I didn't know the meaning of the term fire fighter until Pimlico Rubber,' Armitage would be quoted as saying later, in the official report. 'I thought it was just a term coined by the Victorians, with their taste for melodrama. And because they needed to drum up public funding for the service. How mistaken can a person be?'

The crews were assailed, assaulted, by the stench of burning rubber. The fire was feeding on car and bicycle inner tubes and football bladders manufactured on the first and second floors and then packed in cardboard boxes and stored in wooden crates stacked on the ground floor to await delivery. Armitage and Gaines agreed that the fourth floor was given over to administration and was therefore stocked with nothing more combustible than paper-stuffed filing cabinets, furniture, adding machines and typewriters. The fifth floor was given over to a staff canteen and the boardroom. There was pure fat in the belly and sump of the big kitchen chip-frier and cooking oil stored in gallon drums in the stockroom at the kitchen's rear. The fat and oil were volatile and Finlay had a team outside the building looking to cut off the supply of gas that fuelled the canteen kitchen's three massive cooking ranges. But it was the third floor that gave Finlay his biggest cause for concern. Ten thousand gallons of raw latex sat up there in six fat copper vats, surrounded by the volatile chemicals and the machinery used to process the stuff into various compounds of rubber.

Evacuation was progressing well. The density and height of the column of smoke stretching upwards into the windless sky from the factory provided a compelling case for the people occupying homes in those streets neighbouring the building to get out.

Anyone local left the area urgently enough. Pimlico Rubber was flanked on one side by a railway embankment, which was good for Finlay's fire crews because it meant they could attack the blaze on that flank with accuracy and from a secure footing, bringing to bear greater force of water than they were able to do from ladders. But the rubber factory was flanked at its other end by the Pimlico Paintworks. Paint, varnish, paint thinners; they would explode in their tins once subjected to heat. They would scatter and spread and burn ferociously. They would form rivers of liquid fire impossible to dam. Armitage and Gaines between them could only guess and speculate until the shift foreman from the paintworks breached the police cordon surrounding the blaze and confronted Finlay direct. Paint deliveries to their wholesalers were done fortnightly and the fleet of lorries and wagons that would do the delivering were due the following day. So the works contained thirty thousand gallons of finished product and the ingredients in their vats and tanks and barrels for a similar amount.

Phil Carter was the first fire fighter to die in the conflagration that subsequently became remembered simply by the two words Pimlico Rubber. Radials positioned on the embankment alongside the burning building forced back the flames sufficiently for two crews on the ground to get within feet of it. They played their hoses on a side exit, wood banded by steel, its boards charred and splintered and the strengthening metal warped and bellowed outwards with heat. Carter encroached and swung his axe. Wood crumbled and he flattened himself against the factory wall. The execution of his second swing was almost complete when something within exploded and the full furious force of the blast found its exit through the ragged hole Carter's axe-blade had contrived a few seconds earlier. He was blown off his feet, out of his boots, jerked twenty feet back by the explosion like a strung puppet, with his neck snapped. Carter was twenty-four years old and saving to get married to a girl called Eileen he had met serving on her father's vegetable stall at the street market in Lambeth Walk.

A deluge of water from pumps all around the building began to starve the outer extremities of the Pimlico Rubber fire of the oxygen on which it depended for life. Long shots would not defeat the blaze, but could diminish it, enabling the fire fighters to encircle and begin to tackle it, thoroughly and with a strategy, without their uniforms, boots and the hair on their heads simply combusting in the fierceness of the approaching heat. On the ground floor, at the perimeter of the building, fire was spitting and dwindling in stubborn reluctance in pyres of stinking burn. The first-floor fire, through the windows, was diminishing with an unsteady, almost petulant reluctance, its flames forced through grey smoke back to their incendiary seat at the centre of the building. On the fourth floor, there was a wisp and suggestion of smoulder through those windows left open by the last working shift, for ventilation. But the third floor was Finlay's concern and the latex, bubbling and restless with heat in its copper pans, the concern of all of them.

Eagan and Tooley were the next to die. They breached the building at the Paintworks end and entered after giving the thumbs-up to the crew they had just left. Neither man was seen alive again.

'We believed they were entering a corridor eight feet wide and nine high with large exterior windows sited every five yards along its length,' Finlay said in submission under oath. 'Later we learned that their progress would have been severely hampered by steel girders stacked sideways along that corridor for the planned construction of a warehouse building. Planning permission had been sought and granted, but we didn't know about the girders. They had been put there because that entrance was seldom used, though it was officially designated as a fire escape and entry and exit should have been possible unimpeded. I understand the girders had been stored there so that they wouldn't rust in the rain.'

Toxic fumes was the best guess as to what must have killed forty-year-old Edmund Eagan, a widower and father of two girls still at school. He had pulled off his respirator, which may have been faulty, having recently been through the maintenance workshop, the log showed, twice. The position of the remains suggested that Cecil Tooley, thirty-one, a single man who lived with his mother, died trying to haul his unconscious colleague back along the obstructed corridor and out.

Seven minutes had elapsed since the arrival of the first fire appliances at Pimlico Rubber. At this point Finlay handpicked two crash crews and, in the shelter of one of the Dennis pumps, told them what it was he expected them to do.

'Firemen were running around that burning building like a swarm of ants,' said sheet-riveter Tony Malloy, who had watched the blaze from an observation platform at the top of a gasometer across the railway embankment, five hundred yards from Pimlico Rubber. 'The heat was something fierce. I could feel it from where I was standing. And the flames! I couldn't believe my eyes. I couldn't believe what those blokes were doing.'

They went in. Clumsy with breathing apparatus and fighting to control their breathing, they went in at either flank of Pimlico Rubber; through a service entrance on the embankment side and, on the side neighbouring the paintworks, through the entrance senior management used. Each end of the building was equipped with a stairwell. Both crews were working blind in the black, noxious limbo. At least the respirators guard us from the stink, Finlay thought, leading the paintworks-entrance crew. At the other extremity of the building, he knew that Gaines, Lampetter and Cooper were groping through the same billowing filth. They reached the first floor, hauling the hoses after them, heavy over their shoulders. They climbed towards the second floor, groping upwards, labouring for breath.

'Visibility was very poor,' Albert Cooper said in a submission dictated from his hospital bed. 'They were just about the most difficult fire-fighting conditions I have come across. We had no choice but to try to contain the blaze because of the adjacent paintworks. But we were working practically blind in toxic smoke. If the latex vats had been vats, like we were told they were, it might have been a different story. But they were airtight tanks. Either way, we fought the fire at Pimlico Rubber the only way we could.'

Finlay's stairwell was obstructed by blown-out and still fiercely burning debris outside the second-floor entrance, a double door blasted off its hinges and itself forming part of the obstruction.

As he and his men struggled to climb through and over, using the play of their hose and their axes, at the other end of the building the second crew gained the third floor and got the first direct jet of water on to the latex tanks.

By now, support crews were clambering after their colleagues at both ends of Pimlico Rubber. Crews were readying branch hoses which would suffocate flames with foam once water had sufficiently subdued the surrounding heat. All around the building, hoses, like a plague of restless worms, pulsed and twitched with pressure in heaps on the puddled ground. Water played on Pimlico Rubber from a dozen extension ladders, but the seat of the fire still roared in white defiance through the blasted windows at the building's centre.

Latex in the five sealed tanks had heated far beyond the temperature at which it would ignite. At the base of the tanks was water, always present in the sump of stored liquid. As the water heated, it turned to steam and its vast, gaseous expansion ruptured a tank, sending its contents skywards in a bucketing, volcanic spew, twelve seconds after Cooper and the two men with him gained the third floor. Cooper was on one knee by the door, hauling hose up the stairwell, when he realized that it was raining latex. He turned to see Gaines and Lampetter struggling on the floor through smoke, swimming in agony, screaming through masks they were trying to tear off with hands turned to mits by the deluge of boiling rubber. Dicky Gaines was a father of five and a grandfather, two months away from retirement. Sid Lampetter was twenty-seven and due shortly to become Dicky's son-in-law. Cooper, his tunic and helmet on fire in fierce splashes of rubber flame, never knew until the day he died how he got out. Fourteen ascending men were burned on the stairwells by rivers of descending fire. Three of them never worked again. But they put Pimlico Rubber out, extinguished it, before the danger to the adjacent paintworks grew to be acute. The newspapers hailed Finlay and his men as heroes. The loss of life meant an official enquiry, which exonerated Finlay of any blame but was distinctly short of anything approaching praise. His own view was that Pimlico Rubber was always going to be as close to a total balls-up as he'd get in his professional life. It was six weeks before he could sleep without seeing the faces in his dreams of the men he had led to their deaths.

The cause of the blaze was arson, the fire set on the first and second floors by the company's owner, a third-generation Italian immigrant called Paolo Cardoza. Mr Cardoza exported the bulk of his footballs and cycle inner tubes to Italy, where he had lucrative contracts to supply schools and sporting and cycling clubs. At least, they were lucrative until Benito Mussolini discovered that rubber goods were being imported from a British manufacturer with an Italian name. Mr Cardoza was offered the opportunity by Il Duce to move his plant to Genoa and recruit an Italian work-force. But with a son at Winchester and a wife born in Shrewsbury, he demurred. Facing ruin after losing the Italian contracts, Mr Cardoza set his fire at the centre of two floors with forty-gallon canisters of an accelerant he declined, when arrested and questioned, to identify. He believed he could retire from business on the payout from his insurance policy. He had never been late in paying a premium. In the event he became the last fatality of Pimlico Rubber when he hanged himself by a braid of bedding from the bars of a remand cell at Wormwood Scrubs. He left no note. The fact that the older brother of Sid Lampetter, who perished at Pimlico Rubber, worked as a warder on the wing in which Cardoza was held, was simply a ghoulish coincidence not thought worthy of investigation.

The looting auxiliary with the talent for jokes was a music-hall stagehand called Pickering, Nevin told Finlay. Finlay went over and pulled out a chair and sat at Pickering's table. A pack of cards lay on the table-top, greasy and scuffed with use. Finlay reached over and picked them up and began, without looking, to shuffle the pack.

'Do you know who I am?' he said, speaking into the silence his presence had provoked, looking at Pickering.

Pickering licked his lips. 'Someone important,' he said. 'Judging by the cap-badge.'

'I understand you've been stealing from the dead.'

'Not me,' Pickering said.

Finlay extended the spread pack. 'Take a card.'

Pickering took one. He turned it over. It was the ace of spades.
'Oh dear,' Finlay said. He recovered the card and shuffled the
pack again. 'Take another.'

'I don't want to,' Pickering said. His mouth was no longer
working with the rubbery facility it had had when recounting
jokes.

'I'm fucking well telling you to take a card,' Finlay said.

Pickering plucked one from the pack. It was the ace of spades.
The man in the chair next to Pickering's whistled. Pickering
dropped the card like it was diseased. Finlay picked it up and
reconstituted the pack and gave the cards to the man who had
whistled. 'Here, you shuffle them,' he said. The man did. Finlay
fanned them in front of Pickering, who took one this time
without prompting. He closed his eyes when he turned it over
and saw for the third time the black blossoming of the ace of
spades.

'We don't steal from the dead,' Finlay said. 'The dead take
exception. This is a proud service, and sensible. Nobody sullies it
for very long. If you get my drift.'

Pickering was staring at the cards. He appeared to get Finlay's
drift. Outside, in the autumn sunshine, Finlay remembered Kevin
Pilley, a real artist at three-card tricks and apprentice conman
with whom he had shared a dormitory at Borstal. Finlay had
possessed no great aptitude for the cards. But Pilley had been
patient and they had both had a great deal of time to kill. He had
turned at the canteen door to look back at Nevin. Nevin slept
once more over his breakfast, his recumbent head heavy in the
cradle of his hands.

'They're bombing Liverpool,' Finlay said.

'And Portsmouth. And Glasgow. And Sheffield and Coventry
and Crewe. And Swansea and Bristol. Frankly, if they weren't
bombing Liverpool, it would be a gross slight on the city of your
birth. Of course they're bombing fucking Liverpool. They're
bombing the entire bloody country. We're at war, Chief Fire
Officer.'

White sat looking at his linked fingers after his short but vivid
speech. The Major sat to his left, surpassingly immaculate in the

freshly blast-damaged room. To their right was Grey, insouciant and nicotined, with a loosely tied silk cravat bright as a wound at his throat. Finlay sipped tea. The most recent bomb had shattered their blast-proof panes and chicken wire was strung across windows dingy now with absence of light. Finlay's tea had been delivered to him cold and there had been no offer, on this occasion, of biscuits. He sensed something significant; a ratchet turn, emphatic and ominous in the spiral towards defeat. His leg ached. He had lost three of his buildings. In Liverpool, the docks were being bombed.

'We've offered to move your mother. To evacuate her. We've offered twice. She's refused,' the Major said.

'She's more stomach for this war than I have,' Finlay said, quietly.

'Not true,' White said. 'Doctrinally, I suppose she might have. Your mother is a militant Socialist and we are at war against Fascists. But at this stage, frankly, I don't think the politics of it make much difference. Anyway Mr Grey says that you conducted yourself splendidly the other night.'

'I have lost more than fifty per cent of what you originally charged me to protect. In a matter of weeks.'

'Hardly your fault.' This from Grey.

'Just don't lose any more buildings, Chief Fire Officer. To lose what's left would be very careless.' The Major smiled. Finlay was more astonished by the smile than the source of the humour.

'Do you think their bombing of my triangle a coincidence?'

White continued to be fascinated by his nails. Rictus afflicted the Major's grin and then, wisely, he withdrew it. Grey lit a cigarette with what Finlay judged to be an attempt at a flourish. But the hands could not remember their choreography and the result was almost palsied. The cigarette was successfully lit, but Grey fumbled the lighter on to the desk-top. It was a type Finlay had not seen before. It was nickel, chunky and rectangular, where he had expected to see sleek gold. Rebecca Lange, crimson-lipped, invaded his mind. But he expelled the image.

'My mum says they bombed Liverpool in revenge. She says it was because Churchill ordered Berlin bombed and we hit civilian targets.'

'Well,' White said. 'As the Whitstable incident demonstrated so vividly, your mother is no great admirer of Winston.'

'She blames him for Gallipoli.'

'No more than he blames himself for Gallipoli, I can assure you.'

Was Finlay ageing like the men in front of him? They were hunched and bled of colour. Blood, atrophied and blue, shaped veins like a trellis of dead vines on the back of the hands White so scrupulously examined. The Major's face was as pale as the skin exposed whenever he raised his gloved hands and deposited scabrous drifts of it on to the desk. Grey seemed shrunken, receded. He looked as though he were emptying into some dark vacuum. Finlay thought of Nevin; of how the flecks of grey in his abundant hair had turned to pale ravages framing the Watch Commander's gaunt features.

White cleared his throat. 'There are those who will tell you that government intelligence is a contradiction in terms. At least three of the four people in this room are at odds with that view. But as we have explained to you before, there were many Nazi sympathizers in this country at the outbreak of war and there is no earthly reason to suppose that all of them have left.'

'Having said which,' Grey said, 'the bombing of your buildings could merely be unfortunate. Most of the personnel from the financial institutions fled to the suburbs during the phoney war. But Jerry doesn't know that. If they cripple the economy, nobody in the munitions factories gets paid. That could be their thinking. Their logic. Couldn't it?'

It took a moment for Finlay to realize that the question wasn't rhetorical.

'Why did you let Rebecca Lange go to Scotland?'

Grey leaned forward and looked towards the Major, also leaning forward, across the sedate sheet anchor of White.

'We couldn't really stop her,' White said. 'She is a civilian.'

'She's an alien. What's she doing there?'

'Gone to see some architecture. Built by some Scots chappie named after a raincoat.'

'Mackintosh.' Grey said.

'That's the fellow.'

'Is there anything that we can do for you, Chief Fire Officer?'

Finlay thought about this. 'For me, no. Babcock makes me very comfortable. In the circumstances I'm a lot more comfortable than I've any right to be. But you could put me in the picture. How are things generally?'

White shifted in his seat. Grey and the Major both had their eyes somewhere near the point behind Finlay at which, in elaborate scrolls of blast-damaged plaster, the wall met the ceiling of the room. It was White who spoke.

'The bombing has so far made a quarter of a million people homeless. In Stepney, the figure is almost fifty per cent. The slum dwellings of the East End have no resistance to bombs and have proved impossible to repair. There are pockets of disaffection, of course. But Mass Observation tells us that large-scale civil insurrection is still unlikely.'

'The general feeling is that we can take it,' the Major said.

'The invasion of the Underground is a worry,' White said. 'Last month, four Underground stations took direct hits over the space of three nights and at Balham there was carnage. People have light and company down there and they can't hear the bombs, so they feel safe. But they are very far from safe.'

'How many are down there?'

'We estimate close to two hundred thousand. And we know that some of them stay down there. A hefty minority aren't coming up at all.'

'So your deep shelter mentality does exist, then.'

'Very much so.'

'We rather encouraged the climate for it when we allowed surface shelters to be built without cement in the mortar that bonds their bricks,' Grey said.

'There's quite a community on your own doorstep, Chief Fire Officer,' White said. 'An uncompleted extension tunnel runs east underneath Liverpool Street. Every night it is home to around ten thousand shelterers. A cramped tunnel city of sweat and lice and the stench of excrement and carbolic soap and tea and rumour stretching for miles.'

'Sounds like a trench,' the Major said. 'Except for the carbolic soap. Never was any soap, to speak of. Not in my part of the line.'

There was a silence.

'What are you thinking, Finlay?'

'About those big thousand-kilogram mines they drop, Mr Grey. If they drop one of those over a tunnel under the Thames, all the people on the Underground platforms will drown.'

'The odds are against that happening,' White said. 'Disease is actually our biggest fear. We fear the spread of epidemics. So far, all we've recorded is a serious increase in scabies and impetigo. But a child has died of meningitis on a tube platform.'

'And none of the hospitals in London can boast the luxury of running water,' Grey said. 'Not all the time.'

'Can you confirm that my brother is safe?'

'We can,' White said. 'He is as safe as anyone can be in a naval vessel serving a country at war with a major naval power. His submarine has not been lost, if that is what you mean.'

There was another silence.

'The feeling is that we can take it,' the Major reiterated. 'But the work being done in the two of your buildings still intact can help shorten this war. We urge you to do everything you can to protect them.'

'I am doing,' Finlay said.

White stood. 'We're sure you are. Though I have to confess, Chief Fire Officer, that we fail to see any but the most oblique connection between fire prevention and brawling with Irishmen.'

Finlay did not believe that Rebecca Lange had been allowed to traipse off to Scotland merely to look at architecture. Travel was too difficult. Every major road was cratered and petrol was in terribly short supply and so the burden on the rail network, of passengers and of freight, was huge. Most of the main-line stations had suffered bomb damage. Millions of tons of rolling stock had been destroyed in the raids. There was nothing about it in the newspapers, or not much, but he had witnessed for himself the damage inflicted by a single raid on the main-line terminus at Liverpool Street. He could vividly recall how laboured, how tortuous, had been his own seventy-mile return journey to the Kent coast. The trains were teeming with troops, unwashed and uncouth, and Rebecca Lange just did not seem the sort of woman to endure sharing cramped space with them, clanking wearily over the slow miles to Scotland, only to look at cleverly embellished brick.

He walked along Whitehall towards Trafalgar Square and the Strand, where he intended to visit his gymnasium. He had packed his kit when they had summoned him by telephone early in the morning and carried it now in a canvas grip. He would have to amend his regular routine to accommodate his injured leg. But Finlay felt a deep need for exhaustive physical exercise; not the kind that came incidentally, with wielding the heavy nozzle of a pressure hose to fight fire, but the controlled, choreographed kind of exercise that spent muscular strength and energy in a manner that nourished even while it was depleting those resources. He was still deeply troubled by the dream he had dreamt of Tom and in the absence of concrete assurance about his brother, needed at least to dissipate his energy to a point that would enable him to relax physically. He thought that mental calm might return to him over a period of time, as the dream itself, his having had the dream, became less of an abrupt, assaulting shock to his mind. His wish was more in hope than expectation.

After his gym work and a massage, with the burn of embrocation deep in his muscles, Finlay went to a pub called The Lemon Tree close to the gym, off Bedfordbury. It must have been a place popular with the theatre crowd, because posed pictures of actors with their signatures and dedications faded to bronze on the prints lined the pub walls in little wooden frames. There were pictures of Gielgud and Olivier and Redgrave in heavily made-up faces and clumsy wigs. The wig Olivier wore in his picture was the same coarse-textured, dead, blonde colour he kept seeing on women in the streets. Only Olivier wore his in bangs that fingered his pained, chiselled face. Finlay recognized Leslie Howard, wearing his own hair under brilliantine. There were some ballet dancers in even heavier make-up than the stage actors, but he couldn't have put a name to them. There were heavily busted women and jowly men with exaggerated expressions and double chins whom he assumed sang opera. There were actresses, too: Flora Robson, Anna Neagle, a couple of ballerinas with long legs and eyebrows plucked disdainfully. Jessie Mat-thews looked ripe, Greer Garson wistful. There was a picture of Greta Garbo with the light searching out her features from below, giving her lips a voluptuous darkness and her eyes a cold, commanding glitter. This picture reminded him of Rebecca Lange. There was no resemblance, feature by feature, to effect the recollection. It was the beauty and the glamour and the hint of disdain. Finlay realized that he was thinking a lot about Rebecca in her absence. And it was an absence, something a part of him persistently and genuinely felt. He was missing her. His eyes alighted on a photograph of Errol Flynn, blandly handsome, absurdly barbered, grinning through his eyelash-sized moustache. Finlay didn't have any feelings one way or the other about Flynn. Errol Flynn was an Aussie movie star who got paid a lot of money for making films dressed up as a pirate, or as Robin Hood. Good luck to the bloke. Finlay just hated Nevin's leaden jokes comparing him with the actor.

There seemed to be a lull in the coming of winter, as well as in the coming of aircraft bearing bombs. Sunlight dappled the street when Finlay left The Lemon Tree and the warmth of it spread across his shoulders through the serge of his tunic. He looked up, blinking, but even the sky was not bereft of the symbolism of war. Barrage balloons, snagged clumsily by mooring ropes, sat large in the sky amid the occasional spit and snarl of patrolling fighter planes. The blue beyond them, though, was pure and blameless. The vacancy of the sunlit sky seen from the streets, its unsullied vastness, made the war seem momentarily to Finlay something small and shifting in the scheme of things; a stain that would fade and vanish from the world the vaunting sky looked down on, without trace.

The West End streets were crowded and eventful in the autumn sunshine. Cordoned-off buildings in danger of collapse, piled sandbags protecting buildings still intact and bomb craters narrowed the once expansive thoroughfares and, alert to the siren, almost everyone walked. So the motor traffic was thin, but the pavements thick with people. Finlay passed men in uniform and bawling street vendors and spivs and tarts and the odd toff and policemen, magisterial and middle-aged in blue gabardine.

Sometimes he would search faces for clues as to how they were taking their war. But most had mastered the look of slight preoccupation people seemed to prefer to the look of anxiety or naked fear. Finlay was coming to the belief that fear was finite. He didn't think that men and women were naturally brave. He had seen too much ungovernable terror to be convinced of that. But fear was so enervating, so exhausting an emotion, he felt that eventually it simply ran out, and when you'd had your ration of fear you had to replace it with something that could pass for apathy, or resignation, something more manageable and less wearing on the visage, less corrosive to the soul.

On Charing Cross Road, for no reason he could have explained, he stopped abruptly in the middle of the street and turned around. Thirty feet back along the pavement, facing him, Grey's silent prize-fighter stood staring into Finlay's eyes. He was wearing a sand-coloured overcoat with braided leather buttons and epaulettes. He rocked on his heels and continued to stare. His hands were thrust like bulging clubs into his pockets. And then he smiled. And the smile was the most dismal, empty-eyed mockery of a smile that Finlay had ever seen. And dismayed, confused by just how crestfallen that smile made him feel in the bright day, in the populous sunshine, he crossed the road and entered a ramshackle lane full of shops selling antique books and old jewellery, intent on twisting this way and that through London's labyrinth, to get away from whatever it was that was signified, or sanctioned, by that ghastly, death's-head grin.

Eleven

S HE HAD lit only two of the gas lanterns illuminating her sitting-room. They hissed and whispered on the wall behind them, throwing light over the sofa on which they sat. She had turned the flame of each down so low that the room did not seem to extend much beyond the sofa. Music reached them from somewhere in this contrived darkness. To Finlay it sounded mournful; a Sunday plod along the paths of a park in the rain, trees leaf-soaked, bowed under their burden of water, dripping.

Rebecca smoked steadily, as she had since their arrival at her flat.

'Do you object to listening to this?'

Finlay shrugged. He did not want to sound unintelligent. 'It's all right,' he said. 'A bit melancholy.'

'Melancholy?'

'I don't think I'd like to have been the person who composed it.'

'Claude Debussy,' she said.

'Sounds French.'

'Very,' Rebecca said. 'I don't think he could have been anything else.'

'Not with a name like that, he couldn't,' Finlay said.

It was a question of momentum. He wanted to take her in his arms and occupy that crimson mouth with his; peel off her blouse, haul her skirt up the length of her thighs. In this light her skin would have the yellowy colour of cream. But his first and last attempt had taught him that Rebecca did not welcome clumsiness. So instead, he sipped from his glass of wine as she ground out another cigarette. And he listened to Debussy. A man entirely unaccustomed to doing so, he waited and hoped that the mood might alter and develop of its own accord. He didn't think it would. The only thing he knew with any certainty was that, with Rebecca, he was out of his depth. Her lighter flame flared and he became aware of being studied, scrutinized, in deep shadow and inadequate light.

'You are such a beautiful man,' she said. 'Of course, you must have been told so many times.'

'No.'

'Liar.'

'I'm not a liar,' Finlay said. 'Beautiful is not a word used in English to describe men.'

'Not even by women?'

He thought about this. 'My mother said I was a beautiful baby. My Aunt Cath agreed. I think there was some bias there, though.'

'And your father?'

Finlay smiled.

'Dad used to hold me high, throw me in the air and catch me. He used to call me bonny; his bonny, bonny boy. I think bonny is a Scottish word.'

'Meaning beautiful?'

'Meaning plump.'

She reached over and punched his bicep and her hand slipped along his arm to the elbow and she paused, perhaps aware of his density in the dark, his musculature, his defining weight and stillness. The tip of her cigarette, in her other hand, burned comet-bright above them both.

They kissed, a long kiss, until Rebecca broke it.

Finlay groaned.

'It's trust,' she said. 'I have to know that I can trust you. You cannot imagine how alone I am, Jack.'

Finlay thought that he could.

'What can I say? How can I justify your trust?

She was silent for a moment.

'Tell me about your father.'

'On condition that you tell me about yours.'

He could almost hear her thinking. Then she nodded.

'Go on,' she said.

'He was a war hero,' Finlay said. 'He killed Germans. And then one summer afternoon in 'nineteen-sixteen the Germans killed him.'

Finlay almost heard the click of calculation in her brain.

'Do you remember him?'

'Barely. He was big and kind. He always smelled of coal-tar soap under the smell of whatever it was he had unloaded that day on the docks. He used to bring home an orange every night for me and Tommy. Exotic fruit. Tangerines, Mandarins, Jaffas, blood oranges. Sometimes a melon. One time, a big bunch of Jamaican bananas. He laughed and sang a lot, it seemed a lot to me, anyway. And he used to put his arms around my mum and nuzzle her neck at the sink and tickle her with the bristles on his chin.'

'Who is Tommy?'

'My younger brother.'

'A hero, you say. Was your father decorated in the war?'

'Twice.'

'What for?'

'He wouldn't talk about it.'

'But there must have been a citation?'

'A citation. Of course. Christ, your English is good.'

'The citation?'

'He led a small party charged with taking a trench. They took the trench. My father was armed with a light machine-gun. He got into the trench undiscovered, through a shell crater that went under their wire where our side knew from aerial reconnaissance there was a fire break. So he was able to slither into the trench, round the fire break, and come at the men defending the trench from their unprotected flank. The second medal was for bringing a wounded officer back to our lines after a failed assault. He volunteered for that job.'

'Why wouldn't he talk about it?'

Jack coughed to clear his throat.

'He said he saw men do braver things practically every day. Said medals, gongs he called them, were awarded pretty much at random. My mum says none of the men who were there talked much about what went on at the front.'

Rebecca twisted towards the ashtray balanced on her arm of the sofa in the dark. Her movement was urgent. Finlay knew from that and from her tone of voice that this part of his personal history was interesting her.

'What happened, after he died?'

'I went to the bad. And then the bullies came for Tom.' Finlay lapsed into silence, remembering this.

'Continue, please,' Rebecca said. Along an arm he could barely see, her bracelets clattered. Finlay resolved then, should he ever see her naked, it would be utterly naked. He would take the clips and horned combs from her hair, tease the rings from her fingers and slip the amulets over her wrists. All she would wear for their coupling would be her scent.

'Tell me what happened after the death of your father.'

'On every last Friday of the month, there was a fight on the docks. Sometimes it would involve a seaman from one of the visiting ships. More often it would be two dockers. Sometimes a Catholic might fight a Prod. A Mosleyite might be matched against a Red. But no pretext was needed, really.'

'This with bare knuckles?'

'Never. A docker's hands are the tools of his trade,' Finlay said. 'They'd bind their knuckles in rags secured with tape for protection. Biting and gouging weren't allowed. In summer they'd fight on the quay and in winter in a warehouse with braziers supplying the light, because in the winter months they'd not finish the shift until after dusk. Anyone wanting to watch was charged a threepenny bit. There was plenty of betting, obviously.'

'Obviously.'

'Bouts were refereed and rounds timed. The referee was there to see that none of the losers got kicked to death by a vindictive winner.'

'And to stop the biting. And the gouging,' Rebecca said. 'Your father fought?'

In darkness, Finlay nodded. 'Often. It was winner take all and all those threepences added up. I think he may have bet on himself as well. It meant we could go on a holiday to Ireland every year and see Mam's family at Christmas.'

'So he was successful,' Rebecca said.

'He only got beaten once. A Thai stoker fractured his jaw with a roundhouse kick. My dad beat the stoker so badly in the rematch they had to stretcher him back aboard his ship.'

Finlay thought about his father's hands, gently chucking his chin, taking his own hand to safely cross a road, fastening the stiff toggles of his Sunday coat. Patrick Finlay had never laid a finger on his son. His mother had done whatever smacking had been deemed necessary in their household. When it came to disciplining Jack, a frown of disapproval was as close as his father was able to come to physical chastisement. It had been enough. Young Jack had an abiding dread of disappointing his dad.

'The sons of local men my father fought and beat fair and square on the docks would chance their arm with me,' Finlay said, 'egged on by men who should have known better than to single out the children of a widow. It was all right. I could hold my own. I didn't always come out on top against lads older than me, but I made bloody sure I was no fun to fight. Then, like a wanker, I started setting fires and I got locked up for a couple of years and so of course they began to pick on Tom.'

'What's a wanker?'

A beat of time passed. And then Finlay laughed out loud.

'How crucial is it for you to know?'

She tapped his side with her knuckles. 'I'm pulling your leg, Finlay.' And then sober and serious: 'tell me about the bullying.'

Finlay sighed. Even to himself the sigh sounded painful, the soughing of abject sorrow through unseen shapes, through the fabric of the room.

'Tom was the best athlete I've ever seen. Even as a toddler, you could see it in him. He would run as a toddler, I never once remember seeing him content to walk, and he'd move so fast and so lightly that you'd swear his little feet glided weightless across the ground. By the time he was eleven, he'd broken every under-sixteen record in the north of England from the hundred-yard dash to the mile.'

'They would not have bullied such a boy in Germany,' Rebecca said. 'Is your little brother dark or is he blond?'

'He can run like the wind, our Tommy. He can do pretty much anything with a football. Any kind of ball. But he couldn't fight a cold.'

'He couldn't what?'

'I got enough of my father's strength and belligerence to be able to fight. The honest truth is that I enjoy fighting, especially when the bloke on the receiving end deserves what he's getting.'

'Like my Irishman.'

'Exactly like your fucking Irishman. But Tommy couldn't fight. And his pride wouldn't allow him to tell my mum. And so every single schoolday for the two years I did in Borstal, a sadistic fourteen-year-old bastard called Hangy Todd made my brother hand over the money my mum used to give him for his school dinner. And if Tommy didn't have it, Hangy would hawk and spit in Tommy's mouth. And sometimes when he did get the money, he'd spit in Tommy's mouth just for fun. For two years. Until Tommy started skiving—'

'Sk—'

'Playing truant. And my mum confronted him and he broke down and it all came out.'

Rebecca was silent.

'What are you thinking?'

'That Hangy is a strange name for a boy.'

'A nickname he got from wearing handed-down jumpers. His big brothers were really big. So was his dad.'

'But not big enough to best your father,' Rebecca said. 'When you were released from reform school, did you confront Hangy Todd?'

'That isn't the point,' Finlay said. 'The point is that my brother had the joy taken out of his childhood. And it was my fault.'

Rebecca was silent. Finlay could hardly hear her breath. 'What are you thinking?'

'How passionate you sound. What did you do to Hangy Todd?'

'You don't want to know,' Finlay said. 'Blond, by the way. Our Tommy is blond.'

She was silent for a long time. Debussy had stopped his maundering on the gramophone. From darkness there came the sibilant hiss of the gramophone needle. There was a clock, too, ticking at either end of a pendulum swing.

'Did you never think, Finlay, that you, too, had a right to joy?'

He thought about this.

'No,' he said, truthfully.

He had met her with flowers from the train at King's Cross. The late afternoon was bright with autumn sunshine. Columns of men in greatcoats, wearing packs, obstructed the concourse with resignation on grey faces and cigarettes crimped between their fingers. Steam rose aromatic from tea wagons and belched and billowed from locomotives on the platforms. Bomb blast had taken many of the panes from the great glassed arches that formed the station roof. Golden light shafted through them, thick with tremulous motes.

'Jesus wants me for a sunbeam,' a soldier said, bathed suddenly in one of these pillars of lambent light, and his mates laughed. The soldier had said the words in a broad West Country accent. Easing through their column and looking at their faces, Finlay wondered which of these pals would not survive the war.

He saw her before she saw him because he was looking and she was not. She walked slowly towards him along the platform with one hand in the pocket of her unbuttoned raincoat and the other carrying an overnight bag. She had on a grey waisted pullover and her thighs moved, alternate and slender, under the tight fabric of a long skirt in a darker shade of grey. Her narrow waist was emphasized by a broad belt that was shiny, like patent leather. Other passengers disembarked around her, spectral in the platform steam. But to Finlay, watching, it seemed as though Rebecca approached him singled out by the light, her lips red and her hair tawny, falling around her shoulders like a shawl threaded from gold. Her face was pale and he knew that what he had said to her on their first meeting was true. She was the most beautiful woman he had ever seen. The stems of the flowers were damp in his fist with his tightening grip and he was forced to breathe deeply to counter his quickening pulse. A steam whistle shrilled and she looked up and now, no more than fifteen feet away, she saw him, looked into his eyes, her own registering recognition quickly and surprise, and then the ripple of a grin broke across her face. She dropped her bag to the ground and ran to him and he hugged her tight, and when he looked into her face, he saw only delight. Until he died, Finlay would be able to close his eyes and remember the perfect pleasure registered at that precise moment by the features composing that achingly lovely face.

He kissed her.

'Lucky bleeder,' he heard someone say, from somewhere unimportant beyond the taste and warm touch of Rebecca.

'I love you,' he said, astonishing himself, when the kiss broke.

'Of course you do,' she said. 'You have from the first. Just as I love you.'

They turned right outside the station, Finlay carrying Rebecca's bag, and walked the length of soot-blackened, sandbagged buildings stretching towards Euston. Traffic on the Euston Road was light. Finlay assumed they were heading for Rebecca's flat; that they would walk along Southampton Row to Coptic Street. But instead they crossed the Euston Road before they got to Southampton Row and Rebecca led them down a little alleyway that doglegged behind a derelict theatre building into Lamb's Conduit Street. She stopped outside an old pub called The Lamb.

'This is what you would call my local,' she said. 'There was no refreshment on that awful train and there's nothing in the flat and I need food and something cool first to drink.'

A few minutes later they were seated at a corner table. She ran her hand down his chest to one side, and squeezed. He was unused to the proximity of her again and her touch was a physical thrill so potent that it left a tingling absence when she took her hand away.

'How did you know when to meet the train?'

'A little man I know carries the timetables around in his head. With much other information of far less use. There was only one train today from Glasgow.'

'Are you not supposed to be on duty?'

'They've given me two days' leave. They think I'm exhausted.

They think my morale is damaged. I've left men I've trained and drilled the best I can in my absence.' He shrugged. 'It's only two days.'

'Why are you staring like that at my sandwich?'

'Because there's a fortnight's ham ration on it,' Finlay said. 'And as much butter as you might see in a month.'

'Would you like some?'

He shook his head and sipped bitter.

'I've eaten. After a fashion.'

'The landlord here has a soft spot for me,' Rebecca said, removing a crumb from the corner of her mouth with a finger.

Finlay nodded and shifted in his chair. It creaked. He could imagine the whole world having a soft spot for her.

'How was Glasgow?'

'A miserable place. It's good to be back. It's good to see you.' She put a hand on the back of his and picked his hand off the table and squeezed. He squeezed back. Her skin was soft and cool and he was still shockingly sensitive to the thrill of her touch. He was tender to the touch of her, he realized. Like somebody burned.

'Let's go,' she said, gulping the last of her drink. 'Before we start to speak like two people with tennis racquets in the second act of one of your dismal English plays.'

It had been White who had insisted on the leave. Grey and the Immaculate Major had detached from either side of White and left the room through doors in opposite walls behind where Finlay sat, closing their doors in careful unison. White sat for so long, still behind his steepled fingers, that Finlay began to feel forgotten about, and wondered if he had missed some subtle signal of dismissal. He listened to the sedate, insistent ticking of a ministerial clock and heard the drift of occasional traffic muffled by the chicken wire covering the windows. He fancied he saw shadows start to lengthen, though there were no shadows actually being cast in the matt, ministerial light.

'I don't care what they say about me when I'm dead, Chief Fire Officer,' White offered eventually.

There was another funereal silence. Finlay wondered whether

the man was growing senile under all the stress. Perhaps his mind was simply capitulating.

'Heard of a chap called Bismarck?'

'I've heard of a ship called *Bismarck*, sir.'

White did not respond either to the joke or his use of the forbidden appellation. Definitely getting senile, Finlay thought.

'Quite. Well,' White said. 'Chap they named the ship after once said that the only true immortality is posthumous fame. Not an opinion I share, frankly. I don't give a tuppenny fuck what they say about me when I'm gone, to tell the truth.'

He looked at Finlay at this point and Finlay, holding his gaze, saw that White's eyes were rheumed with red. 'There's only one detail in my obituary that I will care about, Chief Fire Officer. Only four words of it will have the remotest significance for me.'

Another silence.

'And what are they, sir?'

White was crying. Tears were trickling over the contours age had mapped on his cheeks. 'At the end they will write, "His son predeceased him",' White said. He sniffed and then coughed to regain composure. 'Four saddest words in the language,' he said. 'Excuse me.' He took a handkerchief from his pocket and dabbed at his eyes. 'I'm sorry.'

'Please don't be, sir.'

'A sniper bullet. Arras. Two days before James would have celebrated his nineteenth birthday. They said it was instantaneous, but of course they would say that to me, wouldn't they? Look what they told Kipling about his boy.'

Finlay assumed White must mean Kipling the writer. He did not know what 'they' had told Kipling about his boy. He had been obliged to learn by rote the poem 'If' at Borstal. Recalling the poem, he was pretty sure that Kipling must have written it before learning whatever it was they had told him about his boy.

'What rank do you hold, sir? If you don't mind me asking. You are in the military, aren't you, sir?'

White looked at him for a long moment. ''Course I'm in the bloody military. I'm a bloody General. And my name isn't White.' He sniffed, mightily. 'I was a Major on Haig's staff when they brought me the news about my son. I requested a posting at the front. Wanted to kill Germans. Would have done it with a bayonet. Haig wouldn't hear of it. Said he valued intelligence.' White dabbed his eyes again. 'Bloody ironic for a man who didn't have any.'

Finlay looked at the carpet and smiled at the thought that five minutes ago he had suspected this man of senility.

'I want you to take a couple of days off, Chief Fire Officer.'

Finlay took this in.

'And if they bomb my buildings?'

'There will be no break in the bombing this side of Christmas. Probably not until the spring. Perhaps not even then. They have the capacity to go on bombing us for ever. I'm suggesting two days' leave, not unconditional surrender. If you don't take a rest, you will break down. Everyone does, you know. Eventually. I dined with Winston last night. He very nearly came apart after Gallipoli. Told me so himself.'

'And how's he bearing up at the moment?'

'That's an impudent question,' White said. 'But he's bearing up very well. In the pink. Spoiling for the fight.'

And that means you're in the pink too, Finlay thought. Whatever White and Grey and their bellicose little band of army brass were up to now had official sanction. Churchill surely wouldn't share tales of how close he once was to a strait-jacket over dinner with a man he didn't trust.

He looked at the pattern on the carpet and thought of Nevin.

'I'm hardly at the end of my tether, sir.'

'Frankly, you'd be the last to know if you were,' White said. 'Enjoy yourself. See the Lange woman. Fornicate and get drunk. Try to forget for a while that you were brought up a Catholic. Don't, for God's sake, go to Whitstable. Stay away from Irishmen.'

Finlay got to his feet, saluted and wheeled about.

'Sit down.'

Finlay sat.

'You've a distinguished record, outside of your unfortunate tendency to assault Fenians.'

'Sir.'

'But there's this story that's followed you about. Something that dogs your file with the nagging persistence of truth.'

Dread invaded Finlay. Dread engulfed him in its shivering chill. He believed himself innocent of any real crime. But he knew that the man confronting him was much cleverer than he.

'Sir?' Finlay said.

'Ladders,' White said. 'Apparently you have a problem climbing them. Somewhat unfortunate, no? In the circumstances?'

Relief surged and settled through Finlay.

'The story stems from an event long before I achieved my present rank, sir. I attended a tenement blaze. Fierce heat, wooden ladders. Evacuated a toddler from a fourth-floor bedroom, sir. When I tried to exit the bedroom window, I realized that the toddler was too small for safe evacuation by means of a fireman's lift. Matters were further complicated by the fact that the ladder I had climbed was made of wood and had caught fire, sir.'

'My God,' White said.

'So, sir, I gripped the baby between my legs and descended the ladder hand under hand down the rungs. They were intact. It was the rails of the ladder that had caught and were burning. Sir.'

'I see. So who was responsible for the story?'

'I believe it was fire fighter Albert Cooper, sir. A first-class man. But a man with a mischievous sense of humour.'

'The man who perished in the school fire you fought in Kennington?'

'You have an excellent memory, sir.'

'I do,' White said. 'It's my blessing and my curse. Dismissed, Finlay.'

Finlay wheeled about.

'Chief Fire Officer?'

He stopped.

'We did not have this conversation.'

'Of course we didn't, Mr White,' Finlay said. He picked up his grip and walked out of the room, leaving its occupant to war and to the memory of war.

*

It was after ten in the evening when Finlay and Rebecca finally left her flat and walked the dark, sand-and-canvas-damped distance to the antic light and bustle of The Fitzroy Tavern. They walked hand in hand, Finlay in thrall to emotions which for him were unfamiliar, feelings he had not come close to having for a woman before. Anticipation was a part of it. She was gorgeous and strange and yet he felt now that the intimacy he longed to share with her was not beyond him. All around them, night and even day, the life-and-death lottery of the bombing impelled strangers to frenzied bouts of fucking one another in blind alleys, in the doorways of closed shops, on random street corners. In the Moorgate canteen, they even ran a book on who'd be the first fire fighter to knee-tremble his way to a dose of the pox. Finlay felt frustrated by Rebecca's reluctance, but flattered by it too. The talk about trust meant that the thought of his betrayal of her trust was painful to her. He was unused to having someone care about what he did, someone not linked by blood to him, someone not bloodied by the betrayals of his delinquent past.

He had lied to her. The bull screw who tried to sodomize him on his first night at the Portland Borstal had called him beautiful as he cornered Finlay in the bathhouse. To Finlay, this seemed a lie without significance. He had butted and punched and finally stamped the man into bloody, pleading submission. A lashing with the cat, the several beatings he subsequently endured and four solitary months in the punishment block had left him with no particular regard for the man's opinion in consideration of his looks.

She had honoured the tit for tat of their trade. He had told her truthfully about his father. And she had told him truthfully about hers, he believed. He could not know. But her story had been heavy with the pain and bewilderment of unreconciled truth.

'My father was queer,' she told him. 'Queer for Richard Frentz, as Richard Frentz had been queer for him.'

Her language was clumsy now, rather than fluent. Her tenses were not certain. She was failing to find in the certainty of a foreign grammar a chronology which seemed to be unclear to her.

'Had been?'

There wasn't even the clatter of bone sliding down skin now to punctuate her silences. She had run out of cigarettes.

'My father's . . . predilection.'

Finlay shook his head, unfamiliar with the word.

'His sexual preferences?'

'We call it perversion,' Finlay said.

'Don't be a total bastard to me, Jack. Please?'

'I'm here wringing water out of a dry rag,' Finlay said. 'I feel a fool for having blabbed on about my past. I tell you things I've told nobody. I get back riddles.'

An intake of breath clattered through her. And beside her, Finlay considered. Was he angry at her, or at himself for having articulated to her a pain he kept private? Was she playing him like a tinker's fiddle, or was she simply telling the truth about the reason for her father's disappearance and death? The Nazis did not like queers. That much was the plainest logic to the simplest fool.

'Go on,' Finlay said.

'I don't know when they stopped being lovers. I suspect it was considerably after what happened in Düsseldorf.'

'Jesus.'

'Love is not contingent, Jack. Even among queers.'

Contingencies to Finlay were what the fire-fighting manuals taught you by heart to prepare for and guard against.

'I shouldn't be here,' he said. 'Our countries are at war.'

'You shouldn't be here because our countries are at war. That's perfect, Jack. Only hours ago, you told me you loved me. Love me: you told me that you love me.'

He said nothing.

'And if you had your way, you'd have fucked me. You'd be fucking me still,' she said, her throat catching. Finlay waited for the theatricality of a sob. It did not come. 'You'd better go,' she said, her accent Germanic now. 'Go, Finlay. *Schnell*.'

He turned from the hip and found the round warmth of her shoulders spreading indignant heat under the fingers of each of his hands as he held her gentle, insistent.

'I'm sorry,' he said. 'I'm sorry, Rebecca.'

She settled back. She closed her eyes. He listened to her breathe for a while. It was possible to forget how solitary she must feel, he thought, in a land at war with the country of her birth. He thought of her emerging from steam on the railway platform. He remembered a poster he had seen at the station, pasted on to half a dozen prominent places along its walls. *Is Your Journey Really Necessary?*

'Why did you go to Scotland?'

'To interrogate a man.' She coughed. 'The people you work for have captured a U-boat captain. His submarine collided with a mine and foundered off the Scottish coast. The crew set off distress flares in the water and they were spotted by some trawlermen.'

'Bloody lucky for the Krauts.'

Rebecca barked laughter.

'Yes, and no. Some of those trawlermen have relatives and friends on your Atlantic convoys. By the time I got to the captain of the U-boat, he had been quite badly beaten.'

'I'm surprised,' Finlay said.

Rebecca laughed her bitter laugh again.

'Are you? Didn't you fight under a Scot?'

So the gloves are coming off, Finlay thought. We're getting to the meat. And to the bone.

'What did he tell you?'

'It was the manner of the telling, Finlay. Perhaps he was a relative of your unfortunate brother's Hangy Todd. The Captain waited until I opened my mouth to speak and then he spat blood from his broken teeth and phlegm industriously stored from his broken nose accurately to the back of my throat.'

'Did he tell you anything?'

'When he revived. A Company Sergeant Major from the Black Watch was acting as my escort and took exception to the spitting.'

'So what did the spitter tell you when he came round?'

'That I was a traitor and would hang when Germany has won the war. That I would be fortunate to hang.'

Finlay thought for a moment.

'And you were able to identify this CSM's regiment from his tartan?'

'Of course I was not,' she said. 'He told me himself when I mentioned that he was the first soldier I had seen dressed in a pleated skirt.'

Finlay laughed. 'No wonder he belted the Kraut. Which one of them sent you to Scotland?'

'The one you call Grey. He is my godfather.'

'How did he get to be your godfather?'

Rebecca shifted on the sofa at his side.

'I need a cigarette.'

'Not as much as I need an answer. How did Grey get to be your godfather?'

'Grey was a mathematician at Cambridge. He was brilliant, creative, precocious. He would have been the youngest professor of mathematics in the history of the University. He published as a postgraduate student and some of his papers in the field of theoretical physics are still standard works. My father read Grey and was excited by what he discovered. He thought that much of Grey's thinking had practical applications in engineering. Specifically in propulsion. In power.' Rebecca stopped talking.

Somewhere beneath them, Finlay fancied he heard footsteps and then a door slam.

'Go on.'

'They corresponded. When my father studied in London with Frentz, they met with Grey and he and my father became friends. Perhaps they became more than that. I don't know. Certainly they were friends.'

'And they worked together on their theories about propulsion?'

'No. They did not. Shortly after war broke out in 1914, in common with almost every other young Oxbridge man, Grey volunteered for the army. He was at the front pretty much continuously for almost two years. And then he had some sort of breakdown. He recovered as a soldier and continued to serve. But he lost his gift for abstract thought. Or perhaps he merely lost his enthusiasm, his ardour for it. Either way, by the time the armistice came, he was finished as a creative scientist.'

'There's a secret floor in Absalom House. A space not accessed by the lift or by stairs. Your father was gifted at proportion and it's cleverly concealed. But it is there, isn't it?'

For a moment, she just sat, head bowed, a beautiful woman diminished into silence by the pain of memories. Finlay felt an almost visceral urge to console her, to protect her, as if the strength of his embrace alone could exorcise her shame and end her isolation. He took her head between his hands and kissed her mouth, her throat, her hair.

'I'm sorry, Rebecca. It isn't my business. I'm sorry. Forgive me. Trust me. Please, please trust me.'

'The place you're talking about isn't a secret,' she said. 'It's more a conceit. It's a space in which my father stored things.' She was silent for a moment. Then, reluctantly, 'I suppose you could say he concealed things there.'

'May I see it?'

'Yes, Finlay. You may. I'll give you keys and tell you how to find it. If you like, I can show it to you.'

Bravado brought singing to The Fitzroy Tavern as the streets surrounding the pub shuddered under an onslaught of evening bombs. The siren had sounded the warning and the bar staff had donned their tin hats and simply kept on serving. Nobody left. The door opened only on people continuing to arrive, risking the rubble and craters and blast on the route for the sake of drink and the mood of abandonment present only in the face of appalling danger. Loudly the gathering groups sang; raucous, laughing, bright with gesticulation, the women emerging gaudy from dark coats and wraps and shawls which they shed once inside; many of the men dapper, precisely attired in black tie and tails or pressed into uniform. Outside, the crump and roar of high explosives sounded like the rumour of battle against the din of the pub interior. But when Finlay placed the flat of his hand on the varnished bar, he could feel the bombardment thrum through vibrating wood. And when a cluster of bombs landed close, the shock sent ripples through beer puddled on the bar in places and the ceiling of the room seemed to shiver above its cluster of bouncing lamps.

They found a table. Rebecca unpicked the knot of a scarf she had put on before leaving her flat. She looked around and Finlay caught a pensiveness about her eyes and mouth, a paling of her complexion, before she willed herself into what the world saw, shaking out her hair, smiling only for him.

Alone, Finlay thought. Alone.

'I once put out a fire at a factory called Pimlico Rubber.' She took a sip of her drink.

'I know. My godfather told me all about your depressingly brilliant record when I complained about your instructions concerning the Absalom dome.'

'One of the men who died at Pimlico was shortly to get married. He perished with his prospective father-in-law. The older man was saving hard to pay for a wedding. The younger was saving just as hard in the hope of starting a family.'

Rebecca looked confused.

'Are you with me so far? In this country, it's the custom—'

'—I'm with you so far,' Rebecca said. 'I've just never seen you look like this before.'

'When we were called to Pimlico Rubber, both of these men were well into their third consecutive shift. Without a break. Wholly against regulations. An outrage to common sense. Contrary to the professional ethics of anyone who has the right to call himself a fire fighter.'

'Why?'

'I was cajoled, kidded, pressured. They needed the money. I still don't know why I connived in it. I suppose we all want to be popular.'

'And did fatigue contribute to the way they met their deaths?'

'They shouldn't have been there.' Finlay was staring into his linked hands, under their table, on his lap. He looked up through his eyebrows at her. 'Nobody sleepwalks his way up a stairwell into a factory fire. They'd been on the job for over twenty hours. They must have been tired and that couldn't have helped. But the fact is that they died somewhere they should not have been.'

'This never came out.'

'An old fire fighter friend of mine altered the worksheets and doctored the station log,' Finlay said. 'So no, it never came out. But it happened.'

Rebecca's Irishman strode in, patting clouds of lathe dust from the great plains of his overcoated shoulders. Sober, Finlay observed that he moved nimbly enough, easily through narrow and shifting channels, on his patient approach to the bar. Finlay felt the tightening of his stomach that he always felt in the proximity of dangerous people. The Dubliner was dangerous, he had no doubt whatsoever of that. And this was the soberest Finlay had seen him. But it was not fear that Finlay felt, more a sort of careful excitement.

'Becks,' the Dubliner said. He lifted one of his heavy hands and curved it around one side of Rebecca's face and touched her cheek with his fingers. It was a gesture that surprised Finlay, watching, with its tenderness. The hand dropped. Finley tensed. 'A pint of plain,' the Dubliner said to a waiting barman. He turned to Finlay and began to unbutton his coat. Dust and grime ringed his eyesockets and lathe dust had turned the dark ringlets falling over his forehead white. He looked like a member of an opera chorus crudely aged by panstick and wig.

'Just saw one of your fellows killed,' he said to Finlay. 'Poor bastard was ripped in half.'

'A fire fighter?'

A nod of the head.

'Where?'

The Dubliner picked his pint off the bar and sipped. 'Chiswell Street.'

'That's Moorgate's ground,' Finlay said, redundantly.

The Irishman just nodded and sipped stout.

'Auxiliary?'

'I'm no authority. I don't think so, though. Had on a uniform like the one you wear.'

Finlay felt the temperature against his skin lower several degrees. He licked his lips. But they were dry delivering his words. 'Ripped in half?'

The Irishman sipped stout and swallowed. 'Strafed. He was standing in the middle of Chiswell Street directing fire crews and they were being strafed, I think by a Messerschmitt cannon. A heavy-calibre weapon, anyway. It tore up the road the way a plough blade turns the earth. It tore up hoses and it tore your man to pieces.'

Finlay was at the scene in fifteen minutes, sprinting full-pelt through fire-daubed streets, flames painted in orange and gold, through Bloomsbury and into Clerkenwell and then the edge of the City. They had put Nevin on a stretcher a few feet down an alley and covered him with an oilskin cape. It was raining softly now, through the thunder of bombs and the scream of fighter aircraft and the percussive thump of anti-aircraft batteries, on to the undiminishing fires. By firelight, Finlay could see raindrops gathered like dew in the hair on the back of one of Nevin's hands, which had slipped from under the oilskin covering him. Kneeling, Finlay knew it was Nevin from the thick wedding band the Moorgate Watch Commander habitually wore. He would have known it was Nevin anyway, would have recognized even under his makeshift shroud the familiar, stoic bulk of the man, finally finding repose. Finlay lifted the exposed hand, which was still warm, and kissed Nevin's wedding ring.

'I'm sorry, comrade,' he said. 'I'm so sorry.'

Finlay rose and walked to the end of the alley and tried to assess the reeling violence of the night's airborne assault. The sky was alight with tracer rounds and the firefly trails of damaged aircraft. The ground was chaotic with girders, gantries, rubble; the huge, spilled entrails of buildings gutted by bombs. Flames guttered and flared in bewildering pockets of deadly fire. Fire crews toiled and Finlay could see in the coil of their tense silhouettes the dread of strafing cannon-fire a diving fighter engine would signal. Away to the east, through the cooling drizzle, fire burned all around St Paul's. And further east, Finlay could see smoke billow, petroleum-fed, from fires on the docks.

'It's a fucking mess,' someone screamed in his ear. Finlay turned and saw the Lead Fire Fighter B Watch, who had alerted him in the Moorgate canteen to the nature of Nevin's vigil. The man – Finlay was pretty sure his name was Pearson – would be Acting Watch Commander now in Nevin's place. Finlay knew he could do nothing more in fire-fighting terms than the man was doing, so he simply nodded in agreement.

'Give me your torch.'

Pearson looked blank. 'But you're in civvies, sir.'

'Just give me your torch. You've got spares on that pump?' Finlay nodded towards a Dennis appliance parked at the near end of a column of appliances to Pearson's rear.

'Here,' Pearson said, unclipping the torch from his belt.

Finlay was walking away when he remembered the thick wedding band adorning the finger of Nevin's corpse. He walked back to Pearson and turned him around.

'That looting cunt, Pickering—'

'Is dead, Chief Fire Officer. Crushed under a collapsing wall. Killed his first shift after you dealt him the cards.'

Finlay took a step back. Through a soot-black face, Pearson blinked at him.

'Sooner you get off my ground the better, with respect, sir. Tonight, leastways. The wags among my lads are calling you the angel of death.' He smeared soot around his firelit features and blinked, his eyes raw with soot. 'Like I said, sir. It's a fucking mess.'

Twelve

FINLAY WALKED eastwards almost without the realization that he was doing so. He paced through flayed streets under the screech of dogfights and the unrelenting deluge of bombs, navigating London like a sleepwalker. He had known it would be Nevin as soon as the words were out of the Irishman's mouth. Dimly, he was aware of his destination.

Absalom House was intact. Finlay had known that it would be with the same certainty that had told him it was poor Nevin's exhausted body out of which a Messerschmitt's twenty milli-metre cannon shells had so recently torn the life. The German bombing seemed indiscriminate tonight. Vicious, damaging, but random in the application of its destructive force. Usually they had strategic targets. Always they chose as secondary targets those landmarks that they felt defined London in the minds and hearts of the city's population. But tonight was different. The sustained spite, the sheer quantity of explosive force spilling from the sky seemed like an attempt to flatten the capital, to bury it in an avalanche of flame and rubble. The air was hot and harsh with the stink of fire, incendiaries, bombs, spent ammunition; in places the dank steam from Thames water pumped through river-fed hoses.

But amid all this chaos, Absalom House rose massive and intact, as if in brooding indifference to the carnage visited around it. Inside, under the noise of the bombardment, Finlay could hear the guttural rumble of the diesel generator in the basement, powering the rows of machines he had seen on the ground floor, wheels spinning under the glass panels in their fascias like nothing so much as the displays on the one-armed bandits his aunt had played on holiday afternoons in the amusement arcade on the seafront at Bray.

Lange's conceit was sited between the second and third floors. Wood panels decorated the ceiling of the second floor. Finlay counted back thirteen panels from the entrance to the second-floor room Rebecca had described to him and then dragged over a tall bookcase, denuded of books at his own insistence, and climbed the shelves and peered at the panelling. Sure enough, he saw a keyhole. Twisting the key to the right and then pulling it when it gripped the lock would suffice, she had told him. The panel lowered smoothly on its hydraulic mechanism and a ladder slid down from behind it, articulated sections clicking in the bomb-battered night, slick with lubrication.

Pearson's torch revealed a windowless room about eight feet high that ran the length and width of Absalom House. Below, Finlay could hear the hum of unseen machines. Here, though, all was quiet. There were pictures stacked under dust drapes against the walls, and old scientific instruments – astrolabes, globes, intricate cosmologies constructed from brass and wire, gyro-scopes, compasses, sextons, telescopes – crowded together on table- and desk-tops and filling large areas of wall-mounted shelves. The room smelled of oil paint and metal polish. Finlay swung the torch and the beam picked out an umbrella stand filled with antique swords, heaps of furled, yellowing charts on shelves, a closed violin case. He wondered why a man obsessed with scientific progress would fill clandestine space with the booty of a distant past. It was more pirate's lair than studio, or laboratory. There was no evidence of plumbing in Lange's conceit. There were no power points. There wasn't a hurricane lamp, not so much as a candle stub. It was clear to Finlay from the dust and pervasive odour of age and decay that this was not a place of work. He exited it knowing little more than he had about anything, his curiosity anyway dulled by the impact of Nevin's death. Nevin had survived the Ypres Salient and been torn to pieces by German cannon-fire on a street in the city of his birth. There was no comfort in the thought that he was finally resting.

He was not resting. Finlay's final memory of the man would for ever be of pieces of mortified flesh leaking blood into a gutter.

Babcock was in Finlay's cell, sitting cross-legged on the cot, buffing some piece of kit Finlay saw at closer inspection was the knuckleduster he had taken from Rebecca's Dubliner. It gleamed like malevolent gold between folds of polishing cloth in the old batman's industrious hands. Babcock uncoiled off the cot, giving its top blanket a straightening tug.

'Making myself useful, Mr Finlay,' he said. 'Conflict never being resolved without initiative.'

This gambit got no response from Finlay.

'Sounds like it's gone off good and proper tonight,' Babcock said, lifting his eyes momentarily to the ceiling.

Finlay looked at his wristwatch. 'It's ten o'clock at night, Babcock. What the fuck are you doing here?'

'My bit, Chief Fire Officer. We all have to do our bit.'

A bomb detonated almost directly above them then, the first of a cluster that set the metal walls vibrating with a low moan and the rivets clamping the walls to their supporting girders singing with protest. There was a crack and a gathering rumble and ash emptied in a rush out of one of the air feeds emerging from the ceiling. It stopped as suddenly as it started, leaving a cone-shaped heap a foot high on the linoleum floor.

Babcock whistled.

'Lummy,' he said.

Finlay said nothing.

'That one very nearly had our names on it.'

'Pack it in, Babcock. You sound like a comic turn on the wireless.'

'I'll fetch a brush and pan,' Babcock said.

Finlay removed his jacket and tie and sat on his cot and stared at the telephone, which squatted, still and silent. For some reason he expected it to ring and to hear Grey's voice at the other end of the line. But then he had almost expected to see Grey, raincoated, in the vicinity of Nevin's corpse. The thoroughfares of the assaulted city, between Chiswell Street and Liverpool Street, had been teeming with fire crews, with Heavy Rescue demolition teams, with wardens and ambulance crews and police officers. And among them, at every turn, Finlay had expected to see the gaunt countenance and lean figure of Captain Grey. After a while he noticed that Babcock was back, busying himself on his knees sweeping ash and humming a tune that Finlay knew, with something approaching instinct, was currently on the minds and lips of the cinema-going public.

'How's your wife?' Finlay said.

Without knowing what White had allowed him to learn, Finlay thought he would have noticed nothing in Babcock's reaction. Even so, he wondered if imagination embellished with false significance what he actually saw. But he did see it. Babcock, at the mention of his wife, shrank slightly. For just a moment, the man seemed to shoulder burdens he was incapable of carrying and to shudder under them. Then he recovered.

'The wife is chirpy,' Babcock said. 'Cheerful as you like. Insists we'll muddle through. Reckons we can take it, the wife does, Chief Fire Officer, and that Jerry can go to hell.'

Unwilling, unable to collude in this, Finlay only nodded. He did so emphatically enough. The lights in the cell began to flicker. And he observed the way that Babcock, busy, seemed to move in two dimensions, like a memory, or a motif.

Finlay stripped to his briefs and began to wash with a fat and fragrant bar of Palmolive he found wrapped in greaseproof paper beside his sink. In the small mirror above the sink, Babcock wandered in and out of focus. 'Jesus, look at you,' Babcock said. 'I've seen more fat on a drawing. Look at the muscles on you. No wonder you're frustrated, pointing hoses at buildings on fire. You were constructed to fight. Christ, you were invented to fight, Mr Finlay. My oath. What a waste.'

Finlay was rinsing soap from out of his eyes. Babcock's resilience astonished him. He had never met a man so capable at curtailing the realities of the world to what was tolerable. Some heavy piece of German ordnance erupted above and the metal floor thrummed under the linoleum under Finlay's feet.

'You know, Mr Finlay, we are a long way underground here. Under the Thames. Under the tributaries of the River Fleet. Under Roman baths and plague pits dug in the Dark Ages. Under

God only knows what remnants of tunnelling those industrious Victorians failed to adequately map.'

Rivets pinged in girders warping behind the iron walls confining them. There was the odd, somnambulant sound of steps warping on the metal stairwell winding upwards in the cylinder of steel rising to the street outside.

'You think we should go somewhere else?' Finlay said. He was drying himself with a towel and enjoying Babcock's discomfiture in a manner he knew was sadistic. It was all he could do not to ask after the health of Babcock's boy. The death of Nevin had brought upon him a mood of guilt and viciousness.

'Anywhere else, frankly.' Babcock said. 'I'm an engineer, Mr Finlay. I know about tolerances. And I was in the trenches with Captain Grey and so I know about luck, too. We've both of us ridden ours. Now we're pushing it.'

The walls boomed about them, as if in affirmation.

'This place is for it. Mark my words.'

Finlay was buttoning his uniform tunic. 'Where would you suggest we go?'

Babcock smiled into the mirror, a distorted leer in the limited light. 'I know just the place,' he said. 'Don't you worry about that.'

Just before they left, Finlay plucked the telephone receiver from its cradle. He pressed it to the side of his face and listened. The line was as dead as he had known it would be.

Leaving his cell with Babcock felt for Finlay like a kind of liberation. There was something militant about the man tonight, a cocksure strut in his walk as he led the way, whistling, the sound amplified and harsh through the metal voids of thrumming tunnels. There was a respite in the bombing by the time Babcock and Finlay gained the streets. The Germans were bombing in waves with the intervals between them timed to be deliberately irregular to prevent the batteries of anti-aircraft guns from developing any kind of rhythm or momentum, or properly orchestrated fields of fire from the ground. The ack-ack batteries were far more prevalent now than they had been only weeks earlier when Finlay had first arrived back in London. They occupied highly symbolic strategic sites all over the capital and their belligerent crews fired hundreds of thousands of loud rounds through barrels rendered red-hot by the sheer percussive friction of their rate of fire. They still seldom hit anything. They were actually more dangerous to anyone under the trajectory of falling ordnance than to anything flying in the sky. The battery on the north side of Westminster Bridge looked particularly obstreperous and magnificent as it swung to send shells tearing into the air to miss Junkers by several thousand feet and detonate to the hard-hit east, where most of them landed. But the quantity of metal tearing the sky each night had made the Germans more cautious and cleverer about the way they bombed. They flew higher. They attacked in irregular waves and they strafed more heavily. The lull Babcock and Finlay found themselves in would not last, but it was something. Babcock led the way through Spitalfields terraces until Finlay was thoroughly lost and had to follow the other man merely to find his way. Babcock had stopped whistling. The jaunt in his gait had been replaced by a steady prowl. He was no longer a strutting music-hall act. He moved with the stealth, through the black-out, of some night predator. They stopped at a row of lock-up garages behind a tenement. Finlay could see where they were because a house fire burned unimpeded to one side of the yard in which they stood, about a hundred yards away. Finlay's trained ears listened hard for the sound of anyone trapped by the flames, but there was nothing. The house sagged and heaved as spent supporting timbers surrendered to the weight of bricks.

'One more slum-dweller made homeless,' Babcock said, without looking up. He hawked and spat. He had inserted a key into a large padlock securing the lock-up door. The door opened on a maw of darkness, revealing nothing. Then Babcock rolled out from it a motor cycle on which every flicker of factory chrome had been painted matt black. He sat astride the machine and kick-started it at the first attempt. Either it was regularly ridden, or it was expertly tuned. The engine sounded so muffled that the noise it made was nothing more really than a low rumble, even when Babcock gave the throttle a jerk.

'Get on,' he said.

Finlay climbed on to the pillion seat. Babcock tensed for a

moment and listened to the the sky. But the lull was holding. Even when he kicked the bike into gear, the baffled exhaust made almost no discernible noise. The streets were still wet from the earlier rain, which had held off since, like the bombs. It was interesting, to Finlay, to pass at this pace through the ravaged streets. The experience was almost cinematic, like watching a firelit film of devastation in a land so badly damaged and bleak that it almost insisted to him it was somewhere foreign, and not England at all. The smells rushed in and out of his senses, assaulting nostrils and lungs, and then they were gone, impressionistic in their hot, damp, dreadful seasoning of the chaos. Fire burned dimly in nimbuses of ochre and red behind windows, on roof-tops, in spaces laid to waste. There were no people. Finlay saw not one human being in the dark, alien, wasted landscape through which Babcock rode the bike. They travelled fast, considering the headlamp was blind with black paint and the magneto apparently disengaged. Babcock rode the motor cycle expertly. It responded to his subtlest touch. Finlay supposed that his engineer's understanding of what endowed the bike with power and propulsion had made him intimate with the machine.

Perhaps he had built or rebuilt the bike. Finlay could see him stripping the thing down and reconstituting it with fastidious care, component by painstaking component. He knew nothing about Babcock, he realized, with something of a start. Babcock was one more mystery enabled by his own blinkered, almost sullen response to the job into which he had been so reluctantly forced.

Babcock cut the engine and the motor cycle freewheeled to a stop on gently undulating land bordered by neglected fencing and a wild bank of weeds. He pushed the bike into the weeds, which were wet and high and wholly concealed the machine.

'Won't someone steal it?'

'Tonight's bombing isn't done and everybody knows it. No one is going to venture out. Not to waste land, anyway,' Babcock said, softly. There was just starlight enough for Finlay to see him nod. 'We're going that way. No more than five minutes' walk. But there are one or two bomb craters between here and there and they're at least as deep as a man and filled with standing water. I can't swim and I'm sure you don't want to. So follow me carefully and watch your footing.'

They walked down a long slope of cinders and grass tussocks strewn with coping stones and piles of cobbles and discarded railway sleepers. The gradient was gentle but the going difficult in the absence of light and given what Babcock had said about bomb craters. Gradually, Finlay became aware of something massing in the darkness in front of them. Some formidable structure, darker and with greater density than the night. He could hear a drift of accordion music and fancied that he could hear something sung; like a sea-shanty or maybe a psalm set to music, but he knew it must be merely his ears playing tricks as they strained to discover the roar of engines from above.

Then they were under the edifice and Finlay saw that it was a great railway viaduct giving on to an array of arches, stretching onwards, their vaulted spaces suggesting a dark, cathedral spread. He was aware suddenly of a pervasive stink, like grease grown rancid; and of people everywhere, huddled in small groups and large gatherings, around low fires and feeble storm lamps, wrapped under blankets and coats in the gloom. Babcock led him along narrow paths between the different groups. Finlay passed women giving tarot readings, drinkers of both sexes getting determinedly drunk around crates of beer, men who from their tattoos and rich mix of nationalities could only have been crews from merchantmen moored at Tilbury and Chatham and in the Thames basin. He had not imagined the music. He passed a gang of negroes, at least a dozen of them, swaying cross-legged as they sang some plaintive spiritual. There were magicians and card sharps and tarts and derelicts and fortune-tellers and fruit-hawkers. Over in one corner Finlay saw a cock-fight, fierce betting taking place around the tearing birds in a circle lit by candle stubs. And everywhere, under thin blankets and soiled sheets, couples joined in the unmistakable rhythm of copulation.

'How many people are there here?' Finlay whispered to Babcock.

'Around fifteen thousand, they say.'

'Every night?'

Babcock stopped walking. 'Some of them never leave. The

prostitutes. The drunks. The deserters. There's more at night, because tourists come at night from up West to gawp and dawdle.'

'What is this place?' Finlay said.

Babcock leered in the cadaverous light. Somewhere behind him a bottle smashed and someone stifled a scream. He held his arms apart in a gesture of wide theatricality. 'This is England, Mr Finlay,' he said.

Two hours later, Finlay fumbled his way along the cobbled wharves and into The Prospect of Whitby. Grey occupied a table in a far recess of the pub, next to a window that was heavily curtained against the night river. His man, his driver, Finlay's grinning nemesis, stood massive and at ease about ten yards to the rear of where Grey sat. Smoke rose in a thin spiral from the cigarette between Grey's fingers. There was a whisky bottle and a jug of water beside the drinking glass on his table. Finlay sat opposite the man without ceremony. He removed his cap and put it on the table. Grey looked at him through pale brown eyes.

'Nevin has been killed.'

The look on Grey's face was unreadable. 'I'm sorry?'

'Nevin. Moorgate Station. A colleague of mine. A comrade. A friend.'

'I'm sorry,' Grey said. 'Drink?'

'You met him once,' Finlay said, remembering. 'UXB attached to a parachute.'

'Yes I did. Meet the fellow, I mean. Good chap. Great shame. Drink?'

'Bitter.'

'Don't be,' Grey said. He smiled at his joke and made some discreet signal to his man, who went to fetch the drink from the bar.

'I accessed Lange's crawlspace.'

'Not with one of your fire axes, I hope,' Grey said. 'That's a beautiful building. Panelled with such integrity. Don't you think?'

'It's full of junk.'

'Depends on what you think of as junk,' Grey said. 'Did you have a good look around the rest of the place?'

Finlay nodded.

'Impressed?'

'None the wiser.'

'But you were impressed?'

Finlay thought about this. 'There's some sort of assemblage with magnets on the fourth floor. Ball bearings shooting around between different fields of force. Terrible velocity. It looks very interesting. Ta.' Finlay's pint of bitter had been delivered. 'But it wouldn't down an enemy aeroplane.'

Grey nodded and smoked.

'You are a brave and purposeful man, Finlay,' he said. 'But nobody is ever going to mistake you for the brightest of sparks.'

'Lange's secret room was full of rubbish,' Finlay said. 'Old swords.'

'Forged in Toledo in the sixteenth century,' Grey said.

'Obsolete scientific instruments.'

'One of them used by Galileo. One of them made by John Harrison.'

'An old violin.'

'On which Paganini composed,' Grey said.

'And paintings.'

Grey smiled. He looked tired. He always looked tired. 'Did you catalogue the paintings, Chief Fire Officer?'

Finlay sipped bitter and settled in his chair. Behind the heavy drapes covering the window, he wondered in what condition the barque he had seen moored there on his first visit to this pub would be in now. It seemed an age since then. It seemed he had known Grey, or more correctly, of Grey, all his adult life. In his mind's eye he saw the barque sunk, its hull holed and half-buried in mud, its masts canted and its sails death shrouds, its rigging flapping, frayed, absent of task.

'You are a snob, Captain Grey.'

Grey did not react to this. But his man tensed and almost snarled to his rear.

'Tell me about the paintings,' Grey said.

'A Turner. A Stubbs. A Renaissance painting. Could be a Botticelli.'

'Very good,' Grey said.

'And then a load of old crap.'

'Ah. But I rather think you mean new crap.'

'Two or three all over the place with the geometry.'

'Braque,' Grey said.

'Some slapdash views of the Eiffel Tower.'

Grey sniffed.

'Delauney.'

'And some pictures of boats in a bay that look like children could have done them.'

'Dufy,' Grey said.

Finlay sank his pint.

'Not much scares you, does it, Mr Finlay.'

Finlay thought about this.

'He does,' he said, nodding towards the still shape at Grey's rear.

'Why?'

'Because he's a killer.'

Grey made great ceremony out of lighting a fresh cigarette. Once again Finlay saw the robust nickel lighter with holes drilled into the hood that seemed so uncharacteristic in hands as graceful and adept as Grey's. There was the odour of petrol as he opened the lighter and paused before striking its flame. Grey snapped the lighter shut and slipped it into a pocket.

'There's black and there's white,' he said. 'There is good and there is evil.'

Finlay did not respond.

'And then there is what we might best describe as contingency.'

Contingency was a proving to be a very versatile word, Finlay thought. He could guess its meaning here, more or less, from the context.

'McKay here has twice saved your life. The when and the how are unimportant. But we are approaching the endgame and you should know whose side you are on and who's on yours and you should be properly bloody grateful.'

Finlay looked at the monolith called McKay.

'Where was he when that Irishman gave me a kicking?' McKay snorted. Even his mirth sounded sinister.

'We thought you'd best the Irishman. McKay knew your father, you see.'

'Your old man was a force of nature, sir,' McKay said. 'Begging your pardon.'

'I don't think you've ever begged for anything,' Finlay said.

'It must be very difficult to be the son of such a celebrated hero,' Grey said. 'Difficult enough in peace, let alone in war.'

'Which is why I volunteered to fight,' Finlay said. He was tired. He was feeling the loss of Nevin, despair at what Babcock had shown him, the cold dread of whatever McKay had apparently done on his behalf. He had abandoned a woman to whom he had earlier in the day declared love to say meaningless words over a corpse and attempt to solve a mystery that was none of his business even if it was within his intellectual grasp. Which he doubted it was.

'Why did Lange fill a space the size of an entire floor in Absalom House with junk?'

'That junk belonged to his Jewish friends,' Grey said. 'He bid for it at the forced auctions in Berlin. His intention was to give it back when the political climate changed. But the political climate didn't change. Not for his Jewish friends, not for him.'

'Shouldn't you put it all somewhere safe?'

Grey laughed and behind him McKay gurgled like a drain.

'I wouldn't waste the fuel,' Grey said. 'I wouldn't waste the manpower and I wouldn't waste the space. Safety is for people first, Chief Fire Officer. You call me a snob. You might be right. But I'd rather give refuge to any misbegotten mother's squalling bastard than to a vase or statue. We'll save civilization if we're up to it, I think by the skin of our teeth. Art and antiquity will have to wait their turn in the queue.'

A silence descended then. In the distance, the odd bomb still was dropped or detonated, but there was a quiet in the bar that almost begged the cordiality of normal conversation. They were in a pub, after all.

'Tell me about Gommecourt Wood.'

McKay tensed and Finlay felt the threat of him like a drear and huge foreboding at which he dared not look.

'It wasn't Gommecourt,' Grey said with a smile. 'It was at a place called Serre. Babcock was with me there. And Colour Sarn't McKay, who knew your father, was there also.'

Finlay looked at the obdurate monument called McKay.

'How well did you know my dad?'

'Very well indeed, sir,' McKay said. 'Got to know him intimately. Best man I ever met.'

'Christmas Eve, nineteen-fifteen,' Grey said. 'Town called Albert. Heard of it?'

'Of course I have.'

'Wonderful bout. Best bout I've ever seen and I saw Carpentier fight twice in Paris. Twenty rounds and not a cigarette paper between the two of them. Fair to say, McKay?'

'He was very strong, your father,' McKay said to Finlay. 'And a most single-minded man. I was amazed that fat Paddy bested you first time around. Your old feller must've been spinning in his grave. If you don't mind me saying so.'

'Perhaps McKay can fetch the three of us a fresh drink and join our table,' Grey said, brightly. 'And then I can tell you all about what it is that you are so stubbornly keen to discover.'

Grey had risen that morning at five and shaved at first light, gratified that his hands were sufficiently steady to accomplish the task. He breakfasted on excellent coffee and bacon rashers and biscuits rustled up by Babcock, who sat now in the shelter of the dugout, sharpening the sword which Grey had not the remotest intention of carrying into battle. German snipers had proved more than adept at spotting cap-badges and revolvers. Grey would go over dressed as a trooper. Only the flash on his sleeve would distinguish his rank. But Babcock had already completed his neat job of sewing. And it was Babcock's obsequious custom to make himself always innocently busy.

Grey thought of home. He thought of his mother and father the last time he had seen them, wan, distracted with grief at the death of his brother at Ypres. He thought of Cambridge and his cosy rooms and cosily illicit life. There was pollen in the air, costing him breath, and the scent of summer flowers and the song of birds. He pondered briefy on the sublime indifference of the world, on this particular, epic day, to the machinations of men. To do so was his habitual way of reconciling to himself those appetites he indulged despite the distaste he continued to feel for them. He didn't matter to the world. And then, because he mattered to the moment, in his responsibility to other men, he confronted his fear of failure and disfigurement and death. He thought about the doubts he felt in the hollow part of him about his ability to lead. And for today, he overcame all of these.

'Vanity, of course,' he said to Finlay. 'But then vanity courses through war like blood through the body.'

Serre was a village held by the Germans between Gommecourt to the left of the British line and and Beaumont Hamel to its right. The men chosen to take it were the Fourth Army's 94th Brigade. The 94th was entirely made up of the Pals Battalions. These were young men, boys by any strict definition, who had grown up together in the terraces of neighbouring streets in the towns and cities of the north of England. There were Pals Battalions in the first wave of the attack on Serre that morning from Accrington and Barnsley and Sheffield and Leeds and Bradford and Durham and Hull. Captain Grey was attached to the 16th Battalion, West Yorkshire Regiment, generally known as the 1st Bradford Pals. 'My boys were so disciplined when they went over,' Grey told Finlay. 'They had been through their training at Etaples, endured that BEF training that was by turns so tedious and brutal, and they had been together in the trenches. Time and repetition makes clichés of the truth. But they were comrades, friends, brothers. And when they bedded down on the night prior to the assault, there was not one among them shy of the coming fight.'

Grey stared at the pale amber colouring his whisky glass.

'They went over in three lines with their rifles pointed towards the enemy trenches, their bayonets bright in the sunshine burning through the smoke left across no-man's-land by our artillery barrage.'

'And you went with them?'

'I led them. Proudly. I was damn sorry for the first fifty yards of our advance that I hadn't brought that bloody sword.'

The advance was slow. Steady. The German machine-gun fire that greeted it was a low, distant puttering. It did not sound loud, like violence. But it was persistent. Wincing into fire, Grey could see muzzle flashes from maxim guns dug in at regular intervals behind redoubts strung along the length of the forward German trench. The advance continued. Grey became numbly aware of spaces opening to his right and left as the lines seemed to waver and fall at the edge of his vision. They continued onwards. Men fell silently. They flopped to the ground, the life eagerly leaving them before their bodies lay properly on the earth. Grey walked on, a rifle heavy between his hands, aware of the air being rent to his right and left, above him, on the shuddering undulations of the ground beneath his feet. Still they advanced. There was fire from the woods to their left now and Grey sensed rather than saw the flank wither as men were jerked from life in the murderous crossfield of fire. A lieutenant came over to say something and a burst of machine-gun rounds turned the words to bright blood and he fell clutching his throat. The advance continued. Some of the men were seeking cover and returning fire, a dwindling, staccato sound against the withering fury of the fire into which they continued to walk. And then, with a raucous shriek, the German bombardment began. The air above them turned yellow in flashes and grey with the weight of churning explosive and the burst and zip of shrapnel. Grey was rocked from his feet by a blast of percussion at his back. He crawled, holding his rifle, over the lip of a shellhole. There were men there already, some of them groaning and writhing and red and in parts bone-white with new wounds. On the forward lip of the crater men were trying to fire their rifles and dying in swathes as the German machine-guns targeted them in lateral sweeps.

'It's a fucking catastrophe,' someone said.

Grey looked to his right and saw Sergeant McKay, filthy, blood-encrusted, his eyes wide with anger and indignation, trying with his hands to push bright entrails back into the belly of a boy in a uniform.

'He's dead, Sergeant,' Grey said.

'We're all fucking dead, sir.' McKay said. And he spat at the ground as the world screamed and shuddered in poisonous explosions of bright ochre and gloom above them.

It was after four o'clock in the morning and the night bombardment had finally petered out when McKay drove Finlay back to Coptic Street. Finlay sat up beside him in the front of the car. McKay drove carefully and well, his huge gauntleted hands light on the big steering-wheel. He had shifted seven or eight pints of stout, once invited by Grey to share their table, but it was obvious that a mere gallon or so of beer impinged not at all on the man's sobriety or alertness.

'It's in Stepney, that place Babcock showed you last night,' he said to Finlay. 'There's two of them there. One of them used to be a margarine store before the war.'

'That's the one I was in. It stank of stale grease.'

'I'm sure neither of them is too fragrant. The other one is run by a dwarf who used to be an optician. East End hunchback. Only in England, eh, Master Jack?'

Finlay smiled at the nickname. McKay was being proprietorial presumably because he had once fought Finlay's father to a bloody standstill. Should he, on the same basis, start calling the Government killer 'uncle'?

'Scandal is that neither of them is safe,' McKay said. 'Decrepit railway arches supported by girders that look solid enough but provide no defence against bombs. Anything carrying above eighty kilos of HE and the whole fucking lot will come down around their ears. Not that some of the cunts in there deserve any better.'

They had reached Coptic Street. Finlay put a hand on the door handle and then looked at the Colour Sergeant. 'You'd do anything for him, wouldn't you.'

It was not a question. The engine ticked under the bonnet. Mechanical order was sweet music to his ears, Finlay realized, after the screaming chaos of the raids. The discreet burble of Babcock's Norton; the expensive tremble of a Whitehall Bentley with the transmission in neutral.

McKay sighed to himself.

'You would not believe how hot it was the day it all went to pot. A hot and sunny day, full kit, one water bottle apiece. We were cut from brigade to about battalion strength in less than twenty minutes. Eighty per cent dead or wounded, still under constant frontal assault from machine-guns and mortars. Heavy and accurate enfilade fire from the wood on our flank. Gomme-court, the wood. Imagine it, Master Jack.'

Finlay tried to imagine it, as he had tried many times before. But once again, it defeated his imagination.

'I found myself in a shellhole with about twenty other blokes. The captain among them. Bit of mud in the bottom of the shellhole. It had rained a fair amount in the days prior to the assault. But what scant water there was, it was spoiled by bits of corpses and undrinkable.

'The captain took command. He promised he'd get us back to our lines in the hour before the dawn. He was as thirsty as any of us, as tired, as shocked at what had become of us. But he left that shellhole nine times as we waited for the hour before the dawn and gathered another dozen of our surviving lads in doing so. And then he did as he swore he would and got us home. Nobody else, certainly none of the boys, really thought we would escape from that horrible fucking wilderness of wire and dead men. But we did, thanks to him.'

'How did he find his way back?'

'Took a reading from the stars. Navigated by starlight. Clever man, your Captain Grey. Bravest I've ever met.'

The two men sat in silence for a moment.

'It's probably less common than you imagine, is courage,' McKay said: 'you growing up with it.'

'With the memory of it. With the mementos. Enduring its cost,' Finlay said.

'He went out again after bringing us back to our lines,' McKay said. 'He could not believe that so many had died. Just over a hundred men returned, out of the entire battalion. He found them lying in rows, he said. Row upon silent row in the darkness, like sleep. And he came back and wept. Cried like a child.'

'How were the other officers?'

'There were no other officers. None of the other officers survived it. The captain was the only one.'

It had begun softly to rain. McKay switched on his window wipers and they swished fan patterns on to wet glass in darkness.

'Did he say anything?'

'Not to me. He said one thing to Babcock, when Babcock went to fetch him a bottle of whisky. He told Babcock that nature abhors a vacuum. That was all he said. And I've never known him talk about it again until tonight.'

McKay looked at Finlay.

'I grew up a workhouse foundling. You grew up in the shadow of your father. But I've seen you walk into burning buildings, Master Jack, like it's a regular occurrence. Me, I didn't know what courage was until Captain Grey showed it to me in a shellhole in France. And you're damn fucking right. I would do anything for him.'

McKay pulled off a gauntlet with his teeth and reached across Finlay into the glove compartment and pulled out a booklet, tearing a chit from it.

'That's your travel pass,' he said. 'If neither of us has any luck, I'll be seeing you again.'

She was asleep. He had half-expected an angry vigil of Scotch and Benzedrine with records spilled across her rugs and the Irishman snoring on a sofa to a jazz soundtrack, but there she was, tucked up in bed, the counterpane revealing bare shoulders and her hair pulled upward in sleep behind her head, exposing a filigree of fine blonde curls under its weight, at the nape, when he found her lighter in the darkness and ignited its flame to look at her. She turned, awakened by the light, reaching for him.

'In a few hours I have to go away.' He held her.

'Where?'

'To a place called Barmouth. Just overnight. It's in Wales. On the coast. A train ride.'

'Why must you go?'

'To see my mother. Her house was destroyed in the raids and Grey has sent her there.'

'When?' She was awakening, pulling strands of hair from her face with her fingers.

'A few hours.'

'Then we have a few hours.' She was unbuttoning his tunic, fumbling with the buckle of his tunic belt. They had a few hours. Beyond that, nobody really knew how long anybody had. Under the covers, Rebecca was warm, tawny, naked. Finlay undressed and slipped into bed beside her feeling that he would live more through the coming hours than he had in the whole of his life. He felt a lifelong solitude slip wearily away from him. He was with Rebecca. It had taken Rebecca to bring to him the overwhelming need, he felt now, truly to share.

'Do you love me?'

'I love you,' she said.

'Do you trust me?'

She murmured something in her own language and then her mouth found his.

Thirteen

Frail snow petals formed in the freezing air outside and melted on the warmth of the train windows. Melting snow petals bleared the landscape, falling down the glass in ripples, like waves on a seashore of visiting grief. Finlay drew a line through grimy condensation in an effort to see further. It was sunset and the train rocked and moaned through a mournful passage of hills. The carriage in which he sat was almost empty. The train was a short hybrid of freight and passenger transportation. The freight was a cargo of torpedoes. Finlay had recognized their cylindrical shape under taut tarpaulins, their tiny propellers wrapped in greased paper tied with wire. Perhaps the cargo carried by this particular train had put passengers off travelling on it. Trains were frequently enough strafed and bombed.

Finlay had always thought the orange sunsets of October, incandescent with diminishing fire, one of the compensations for the losing of summer light. Even after his reluctant return to England, amid the raids, he had taken solace of a sort in the gorgeous auguring of the autumn nights.

A single soldier had guarded the wagon stacked with its cargo of torpedoes. He stood in his greatcoat and tin hat, motionless on the railway platform, the butt of his bayoneted rifle planted between his feet, his face lost to shadow. Rain edged the blade of his bayonet and dripped in heavy droplets from the rim of his helmet. He was as solid and lifeless as a statue, this sentinel, the folds of his greatcoat as dignified as bronze. He reminded Finlay of memorials familiar in many a town and city throughout England of what everyone now called the 'fourteen–eighteen.

And so it was as the miles whiled wearily by, the spectre of this sentry lulled into Finlay's restless mind Grey's boys, slumbering in death outside the village of Serre in no-man's-land.

They had died on a July morning twenty-five years ago. Through a quarter-century they had never seen the diminishing fire of another autumn sunset. They had died as boys, he thought, who would never ride bicycles or fish ponds again or put their coats down for goals in a game of football on the park.

But the boyish things were small, insignificant, in the scale of the adulthood they had been robbed of. They would never know the mad intoxication of attraction. They would not know intimacy and its slow, delicious nourishment of the soul. Rebecca had insisted on assembling in the morning what scant provisions she had and making them into a meal for his journey. She had fumbled on a dressing-gown and moved drowsily about her dark kitchen, hair in unravelled ropes of gold across her shoulders, eyes watchful of his. Now, without appetite, he unpacked his food. She had filled thick slices of black bread with cheese rinds and pickled cabbage. She had found from somewhere a half bar of chocolate. Finlay had refused her offer of a bottle of wine and bought ginger beer from a kiosk at the railway station. She had slipped a pewter flask of whisky into his coat pocket as they kissed goodbye. And it was from this that he drank now as the train rocked and the darkness encroached outside and the carriage filled with the bitter aroma of pickling vinegar.

Finlay walked the couple of miles from the train station to where his mother had been lodged, the route mostly along a coastal path, with the sea booming to his right like artillery fire in the darkness. She let him in herself and led the way up the stairs by candlelight to her rooms. They were warm and Finlay could see that they were spacious, even in the confining light allowed by candle wicks. Grey had done her proud.

'Would you like tea, son?'

He shook his head.

'A drink? There's beer—'

'Sit down, mum.'

Margaret Finlay sank into a chair.

'He's dead, isn't he? Our Tommy is dead.'

Margaret Finlay's face swam in agony. She gripped the arms of the chair that held her with swollen knuckles and she bowed her head.

'You should have told me,' Jack Finlay said. His voice broke. 'You should have told me, mum.'

When she lifted her head, her face was wet with tears. 'They asked me not to. They told me that your job was very important to the war effort. We cannot lose this war, John.'

'When did he die?'

'August.'

Finlay had his head in his hands.

'I've had letters from him written since then.'

'I wrote them,' his mother said. 'Grey suggested I should and God forgive me, I did.'

Finlay rocked and shuddered with his head in his hands.

'Oh Jesus. Jesus.'

'They needed you to fight fire. You'd have been no good to them grieving. They're not bad men. They're better than you think. Stronger.'

Finlay said nothing. He moaned and rocked and the salt stung his eyes, closed against the heels of his hands.

'Tommy didn't suffer, John. It was all over very quickly. There was no suffering.'

It hit Finlay like a blow, then, that this was his mother, who had lost her husband and her baby to war, trying to comfort and apologize to him. He got up and went across to her and, kneeling before her, hugged her hard, gathering her hair in his hands and pulling her head to his chest. They were like that for a long time, while candles guttered in the room and surf from the sea boomed like a barrage down on the shore.

Grey was waiting on the platform when his train pulled in to Paddington.

'I take it you are rested after your leave.'

'In the pink, Captain,' Finlay said. 'Never better.'

'Topping,' Grey said. 'We understand Jerry is about to put on a really big show.'

They had been walking the length of the platform, weaving

between files of troops towards the ticket barrier and concourse beyond.

'You mean bigger than that raid the other night? The one you spent in The Prospect?'

Grey stopped. It was late afternoon and in the last, feeble light through the vaulted station roof he looked almost translucent with fatigue. But Finlay no longer worried about how tired, or gaunt, or desperately in need of rest and nourishment Grey appeared to him. Grey was unkillable, he realized now. By all the laws of physics in which he had once so delighted, Grey should have died in the storm of metal that greeted his battalion outside Serre. But Grey had lived. Grey was indestructible, Finlay had decided, his frail and sometimes louche appearance only nature's ironic joke.

'You can't go back to Liverpool Street,' Grey said. 'Your quarters there are a tomb under forty feet of water.'

'Babcock was right then.'

'Babcock?'

'About that tributary of the Fleet,' Finlay said.

Grey laughed.

'Since the Fleet's nearest course is a mile away from where we put you, it would have to be some tributary. We don't know where the water came from, frankly. But since you are above rather than beneath it, it's of no importance now. Go to Moorgate. Talk to Pearson, who is expecting you. They'll feed you there. Wait for the air-raid warning. Concentrate on Absalom House.'

'Just Absalom?'

'Just Absalom, Chief Fire Officer. Absalom House is the only one of your buildings left.'

Grey did not offer Finlay a lift to Moorgate and the warning siren sounded when he was still trying to struggle through queues for a bus to take him in the direction of the City. As people scattered and the streets cleared, he simply took off his coat and discarded his gas mask and started to jog through the streets eastwards, towards the rumble of approaching aircraft. He was at the junction of Oxford Street and Charing Cross Road when he saw a motor cycle half-concealed under a rain cape in an alleyway. The engine, when he touched the cylinder head, was still warm. He kicked the bike over and it rumbled into fitful life and he rode it as fast as it would travel to the Moorgate station.

An ARP warden brought the news that Absalom had been hit by incendiaries as Finlay changed into a uniform. Bigger bombs, high explosives, were detonating by the time he reached the scene aboard the first fully manned appliance. They seemed to be targeting Liverpool Street again. The Absalom blaze lit up the third and fourth floors in twin necklaces of fierce yellow and ruby light through its windows. Two more appliances arrived. Finlay got three hoses playing on the burning floors from the pavement and brought two extension-ladder-mounted hoses into play before going in with hammers and axes at the head of a crash crew on the ground floor.

Black, noxious smoke, chemical in its intensity, met and assaulted them, forcing their retreat back to the building's high marble vestibule where they tumbled, blind and choking, through the main door. A lead fire fighter ripped off his ventilator and looked at Finlay, shaking his head. Finlay tried to think what it was he had seen in Absalom that would trigger such lethal fumes if it burned. His mind was blank with bewilderment. Pavement danced beneath their feet as the big diesel generator in the basement blew with a moan that became a roar, blasting off manhole covers and spewing through ventilation grilles into the street.

Finlay could feel panic threatening to engulf him in vast waves that passed over and through him with increasing frequency and force. Was she in there? What if Rebecca was in there?

He heard a huge, caterwauling crack as the glass summit of the building shattered in the rising heat and great shards of ornamental glass began their descent through the fabric of Absalom House. Two great pieces tore through the tarpaulin that had covered them and slithered down to the street where they smashed and sent fragments exploding through the air. One punctured the tyre of a Dennis pump and another tore through the canvas skin of a mobile water reservoir mounted on a wagon. A third fragment passed through the shoulder of a fire fighter, missing his lung, but leaving a hole in him the size of a baby's fist.

Finlay had an extension raised at the south-east corner of the building and climbed it faster than he had ever climbed a ladder in his life. Here the play of one of the platform jets had seemed to make some headway against the fierceness of the flames. A crew spotlit Finlay from the street and he used hand signals made rusty by absence of drills to point to where he wanted to go. He got close enough, behind a heat shield, to see into a corner of the atrium. Then something gave with a snap of steel cables and a shunting screech of sound that ended with a thud at the building's base. Finlay knew it was the lift. And it had descended from the top floor. It meant that she was here.

He took a breath and stepped on to the window ledge in front of him, the glass pane long shattered, the granite smeary with heat under his boots. Heat singed the bristles on his face and made his eyeballs sting and shrink in his head. The body shies instinctively away from fire. Finlay overcame this instinct and was about to step down into the inferno of the atrium when its floor gave with a crump, starting a chain reaction of collapse that would leave Absalom a granite shell. Finlay swayed as the vacuum rush of collapse pulled him in. His hands reached for purchase, vainly, because he could not span the window with his arms. And then he was hauled backwards out of the building, as he clawed, one hand gripping a rung, by Pearson, black-faced and grinning on the turntable ladder above him as they swayed away from heat and chaos.

'Reckon you owe me one,' Pearson shouted, clipping Finlay through his harness to the ladder, securing him. 'Heard about you and ladders, sir. Wouldn't have believed it if I hadn't seen it for myself.'

Then he saw the look on Finlay's face and his grin vanished. He chopped signals in the spotlight glare with his hands and the crew at the turntable base wheeled them away from Absalom and down.

Finlay, swaying in his clipped harness, stared, abject, through his descent at the building's burning husk, his body slumped, turning occasionally, as might a corpse on a gibbet.

'Are you all right, sir?'

Two men were unbuckling him, easing the breathing apparatus off his back.

'Are you all right, sir?'

'You're a good man, Pearson,' Finlay offered, mechanically.

Pearson looked back at the ruin of Absalom, its flames reflected crimson in his eyes. 'Poor Ricky Nevin used to say there's no call for any other sort just now, sir.'

But Finlay was already walking away.

The assault was as heavy as Grey had warned it would be. It was as heavy and seemingly indiscriminate as it had been on the night that Grey had sat chain-smoking at a table in The Prospect of Whitby, sipping Scotch and telling Finlay about Serre. Over in the west the rolling thunder of bombs unburdened themselves from high formations of aeroplanes, provoking the melodramatic response of useless, pulverizing ground fire, giving the ignorant something to cheer between sips of beer and bouts of fucking strangers in their shelters. Searchlights lit the sky to the west and in their beams was visible the odd, marauding shape of a Messerschmitt as it dived to strafe fire fighters, destroy rolling stock, hamper a heavy rescue or ambulance crew with cannon fire.

When he entered The Fitzroy Tavern and saw the Irishman among friends at the bar, the odds of four or five to one meant nothing to him. The odds would have meant nothing to Jack Finlay anyway. He had never really been a betting man.

Still streaked across his face and neck with soot from Absalom, his tunic torn and singed and his eyebrows burned clean off, Finlay was a sight even by the pub's traditionally picturesque standards. But fewer people than usual observed the spectacle, the sheer intensity of the latest German onslaught perhaps eating away at bravado, eroding the general mood of recklessness and thinning the evening crowd. An audience being the last thing on Finlay's mind, he walked straight over to the Irishman, four-fingered him in the eyes with a jabbing right and then butted him twice, hard, on the mouth, before sweeping the man's legs away with a kick and dropping to finish the job. Finlay was fast and landed three good kidney punches before one of the Dubliner's companions smashed a beer mug over his head. Finlay shook glass and stout from his hair and sank a double hook into the side of the Dubliner's jaw. He felt something explode against his own cheekbone and shook his head again and rose and stamped on the Dubliner's ribcage. One of them grabbed him from behind then, taking all the momentum out of the kick with the heel of his boot that Finlay had intended to grind into the Dubliner's groin. Frustrated at being so impeded, he slammed his head back into the man's face, hearing teeth snap as another man grabbed his legs and lifted him and a fourth swung a bar stool down from above head height into his body. The men holding him did not loosen their grip. They carried him to the alley outside. All the time they were kicking him, Finlay never lost consciousness. He had the clarity of thought to know that they were killing him. So, through the pain and the blood and mucus, when the assault faltered, he knew they were being interfered with rather than losing heart. He looked upward through a gap in his hands. All four of them stood with their backs to him. McKay faced them, grinning as they attempted to surround him. McKay's fist came out from his side with cartoon swiftness and he jerked the nearest of them off his feet by his coat lapels and smashed the heel of his free hand into the man's chin. The blow sounded like a pistol shot. Its recipient sagged unconscious in McKay's grip, only the toecaps of his shoes trailing the cobbles. McKay dropped the man and the other three fled. Finlay's only thought at that moment was that his father had once fought this creature to a standstill.

McKay unbuttoned his greatcoat and dropped to his haunches and gathered Finlay gently under his shoulders and behind the crooks of the knees. He lifted him smoothly off the ground.

'You're coat's getting ruined,' Finlay said, tried to say. There was something wrong with his mouth and the words came out cushioned and distorted.

'Sshh,' McKay said.

Grief came to Finlay then. Grief shuddered through him. An image of Rebecca's bed, empty, unmade, still warm with her, arrived uninvited in his mind as his body shook with the pain and cleaving suddenness of her absence. He tried to say her name, tears blinding him, but his mind failed to conjure her face and his mouth seemed unable to shape the single word.

'Sshh, Master Jack,' McKay said. 'You're bubbling blood. Save your breath. You've broken a rib and it's gone into a lung. Stay awake now and I'll get you to a hospital. Stay awake and trust your old Uncle Charlie. I'll get you to a hospital and it will all be as right as rain.'

In the cradle of the killer's arms, Finlay wept at his loss and shivered.

'Right as rain, Master Jack,' McKay cajoled and promised.

Fourteen

FINLAY AWOKE and felt nothing but the insidious creep of numbness under the bandages wound tightly around his torso. They had arranged the bed head at a steep incline, supporting him from the waist. He could feel the weight of his shoulders and chest when he tried to fill his lungs in taking a breath. Some kind of contraption had been clamped around his head. He could see the steel bolts at its extremities, blurred by peripheral vision. There was a large ceiling fan above him, its blades like those of a fighter propeller, and he was aware of its persistent revolution in a brush of breeze against his lips. He smelled antiseptic cream and lint. He realized that his sight was still intact. He heard someone settle into a chair at the side of his bed. But he could not turn his head and look at them. The contraption on his head prevented the manoeuvre. He wondered had he broken his neck.

'My boy never had a hope in hell.' The voice belonged to Babcock. 'They still won't tell us the truth about the *Glorious*. Obsolete. Outgunned. Didn't even get to bear its bloody guns. Sunk by the *Scharnhorst* in a few cold, miserable minutes off Norway. Won't even tell us what it was doing there, steaming around with no strategic role to play of any conceivable bloody use.'

Finlay said nothing. His mouth was dry and his tongue had been split, he realized. He could feel the stitches sewn into its tip, rough against the roof of his mouth. He remembered that Babcock was a dab hand at sewing. Babcock had sewn together the wound in his leg.

'Might as well have sent them out blindfolded and handcuffed, roped together on Thames barges, those three crews, for all the chance of survival they had. Three ships of the line blown out of the water and not a man to tell the tale. Sorry fucking tale it would have been, Chief Fire Officer. Classified. Classified fucking Admiralty cock-up.'

Finlay wondered why there were no attendants on the ward. It seemed to be deserted. Were there other patients? He could not turn his head to look. He strained to hear the hubbub of conversation from other visitors. But there was none. He sensed the space he was in was too big to be a private room.

'Wasn't even time for a wireless signal. They were engaged and they were destroyed. Powder magazines amidships. A few plates of sub-standard steel welded on as extra armour. The *Glorious* didn't have the firepower to frighten off a flock of birds. Great big bloody tub of a museum piece. They didn't find a body. They didn't find a lifejacket or even a single piece of floating wreckage. Blown to smithereens. No chance. I tell the missus, at least it must have been quick. I have to tell you, Mr Finlay, that she takes no consolation.'

Finlay's next visitor was his father. He didn't talk, like Babcock had. He just sat, a massive presence, still on the creaking chair, and held Jack's two hands in one of his on the counterpane. He cried quietly for a while, Jack knew for his other son, and then he squeezed Jack's hands and rose to leave.

'Don't go, dad,' Finlay called after him. But he knew that he was alone again in the room.

Rebecca came to see him. He heard the familiar click of her heels on the linoleum and in his mind could see the switch of her hips as she walked the length of the ward. She kissed his cheek and he inhaled her and felt a lock of hair brush silky against his neck.

'I'm sorry you died,' he managed to say.

Her hands lay on his bed sheathed in black leather gloves. She spread wrinkles from the counterpane with taut fingers. 'We all die,' she said. With cool lips, she reached across and kissed him on the mouth.

Finlay wept then in the wake of her departure. He wept at his loss and waste and failure. He thought about his brother, seated at his wireless post, swaying with the current at the bottom of a dim green sea. He thought of his mother, deprived even of the small consolation given her by the shrine to his dad, lost to the bombing that took their house in Stanley Road. She had been out at a seance when the string of high explosives hit, cajoled by the bereft into seeing things on their behalf that nobody should.

The death of Rebecca was too painful a thing for him properly to contemplate, let alone confront. He was angry that she had taken such a reckless risk as to be in so vulnerable a place at the time of the raid. He was bitter at his own failure to protect her. But he could not dwell on the subject of her loss in the manner that enables men to recover from their grief. He lacked the will. He lacked the strength. It was yet another failing, one that filled him with a sort of weary self-disgust. If he recovered, Finlay knew it would be despite himself.

The hallucinations continued for several days. It might have been several weeks. Richard Nevin visited. And Albert Cooper came and sat and drank from a bottle of beer and told Finlay a filthy joke. Babcock warned him earnestly about the threat of sabotage. White came and grumpily recounted a long poem by Kipling. Pickering, the looting auxiliary, paid a visit, chuckling and throwing playing cards that all showed the ace of spades on to his bed, leaving Finlay shivering in cold sweat under his bandages. The Dubliner came and flashed his kiltie blade, razor-edged, under Finlay's nose, singing 'Danny Boy' in a sweet tenor voice. But Finlay, though he waited, never felt his father's presence again.

When he returned to the real world he was still in a hospital bed and the bed still lay under an indolent ceiling fan. Now there were other patients and nurses and the occasional visit from a doctor, who seemed about the same age as Finlay and had sallow skin and carried a clipboard and whose breath smelled of pipe tobacco. The doctor asked him irritated questions and stabbed at a pad on the clipboard with his pen. Finlay realized that the doctor regarded his injuries as self-inflicted. In a way, he supposed they were. After a while they unbolted the apparatus holding his head rigid and gave him gentle physiotherapy and made him take long salt-water baths. Finlay was able to study the two patients in adjacent beds to his. One looked like he had been trodden on by stampeding cattle. The other had his hands suspended above him in a hoist, bandages like rolls of soft bread thrust over his fingers. Both men were young and each seemed to be sedated.

'What happened to my neighbours?' Finlay asked the sallow registrar.

'Fellow on your right was beaten with an iron bar. Systematically. Fellow on the left merely had his fingernails torn out with pliers. France and Norway; contrasting interrogation techniques. I'm surprised either chap escaped. But when you're desperate, eh?'

'They're agents?'

The doctor sucked his teeth and looked at Finlay with deepening distaste. 'They didn't come by their injuries brawling in a pub.'

As he always had, Finlay healed quickly. His ribs mended. His punctured lung repaired itself. The hospital occupied a requisitioned school building and still had a running track marked out faintly on its adjacent playing field. He ran laps of the track in bare feet until one of the nurses found him some running spikes from a pile of school supplies stored in a loft. Gymnastics equipment had been stored in the loft and Finlay pulled mats and a set of parallel bars out of the pile and started to use them. The days were diminishing towards Christmas. The weather was soft and wet, opaque and misty most days, without wind. Dawn came each morning with greater reluctance and darkness was upon the world by four as they crept through December and the shortest day. Finlay did his exercises in the hour before sunset. He felt vaguely guilty about spending so much time on recreation when every man of his age was fighting a war.

'Every able-bodied man,' the registrar said drily, when he voiced this discomfort. 'We're here to get you able-bodied again. The exercise will accelerate that process.'

And his routine found, from somewhere, official sanction. Harry, the masseur from the gym Finlay used behind the Strand, started to come twice a week to knead strength and vigour back into his body on a rubbing table.

'How do you get here, Harry?' Finlay asked him.

'Round trip takes about eighty minutes from the Smoke in a motor,' Harry said. 'Big brute of a Ministry driver brings me in an official car. It's no hardship, Mr Finlay. I can't say I've ever travelled by Bentley before.'

His mother telephoned.

'I saw dad.'

'I thought you might.'

There was a silence. He could hear his mother breathing into the unaccustomed apparatus in her hand.

'It was the fever,' Finlay said.

'It was the gift, John,' his mother said. 'It's not the first time and it won't be the last. It's how you knew our Tommy had passed on.'

'That was intuition, mum. Nothing more.'

'Are you mending, son?'

'I'm going to be absolutely fine.'

'Yes,' she said. 'I know you are. I've something else to tell you. But I'll talk to you after you've talked to your Captain Grey.'

'Will you visit?'

'I wish I could, John. I'm laid up with my feet. I'll telephone you again when you've talked to Captain Grey. And I'll see you when you're right again. You're on the mend. That's the main thing.'

'He loved me, didn't he, mum?'

'He does love you, Johnny. He always will.'

He had the time to ponder on his buildings and their collective fate of violence and destruction. He tried to puzzle sense out of what he had seen in rooms fretting with forced use and clumsy alteration. The war effort toiled to such slogans as 'Make and Mend' and 'As Needs Must'. But the science he had seen in his buildings had been baffling and sinister. In one, he had seen huge tanks of soupy liquid, coiled power cables twisting in the translucent broth like conger eels. In another, the ceramic housing of thirty or more crackling conductors had risen from a false floor resembling nothing so much as pulled and rotting giant's teeth. The apparatus at the old Hawksmoor priest's house had been the most disturbing. Jelloid and viscous, a warp of matter whirled, suspended there, between unseen fields of force. It span fast, this purple insult to nature. Finlay had been advised to wear earplugs before entering its lair. The sound of its frictive contact with the air was a banshee's scream. And yet none of this stuff had proved truly volatile. London had not erupted with explosive energy, ungovernable, terrifying, when his buildings had been bombed. Almost all of the volatility had come from the ordnance dropped by the Luftwaffe on Finlay's buildings. Their purpose remained a gruesome, disquieting mystery to him.

Except for Absalom. He had studied the random click and whir of the Absalom machines and known because the card sharp Kevin Pilley had schooled him in the subject that they were devices geared to the laws of probability. Pilley's hopeless ambition when they shared a punishment cell in the Portland Borstal had been to become an actuary. Pilley had made a science of chance. Finlay had learned more from him than how to deal the ace of spades to a looting fire fighter from the bottom of the deck. He had learned enough to know that the machines in Absalom House had been dedicated to code-breaking. It was why they had never rested. Despite his elaborate efforts, their component pieces rested in oblivion now.

Over time, Finlay tried to grieve for Rebecca Lange. But he could not reconcile himself. He would walk back from the running track, its oval picked out in faint chalk on the wet grass, spent from effort, steam rising from his shoulders into the dampness of dusk, and he would use the seclusion of the moment to dwell on what had become of her. Still unable to think of it without anger, he would try to see some significance in her death. At this time of day there were always aeroplanes passing overhead, fighters on their way to valiantly defend the innocents on the ground against the random destruction of bombs. Finlay knew that when pilots died, they usually died horribly; the inferno of their cockpits oxygen-fed, perspex raining molten on to them from the canopies that confined them in aerial tombs. But at least they died for something.

Rebecca had been sent to Scotland to suffer vile abuse on a futile mission. She had been used as a pawn by her godfather in a game Finlay still did not believe she had understood. Trapped by fire in the atrium at Absalom House, she would have been forced to wait helplessly for the gruesome manner and detail of her death. Finlay thought of her the first time he had seen her, dazzling; a glowering, exultant cocktail of glamour and sexual mischief. Hers was an obscene loss, a terrible squandering. He thought of the look on her face as she assembled his makeshift meal prior to his departure for Wales. The expression on her face, when he had lifted her chin to kiss her goodbye, was transparent with unexpected happiness and hope. The death of Rebecca, burned, was a loss Finlay did not yet possess the endurance to confront. This perhaps because he believed her murdered.

And he missed her. He had taken to drinking a cup of tea after his exercises in a derelict classroom that had somehow escaped redesignation for some other, dreary, official use by the hospital authorities. The classroom had a large revolving globe on a stand by the teacher's desk. A wall chart showed the continents. Another showed the prevailing currents in the oceans of the world; dark blue patterns of compelling force through thousands of miles of paler water.

He would sit at a desk and think of her. Of her sharpness, of her surprising warmth and her laughter. Of her recklessly generous nature. Of her tearing absence.

Once, when this reverie brought him close to tears he could not risk, Finlay walked across to a bookcase to distract himself. Most of the books had gone, he supposed to be pulped into instructional leaflets and ration coupons. Two or three volumes had escaped the cull and he chose one of these at random. He flicked through the pages and stopped at a landscape photograph of a frozen sea, ice clinging in great blank stalactites to ship rigging, waves petrified by cold in the very motion of breaking.

'Lake Michigan, from the Chicago shore,' the picture caption underneath it read. Finlay shivered. 'Winter is coming,' he said, to the dry geography classroom walls.

*

The sallow registrar examined Finlay on what was to be his day of release. Finlay did not know that, standing naked for his examination, even when a nurse knocked and entered the examination room carrying a pile of clothes, neatly folded, across both hands. He didn't know because the clothes were so clearly the rough woollen serge of an army uniform; the coarse khaki of an army shirt. Army boots topped the pile. Finlay did not suppose that this uniform had been brought for him to put on. He was a fire fighter.

The doctor was using a small light to examine Finlay's left eye.

'The skull fracture has healed completely. There are odd glass fragments between bone and scalp, but they're literally fragments, too small to cause discomfort.'

The doctor spoke in a loud voice, as if dictating. But nobody was taking any notes. Finlay assumed he was showing off to the nurse who stood behind him with a perfect view, Finlay assumed, of his arse. At least his arse was a part of him not scarred.

'The ribs are entirely knitted and the ribcage has resumed its original integrity,' the doctor said, tapping Finlay's flanks. 'Blow into this.' He gave Finlay a balloon. Finlay blew. The doctor pinched the aperture of the balloon and plucked it from Finlay's lips.

'About three and a half litres of lung capacity,' he said. 'You should enter bicycle races. Show me your tongue.'

It was a thorough examination. Finlay's brain had swelled with concussion after the kicking inflicted by the Dubliner's friends and they had also cracked his skull. At University College Hospital, to which McKay had carried him, they had used a hand-drill to bore a hole in his skull and relieve the pressure on the brain and reduce the risk of an aneurism. The treatment had worked and the hole, like the fracture above his left temple, had healed perfectly. Finlay never found out what the brace in which they held his head was for. Perhaps it was a precaution only.

The doctor slapped him on the back.

'Robust proletarian genes. It's the only explanation. Your powers of recuperation are extraordinary. But this was not an average Saturday night set-to, Sergeant Finlay. If I were you, I wouldn't do it again.'

Finlay realized then that the uniform the nurse had brought into the room was for him. He didn't know how to feel about this. In one way, it represented a catastrophic loss of rank and responsibility and accordant privilege. In another, it seemed a kind of liberation. He no longer had an appetite for fighting incendiary fires. He looked at his wristwatch.

'Where am I supposed to get to?'

'They're coming to collect you.'

'What time?'

'Twelve. In about fifteen minutes. Why?'

Naked, Finlay nodded at the kit the nurse had brought in.

'Because I'd better bull those boots. Or I'll be in for a bollocking.'

Behind Finlay, the nurse giggled. The doctor raised his eyebrows in pantomimic disgust at the imbecility of military custom. He could of course afford his disdain. He would never have to fight.

Finlay would not miss him.

McKay was in jocular mood on the way back to London. He had burst out laughing, rocked with laughter, driving gauntlets in one fist, fists on his hips, when he saw Finlay dressed as a Royal Artillery Sergeant at the entrance to the hospital. Finlay ignored the mirth, grateful to see that they had given McKay a spotless new camel coat to replace the one Finlay had spoiled with blood coughed from his punctured lung.

'I'd like to thank you, Sarn't McKay.'

'Get out of it,' McKay said, laughing. 'Going to put the wind up General Rommel, are we? Oh, Master Jack,' he wheezed, 'you kill me. You really do.'

All the way back to London, McKay sang. He sang marching songs and sentimental songs from the 'fourteen–eighteen. He sang sea-shanties and folk-songs. He sang a Christmas carol. He stopped when they reached the eastern extremities of the capital and the bomb damage, grave and appalling in daylight, began to amass its catalogue of weary devastation.

'Can I ask you a serious question, Sarn't McKay?'

'Don't ask, you don't get,' McKay said.

'Do you think we're going to win this war?'

McKay chewed on this and drove. Everywhere people scurried through damaged streets, excavating, salvaging, clearing, hammering and baling spent water in human chains, splashing zinc pails of it from link to link. It was an uncharitable thought, but there was something insectlike about the scurry and sheer zeal of the populace as it struggled to restore order over the chaos of bombs. Here and there on the streets Finlay saw tea wagons, the women staffing them wearing florid turbans of silk print on their heads, or fans of dead, yellow hair falling to their shoulders. McKay pulled up and brought them tea before addressing Finlay's question as they sipped the black brew and the car idled on a street in Walthamstow and young children gawped at it and at the giant McKay, in his yellow coat and gauntlets, sipping his beverage at the wheel.

'If I learned one thing in the 'fourteen–eighteen, it was this,' he said eventually. 'I learned that men can tolerate anything. You can tolerate any amount of rain and mud and rats and cold and marching and corpses. Any deprivation and indignity. It might be the one unendurable thing about human life, Master Jack. No species is so adaptable as ours. We can take anything.'

Finlay sipped tea.

'I don't see how that's an answer to the question.'

'Because you haven't given it sufficient thought,' McKay said. 'You really think that White and Grey are the sort that wave a white flag when things get a bit sticky? You really think that Churchill is going to stand in chains before a cunt like Hitler, begging for a merciful peace?'

They sat in silence, drinking tea. McKay blew on his to cool it and condensation misted the windscreen for an instant and then was gone.

'What do you think will happen?'

'Lap of the gods, Master Jack. Adolf might invade. If it all goes to pot, I've a place in the Brecon Beacons I bought with a bit I put by after the last lot. Under the floorboards I've a Webley revolver and a Mauser sniper's rifle I brought back as a souvenir from France. Both are fully serviced and I've plenty of ammunition. The missus passed on two years ago. Our girl is raised and wed and living on her husband's farm in Rhodesia. If they invade, I'll do some serious mischief in the hills with the Mauser. I'm a fair shot and can live off the land. I'll stand my ground. But if it really goes to pot, I'll save a bullet for the Webley and myself.'

'But you just told me we can tolerate anything. Nothing is unendurable, you said.'

'I did. But can doesn't mean the same as have to, Master Jack.' He winked. 'Now we'd best be off. The General's a bugger for punctuality.'

It was White and Grey. No tea. No offer of biscuits. It was business, without deception or refreshment. Grey wore the uniform of a full colonel. The chicken wire had gone and they had new windows. The windows looked to Finlay like an act of bravado and filled the room with the smell of fresh putty.

'Why did you attack the Irishman?'

'I think you know, sir.'

'I'd like your explanation nevertheless,' Grey said.

'He planted the devices that destroyed Absalom House. I've seen enough fires to know arson from incendiary bombs.'

White and Grey looked at one another.

'Go on,' White said.

'The Absalom blaze had two separate seats,' Finlay said. 'Third and fourth floors. There wasn't enough inflammable material on either floor to sustain a blaze of that intensity. It was deliberately set. That's what he was doing in Chiswell Street the night he came across Nevin's crew. He had set his charges and was on his way back to The Fitzroy Tavern for a well-earned drink. He would have used something slow, an acid fuse, for the flash charges that ignited his accelerants. I suspect he used gelignite on a clock or timer triggered by temperature to blow up the generator.'

'Why would he want to set fire to Absalom House?' White looked genuinely baffled.

'Because it was a building familiar to him from his friendship with Rebecca Lange, sir. Because he had identified it through her relationship with me as a priority target. And because that's the IRA strategy, isn't it, to take advantage of the current circumstances whenever they can.'

'It might be,' Grey said. 'But the chap you attacked is a writer.

And he didn't destroy Absalom House, I can assure you. Because I know who did.'

Finlay sat rigid. There was a knock at the door. An orderly came in and gave Grey a note which he unfolded and read. He dismissed the orderly and passed the note to White. White looked at it and folded it and put it in his breast pocket.

'So it was you lot. You used Rebecca Lange. And then you killed her,' Finlay said.

Grey held up his hands as if to show his clean, white palms. 'The former, certainly. But there's no reason to believe that she is dead.'

'She wasn't at Coptic Street,' Finlay said. 'I checked on my way to deal with the Irishman.'

'You think she's dead because she's disappeared,' White said. 'It's a fair assumption, but hardly conclusive.'

Finlay gripped the edges of his chair. He felt as though the world had shifted, slipping from under him.

'There was nothing valuable to us in Absalom House, Sergeant,' Grey said. 'There was nothing of value in any of your buildings. The research was bogus, the science a deliberate babble of mumbo-jumbo and mysticism.'

'You're a fucking liar, Grey. I know about Rebecca's father and his work on propulsion.'

White smiled indulgently at him. 'Half the boffins in Europe have a theory about propulsion. Lange's work showed theoretical promise some years ago, but in practical terms got nowhere. The suggestion that it did was ours. And it was a fiction.'

Finlay turned furiously to Grey.

'You risked your life and mine getting that apparatus out of a basement. I saw the machine myself. I helped you carry it.'

'Something the Major had his tame chaps at Borehamwood concoct,' Grey said. 'One of their special effects.'

Vertigo was a sensation Finlay had never felt before. Now he was dizzy with it.

'Why?' he said, arms wide, hoarse with fury. 'For fuck's sake, why?'

'We are working on all kinds of genuine projects,' White said. He looked quickly at Grey and then back towards Finlay. 'One of them is an early warning system that should prove an effective means of countering these air raids. It could be operational as early as the spring. The more bogus projects the Luftwaffe target, the thinner they have to spread themselves and the less chance there is of them doing real damage to a genuine facility. The square mile has no residential population. Most of the financial institutions relocated to the suburbs in the phoney war. And the high density of buildings in the City confines blast damage. It was a pragmatic choice.'

Finlay sat with his elbows on his knees and stared at the floor. He hawked and spat deliberately on the carpet.

'Please don't take it personally,' White said. 'There's an entire provincial city, made of wood, on the hills outside Sheffield. These are necessary ploys.'

'And then of course there's Babcock,' Grey said.

White turned sharply towards him.

'Babcock?' Finlay said.

White sagged. 'Oh, tell him, Grey. After what he's been through. I mean, we're hardly going to hamper ourselves now by his knowing.'

'You were right about Babcock, Finlay,' Grey said, 'He really is a Communist. We knew that he was passing information to the Russians. He's been doing it for a decade or more.'

'We're not at war with Russia.'

'No. And neither is Germany.'

'What we needed to know,' White said, 'is whether Moscow is sharing intelligence with Berlin. In the concerted bombing of your buildings, we believe we have our answer.'

'Why those buildings?'

'One of them was built by Lange,' Grey said. 'The Germans knew something about Lange's scientific bent. And together on a map the buildings formed the precise geometric outline of a pentagram. That would mean nothing to Moscow. But we thought it might get the Germans out of their prams. The Nazis are buggers for the occult. Did you know Hitler packed off a team of eminent archaeologists to search in all seriousness for the Holy Grail? That he daily consults an astrologer?'

'I didn't tell Babcock anything.'

'Oh, yes, you did,' Grey said. 'Most of it, we suspect, when he treated your leg. We've analysed what it was he gave you. It was a great deal more than morphine.'

Finlay tried to gather himself, to compose and orchestrate the headlong chaos of his thoughts and feelings. He looked around the familiar room, which was now almost jaunty, optimistic with its smell of putty and repair. His gaze turned to White, finally justified in the general's uniform his breeding had predestined him to wear. He looked at Grey: the louche civilian now so much fictitious history, Colonel Grey far more convincing than any of the matinee idols he had seen in press photographs, seductively tailored into martial costume.

He swallowed. 'Rebecca. Tell me how Rebecca fitted in. Was she just so much window dressing? Was the charred corpse of an innocent woman a necessary part of your necessary ploy?'

'We didn't really have a choice,' Grey said. 'Her father is a prominent victim of Nazi butchery. Her mother is a Polish aristocrat lobbying hard for American involvement in the war. Rebecca wanted to be involved in the war effort and as her godfather, I felt obliged to oblige.'

Finlay had one more question to ask. He asked it of Grey. 'Why me?'

'In the 'thirties Babcock worked for Paolo Cardoza.'

Finlay looked blank.

'The man who owned Pimlico Rubber,' White said. 'We knew that Babcock would remember you, at least by reputation. And that he would grade the importance of your mission accordingly.'

'And we needed a character like you,' Grey said. 'Not just prepared to walk on thin ice, but to stamp all over it.'

Finlay could think of nothing to say.

'Course we didn't know you'd fall for the Lange woman,' White said. 'And we didn't imagine you'd concoct your own plot and blame the Fenian for Absalom House. You'd be dead, you know, if McKay hadn't followed you.'

'That's the first straightforward observation I've heard either of you make,' Finlay said. 'Do you get enjoyment out of all this?'

'Not at all,' Grey said. 'Personally speaking, I'll do anything to end this conflict successfully without boys dying again. You are angry because you thought your leadership dithering and weak. You should be glad that we are not.'

Finlay turned his wounded attention towards White.

'Is it satisfying to play God?'

White shifted in his seat, but said nothing.

'Catholics,' Grey said. His tone carried more resignation than disgust.

'I just wonder, is your boy in heaven or in hell, do you think, Mr White?'

'Enough,' Grey said.

'I mean, do you know?' Finlay said to White.

There was no response.

'Is she alive?'

'We don't know. She's disappeared. We can't be sure,' Grey said.

'You lot make me fucking sick.'

'Enough,' Grey said. 'One more insubordinate word and I swear I'll have you court-martialled and flogged. I mean that, Finlay.'

Tea arrived then and Finlay was grateful for it. He thought about the two men in front of him. He had seen White lachrymose and thought him senile until White had confided the familial sorrow that burdened his heart. He had crawled underground with Grey, risking both their lives in what had turned out to be nothing but a brazenly staged performance.

'I dreamed Babcock warned me about sabotage.'

Grey gulped tea and laughed. 'Your subconscious mind must have an ironic bent, Finlay.'

'Why isn't the Major here?'

White answered him.

'He succumbed to his wounds this morning. That note I was passed?'

Finlay nodded.

'The Major was killed at Vimy Ridge, corporal. It just took him twenty-three more years to die.'

The three men were silent for a moment. For the Immaculate Major.

By now the possibility that Rebecca Lange might not be dead

had started to thrill through Finlay like seismic shock. It was all he could do to stop his teacup from rattling on its saucer in his lap.

'What happens now?' he managed to say.

White answered him.

'Colonel Baxter says he'll have you back. But he doesn't want you in that kit, Finlay. Wants you to take the officer training course and report to him directly when you've successfully completed it. As a subaltern.'

'What about Borstal?'

'Baxter probably thinks it's a school,' Grey said. 'Like Repton or Stowe. He is a Scot, after all.'

Finlay was at the door before a final question occurred to him.

'What will happen to Babcock?'

'He'll hang,' White said. 'Don't you think it appropriate that he should?'

Finlay thought about it.

'He served his country honourably once. He deserves to be shot rather than hanged. You all deserve to be shot.'

From behind the desk, on the other side of the room, they stared at him. Grey said, 'You'll do well in the desert, Finlay.'

It was approaching twilight along Whitehall. He walked without destination towards Parliament Square. He passed lamps, heavy with ornamentation, that would remain through the coming darkness unlit. He passed the pale stone of buildings flushed pink by the setting sun through December cloud. Sound eluded him. The world was silent and the broad thoroughfares of Westminster empty. He crossed the square in the shadow of the great gun battery poised to pulverize empty skies above Westminster Bridge and wandered past the House of Commons. He was half-way across Lambeth Bridge when he came to himself, his eyes on the dimpled complexities of the current below and darkness descending around him. To his left, the winter trees along the embankment of the river formed a still and intricate tangle. To his right was St Thomas's. The hospital described abandonment and ruin in dark geometries of steel and stone. He breathed above the vacant width of the river. The city was growing still and quiet now, reconciled to hiding itself in the lengthening, welcome absence of light.

Later that night he telephoned his mother.

'She's alive, you know. Your young lady. Didn't they tell you?'

'She isn't mine, mum.'

But his mother only laughed.

The postcard finally reached him at a camp in Kettering, a month into his officer training. The number of times it had been rubber stamped was an inky tribute to the tenacity of the postal service. That soldiers liked to get mail was a basic tenet of Government thinking in wartime. It always had been. The reverse side of the card carried no message or endearment, just an address written out in a clear and deliberate hand. Its picture showed an expanse of water under a wilderness of sky. A flight of geese gave scale to its vaunting expanse. At the bottom of the picture a legend was printed in small script that read: 'Lake Michigan, from the Chicago shore.'